I Am Having an Adventure

ALSO BY PERRI KLASS

Recombinations

I Am Having an Adventure

STORIES BY

Perri Klass

G. P. PUTNAM'S SONS / NEW YORK

The text of this book is set in Janson.

Seven of the stories in this volume, some in slightly different form,
first appeared in the following magazines, to whose editors grateful
acknowledgment is made: "Clytemnestra in the Suburbs" in *The Antioch
Review;* "Trivia" in *The Boston Globe Magazine;* "The Almond Torte
Equilibrium" and "Officemate with Pink Feathers" in *Christopher Street;*
and "Nineteen Lists" (as "A Romance in Greece"), "Not a Good Girl,"
and "The Secret Lives of Dieters" in *Mademoiselle.*

The author gratefully acknowledges permission from Howard Beach
Music, Inc., to quote lyrics from "Stealin' " by Gus Cannon, arranged
and adapted by Arlo Guthrie, © copyright 1969 by Howard Beach
Music, Inc. All rights reserved.

Library of Congress Cataloging-in-Publication Data

Klass, Perri, date.
  I am having an adventure.

  I. Title.
PS3561.L248I2   1986   813'.54   85-28175
ISBN 0-399-13146-9

Printed in the United States of America
1   2   3   4   5   6   7   8   9   10

For my mother the writer, Sheila Solomon Klass, with love

Contents

I Am Having an Adventure

How Big
the World Is

I have done a great deal of traveling, probably too much. I am twenty-five years old and I have been in well over twenty-five countries, though perhaps not fifty. I sometimes feel that if I had only had the sense to make, at the age of fourteen or so, a list of "countries I want to visit," I would by now have a respectable number of them checked off, and that might give me a sense of accomplishment.

People sometimes ask me what my favorite place is, and, depending on my mood, I will say Paris and disappoint them with the obvious, or else Penang or Teheran and dazzle them with the exotic. Everyone assumes that I do in fact have one favorite place, perhaps that I travel in a ceaseless search for a place that will be even more favorite.

People sometimes ask me if there is anywhere left that I haven't been. They have no idea how big the world is; I have never been south of Panama, for example, or in any part of sub-Saharan Africa. When I see pictures of countries I have never been to, I feel comforted and relieved, but then I begin to think that one day I will be there.

*   *   *

Picture my mother, yes, at the country club. Sun on the shiny toenails (Frosted Blood? Wild Grape?), better legs than I will ever have, exposing the face that she coats nightly with expensive dishonest creams to the drying carcinogenic rays of the Westchester sun.

"Yes, Michele's off again. Traveling around in Europe with a boy." Sigh and shrug. "You'd think she'd get tired of it, traveling around without any money, and decide to go finish college. Still, better to get it out of her system now, I suppose."

For a long time I expected my mother to have some terrible explanatory justifying secret. An alcoholic, a drug addict. Family members who ended up in insane asylums. A dark and horrible depth.

It was a lie that I was traveling around with a boy. A lie I told her for her own peace of mind, not to upset her by flaunting my sexual experience; she was more or less reconciled to that. I just thought she would sleep better not knowing I was wandering around Europe not only without money but also without company. Alone.

I was eighteen, in Amsterdam, and very very high. Some people at the hostel had included me in their after-lunch turn-on. Then they all drifted off to do whatever it is we do when we are very high in Amsterdam. I was doing it too, wandering along the streets making stoned and inaccurate calculations about what I could afford to buy to satisfy my munchies. I passed a stall where they were selling raw herrings and almost bought one. Shades of Sunday breakfasts at the country club, though nothing was raw there.

In the eyes of the older Dutch people I passed, I didn't even register. Another one. High, of course.

I drifted to the square with the fountain and sat down on the steps of the fountain. I was humming, thinking a very beautiful boy would happen to sit down beside me and we would go back to his hostel together. It had never happened to me quite like that, but I was sure it happened all around me.

Two men tried halfheartedly to sell me hash. All around me people sat in the sun and giggled, or lay back and looked out through half-closed eyes at the tourists who came by and took pictures of the fountain, of the scene.

Then a boy did come and sit beside me, a jumpy boy with long blond hair and bad skin, not that I'm anyone to talk. I knew there was something wrong with him, but I was too stoned to care.

"Hi," he said to me, "how're you doing?" American.

"Been in Amsterdam long?" He kept talking to me, even though I wasn't making very good responses.

"Yes," he said, answering a question I hadn't asked, "I'm here with a group of people, studying the life of Jesus and trying to bring His message into this troubled world of ours."

"A Jesus freak," I said, giggling.

"Why does that make you laugh? Isn't it better to be a Jesus freak than a drug freak?"

I couldn't stop giggling.

"Come with me," he said. "Come and meet my friends, the other people in my group. We have something to share."

"I want a sandwich with some of that liver stuff on it," I said. "And some frites and mayonnaise."

So he walked with me to get them, and then we went back to my room at the hostel and fucked, and then he tried to make me go to "evening prayer session" with him. But I was a lot less stoned by then and I said I didn't feel well, so he went by himself.

*   *   *

The next day at the hostel, a lot of the people were talking about Van Gogh, and how great he was, and how you could tell that he was permanently stoned. I happen not to like Van Gogh; I've never liked Van Gogh. To be honest, I've never really liked any of the impressionists all that much. So a group went off to look at some Van Gogh paintings, though I don't know if they ever got there, and I went to the Rembrandt House. One of my sandals broke while I was walking around there and I was afraid they'd throw me out for being barefoot if I took it off, so I had to limp through the house, dragging my torn sandal along the floor.

Picture my mother, my father, my brother, and me, on the beach at Acapulco. I am nineteen, it is my Christmas vacation from the first year of college I seem likely to complete. My brother Matthew is fifteen.

"Michele," my mother calls, "your nose is getting red. Come put some Bain de Soleil on it." She pronounces Bain de Soleil very well. It is right up there with items on French menus.

Matthew and I are both very high on some stuff I got from one of the waiters at our hotel, who I think has hopes of making it with me. I actually have a crush on one of the other waiters, but I suspect I'm not going to get that one. First of all, it stands to reason that the more beautiful tourists get the more beautiful waiters, and second of all, the object of my crush is probably not interested in females. I am wondering whether I should give up and content myself with the waiter who sold me the dope, even if I don't find him very attractive.

My father gets to his feet, brushing sand down on my mother, who looks up, annoyed.

"Hey, Matthew," my father says, "how about a swim?"

Matthew shrugs, and the two of them head into the water

together; the water is almost empty except for small children who are playing in the shallow part near the beach. The beach, on the other hand, like our hotel rooms, is wall-to-wall.

My mother watches them go in the water, my father's bald head and stocky shoulders, my brother's tall and gangly body, his shoulder-length hair which is a constant source of controversy.

"You know," my mother says to me, "we don't *have* to come to places like this. Not for me. Your father thinks we have to. He's proving something."

"Where would you like to go?" I ask.

She shrugs. "All I know is, I don't have to be tan all winter to prove how much money your father makes. I could go for a vacation somewhere where there's something to do." She pauses for a minute, looking at me. "You really did put on some weight at school," she tells me, as if I didn't know. "I guess it's that dormitory food." As though at home, eating her food, I've always been thin.

Not to make any too-simple connections, but that night I make it with the waiter who sold me the dope. My connection.

I was in Mexico again about two years ago. I had been traveling in Guatemala and Belize, and I came north by bus. Cheap traveling in those countries is very cheap indeed; I had been living on less than two dollars a day and I had a fair amount of money left. I ended up taking a room in a decent hotel, nothing fancy, but I had my own bathroom and the place was clean. The sort of place that gets listed on the "rock-bottom budget" level in grown-up guidebooks. It was like another world after the places I had been staying, suspicious musty mattresses without sheets, five or six to a room, bathrooms out in the courtyard that I had to brace myself to visit.

So when I took this room in the hotel in Mexico City, the first thing I did was take a very long shower, the water actually warm, though not hot. Still, warm was pretty amazing after the places I'd been staying. I came out of the shower naked, glorying in my cleanness, into this small room which was absolutely privately mine. And then I pulled back the covers of the sagging double bed and got in, because I had no clothes that seemed clean enough to put on after that shower. The sheets were stiff and smelled of starch. I fell asleep and slept for almost sixteen hours, right through to the next morning, and when I got up I felt better than I have ever felt before. I still think back on that, that shower, that bed, that sleep, I retreat into that memory like a fantasy, as if it were some glorious sexual experience to be tasted and retasted for the rest of my life.

I spent most of that day in Mexico City eating. I happen to be crazy about Mexican food, and the food farther south in Central America is bland. I had been pretty much living on rice and beans, and that day in Mexico City I bought something at every stand I passed, delighting in the chili taste. *Chiles rellenos. Cochinita pibil. Chorizo.* At the end of the day I was wandering, stuffed and happy, in Chapultepec Park. I stopped and bought a mango from a fat old lady who sat behind a table spread with fruits, elaborately arranged to make the most of their shapes and colors, the yellow of the pineapple slices, the red of the watermelon. She picked up a metal shaker, asked if I wanted chili on my mango. When I nodded, she carefully shook red powder over the mango, which was carved into a delicate pattern of scalloped edges.

I walked slowly along, eating the oversweet juicy fruit with the sharp red pepper. This is a very advanced culture, I was thinking. They would never think of doing this in Westchester.

*   *   *

Somehow I have always expected the phone call that comes in the night to be about my mother. She's taken an overdose of sleeping pills. She's disappeared.

The phone rings one night in the college dormitory room. My roommate, asleep in the other bed, makes an angry noise. I crawl over the body of my boyfriend, asleep in my bed, and get the phone. It is my father, sounding shaky.

"Your brother's been in a car accident," he tells me.

I fly home the next day, Boston to JFK. My father picks me up and I stay for four days, until it is clear that Matthew is going to be all right. The boy who was driving is dead, his closest friend for years. Dead three months before their high school graduation, my father keeps repeating to me, shaking his head. My brother would probably be dead too, except he was in the back seat when the accident happened.

The last day before I am going to go back to Boston, I get a moment alone with my brother in his hospital room. He is able to talk now, not on so many painkillers. I look at the IV tubes and the cast and I don't know what to say. I want to ask: Were you and Kevin very high? Why were you in the back seat, anyway?

Instead I say, "Jesus, I always figured *I'd* be the one in the hospital bed with the family gathered around me."

"Do you want to know why I was in the back seat?" Matthew asks, his voice strange, slow and nasal.

"Yes," I say.

"We were fighting," he tells me. "I jumped over the seat because I didn't want to sit next to him, and that's when he swerved and we hit the other car."

"Shit," I say.

Matthew nods, or tries to nod. He can't really move his head. "We were fighting over some stupid thing of whether he paid too much attention to this girl at this party. I was fucking jealous."

"Whenever I love someone," I say, to my own surprise, "I'm always sure I'm going to end up by doing them some terrible damage."

"I don't deserve to ever love anyone again," my brother says. "I don't deserve to ever have anyone love me again."

"I know," I say. "But it doesn't work that way. I don't mean to come on as older and wiser, but it just doesn't."

"You'll see," my brother says.

There is a brief crisis as my brother starts recuperating, when he announces that he wants to withdraw his applications to Harvard, Yale, and Princeton without even finding out whether or not he gets in. He is persuaded not to. He insists that he wants to go someplace small and far away, but then he gets into Harvard and again lets himself be persuaded.

The following September, when my brother came up to Boston to start Harvard, I took a leave of absence from my own Boston school (so emphatically not Harvard) and used my summer savings to buy a ticket to India. At American Express, Bombay, I got a letter from my brother. "You were right," he wrote. "We get what we don't deserve. But then what do people get who do deserve it? Anyway, Mom and Dad are furious at you, as I'm sure you know. Practically calling me every night to make sure I haven't flown the coop as well. I hope India is wonderful."

I traveled "on business" last year. Or rather, my business was traveling. I got the job, I should probably be ashamed to admit, through someone my father knew from the country club. My job was to accompany American tour groups through Europe. I didn't actually narrate the sightseeing bus journeys;

to do that we picked up a new guide in each city. My job involved helping people change hotel rooms when they didn't like the ones they'd been assigned, recommending leather shops in Florence or watch stores in Switzerland, general trouble-shooting. I was pretty good at it. It didn't take all that much beyond being neatly dressed and polite. It was strange to be so neat in a foreign country, so divorced from the realities of travel.

Once in Rome we had one of our many free days. Everyone could go off and shop. I had recommended stores to shop in and places to get a bite to eat, and even a museum to one misfit couple who wanted to do more sightseeing. I told them to go to the Borghese Gallery. When all my tourists had gone off, I did something very silly and juvenile. I took off my tan gabardine skirt and my blue cotton blouse and I put on a pair of blue jeans which if I had had any sense I wouldn't have packed, since I could never have worn them in front of my tourists, and a faded pink teeshirt. I put on sandals instead of espadrilles. I took the two little barrettes out of my hair and combed it forward so that my face was partially covered. And then I went and sat on the side of the fountain of the sinking boat at the foot of the Spanish Steps, surrounded by all the other traveling kids, some with their backpacks at their sides, all of us cooling our feet in the fountain.

As a group they were pretty clean-cut, those kids. I didn't talk to anyone. Two or three of my tourists wandered by, emerging from the Via dei Condotti, laden with shopping bags. I pulled my hair farther forward, but no one even looked at me.

I held that job for a whole year. I saved a lot of money because the tips were very good. It's funny, but when I think of the places I got to visit with groups of tourists, I don't really feel I've been in any of those places. For example, I feel as if I haven't been to Rome for three years, even though last year I was there a number of times. But three years ago I was there on my own, or rather, with one other person.

I am twenty-two years old and madly passionately masochistically in love. This does not happen to me very often. The man I am in love with is madly passionately masochistically in love with me. This is even rarer.

The two of us are in eastern Turkey. We have spent two months wandering around in Italy and Yugoslavia and Greece, and now we have found our way to eastern Turkey and suddenly we are both very tired, and suddenly we are both sure that we are going to have one final terrible fight and see the last of each other, here in this random town.

We had met, of all places, in the Sistine Chapel, happening to lie down together on the floor to look up at the ceiling, being made to get up by the irritable guard whose job it is to stand there all day and make people get up if they lie down and to make sure no one comes in the exit or goes out the entrance.

So Paul and I got up together, and started talking, and went out together for a slice of *pizza rustica*, and then in the afternoon, after four, when things started opening up, we went to see the church of Santa Maria sopra Minerva, and looked at the frescoes until we ran out of coins to turn the lights on. I looked at Paul and knew that he would feel the need to go see something else and then go eat dinner before he felt right about making a move, so I stood close beside him in the semi-darkness of the church and propositioned him in some coy phrase or other. I wanted him so badly, I think I knew even then that this was going to be mad passionate masochistic love. I think he did too.

*   *   *

So there we are in eastern Turkey, and the weather is much colder than we expected it to be, and our hotel room, needless to say, is without heat. Last night, for a little while, we regained our sexual spark and heated up the room and ourselves to a glow which reminded us that we were young and in love and adventurous. But even last night the cold was returning as I fell asleep, and I woke up very early, stiff and miserable, and with a taste in my mouth that warned me that I was coming down with a cold and a sore throat.

We drink heavily sugared tea and eat honey cakes, our table close to the kerosene heater which makes smoke and smell, but very little heat. I look across the table at Paul and I feel tremendous tenderness, with my mouth full of the comforting sweetness of honey cake. Paul is shaggy and dirty, his half-grown beard, his ragged brown hair. The intelligence in his eyes, the knowledge that on some level he is just like me, an irresponsible child, running off to bum around the world when he should be in college, but also a serious cultured child, crazy about museums and archaeological sites. And what about the wiry beauty of his body, the electricity in his fingertips? I swallow the honey cake and there is a faint ache in my throat, another reminder of impending sickness.

We have our final fight, like so many of our smaller ones, probably like everyone's fights-while-traveling, about money and luxury. He wants to go find a better hotel, one with heat, or better still, take the bus to Istanbul and from there go back to Greece. I say that if I spend the money to go back to Greece I will be at the end of my funds; my idea is to work my way slowly back to Istanbul and then try to get a job, but first to see a little more of Turkey. Paul gestures sarcastically at the shop: This is Turkey, do you really need to see any more of it?

What are we fighting about, anyway? It's so hard to tell.

He wants to spend money, get us out of this cold, avoid what seems to be straight ahead, sickness and discomfort in a very alien place. I, on the other hand, want to stick it out, see it through, as though I think I have something to learn from it. Always my reaction.

We fight on for almost two days, as my cold becomes a reality. Tears in the hotel room. Backs turned in bed. Pointed stalking through the streets, not looking around to see if the other is still there. Finally I realize, somewhat feverish, that Paul is too good a boy to abandon me, sick in a small Turkish town. We fight while I pack my pack. He tells me and tells me that I'm crazy, but he doesn't pack his own, so when I stomp out and head for the bus station he can't follow—his stuff isn't packed. I get to the bus station and buy a ticket for Ankara, since there is a bus leaving for Ankara very soon, if I understand the man correctly. I keep looking around over my shoulder, hoping Paul will be there, knowing that if he is, we will only go on fighting. Knowing that he has reached the end of his traveling, at least for now, and suspecting that if I had any sense I would know that I have too.

Instead I go to Ankara and get a job teaching English in a seedy school and have an affair with a man from New Zealand who is also teaching English there. I decline his invitation to head off toward Asia with him.

"I was in India last year," I tell him.

A couple of weeks after he heads east, I take my small savings and go west and south, down the Turkish coast.

I got a thick envelope from my mother once at American Express in Barcelona. She had sent me three white linen handkerchiefs with delicate flowers embroidered on them, also in white, and she had put so much perfume on them that they still smelled of it. The note in the envelope said, "A little useless luxury. There was a sale." I still carry one of them, wrapped around the stone with the hole in it from the beach near Copenhagen, my lucky piece. I have not, however, ever been able to bring myself to tell my mother this.

I am fifteen years old and my parents have sent me to Israel for the summer on a Jewish youth group trip. A "pilgrimage," they call it. We have Hebrew lessons every morning. My best friend in the group, Lisa Birnbaum from Great Neck, has met an Israeli soldier, and he has this friend, and she wants me to skip the trip to the John F. Kennedy Memorial Forest and come with her to meet them.

I am having a brief identity crisis, in the middle of the prolonged crisis of adolescence. I am toying, briefly and somewhat hopelessly, with the idea of becoming religious. The reason for this is a certain Melanie Glick, whom all the cool boys on the trip are in love with. Melanie wears overalls and embroidered peasant blouses and plays the guitar and the flute, and she is religious. She embroiders challah cloths with vines and flowers and Hebrew letters. She plays her guitar and sings at our compulsory Friday night services. She observes the Sabbath, does not ride or carry money. She smiles and says that she loves having one day a week which is different from the others, set apart for rest and meditation. I try to picture myself saying that. And all the cool boys are in love with her. The ones with longish hair and tightish blue jeans, some with guitars of their own. They sit with her for hours working out harmonies for Hebrew songs.

Anyway, despite my vague leanings toward cleaning up my act, my friend Lisa persuades me, without too much difficulty, to skip the trip to the forest and come with her. We sneak away, knowing our absence will be discovered, planning to say that we went shopping. A good ten percent of the girls skip every trip to go shopping, and since they are by no means the troublemakers, the trip leaders tend to let it pass.

Soon Lisa and I are in this bare modern apartment with these two soldiers, drinking whiskey from the bottle. Lisa is cuddling into the shoulder of her soldier, and I know what she is thinking. I happen to know that she is a virgin, and she happens to know that I am not. To be precise, I have slept with one boy. To be precise, three times. To be accurate, they were none of them among the great experiences of my life. I discover in myself a profound disinclination to add to them with my soldier, who is plump and speaks almost no English. Lisa and I, needless to say, speak no Hebrew at all.

I announce that my head is aching and I want to go for a walk. Lisa looks at me, wondering whether I am chickening out or just getting out of the way, leaving her alone with her soldier. The two soldiers talk to each other in Hebrew for a minute, then mine escorts me out and buys me coffee. By the time he takes me back to the dormitory where my group is staying, I am feeling quite fond of him, especially when we run into three of the girls who really have been shopping, also coming back.

Lisa gets back much later, after the people who went to the forest have returned. She admits that she has been out shopping, is scolded, then comes to the room that she and I share with two other girls who are out at the noncompulsory Hebrew song sing-along. Lisa grins at me.

"Well," she says, "at least this summer won't have been a total waste."

"Did you bleed?" I ask.

"Nope. All those Tampax."

We are, naturally, giggling. I imitate a crass Jewish accent, meant to be her mother, my mother, everyone's mother.

"So dollink, did you get a lot out of your summer? Vas it a vunderful experience?"

Lisa collapses on her bed. "What I Did on My Summer Vacation," she says.

I reach under my bed and produce a pilfered bottle of Mogen David Sabbath wine, sweet and syrupy as liquid jelly. Naturally we minors are not given wine, but the people running the tour take themselves sufficiently seriously to have some on hand to make the blessings over.

"Here," I say. "We have to drink to it."

"Oh, God," she says, "after all that whiskey."

But we do drink to it, and then she begins to feel sick, so I hide the rest of the bottle in my suitcase and Lisa goes and sits in the bathroom in case she needs to throw up.

I hear Melanie Glick's voice in the hall and feel a sudden sadness.

Six or seven years later I ran into Lisa Birnbaum in Boston, at a concert. She told me that she heard that Melanie Glick had gotten married and then divorced. I am ashamed of how gleefully I reacted to that news. Even six or seven years later it seemed to lift a burden off me.

I called home collect once from India and my mother was the only one at home. She told me my father was terribly worried about me.

"How can you do this to him after Matthew's car accident?" she asked me.

"How is Matthew? How does he like Harvard?"

"Listen," she told me, "do me a favor and don't send him any postcards, okay? Leave us one kid who can go to college without starting to think about the Taj Mahal."

I am eighteen, in Copenhagen. I have been stoned every

day for almost a week, and I am a little tired of it. I walk along, enjoying the clearness of my head, the blueness of the sky. Everyone is blond. I buy a pastry. I have been hearing about this beautiful beach nearby where everyone is free and naked, and I have not gone because, even stoned, I am self-conscious about being naked in front of all these beautiful blond people. But now, not stoned, I decide to go and see it; I can always keep my clothes on.

And so I end up lying naked in the sun, having positioned myself near a couple of women my mother's age. I lie on my stomach and read a book, a copy of *Tinker, Tailor, Soldier, Spy* which someone at the hostel traded me for the copy of *Narcissus and Goldmund* which I traded for back in Amsterdam and have been carrying around ever since; I don't like Hesse.

I am blissfully gloriously happy, the sun on my back. At that moment it is perfectly clear to me why I am there. I can even smile at the distant echo of my mother's voice: An English book and a beach? For *that* you go to Europe?

And eventually I get up and go in the cold water and don't feel shy anymore and I meet a group of people. A couple of Danes, some Swedes, a German boy, two American girls. I go back to Copenhagen with them, and we have dinner together and drink beer and then go to a park and get high. I spend the night not with any one of them but with a French boy who joined up with us in the restaurant. And I send a mental smirk to my mother: Well then, how about this? Is this European enough for you?

And of course that was also the day I found the stone with the hole in it.

I am twenty-five years old. That is my age at this very moment. I have a great deal of money saved from last year, when I had that job with the tourists. My family waits patiently to hear where I am going this time; perhaps there is a vague hope that I will announce that I am going to use the money to "set myself up" in some city or other, to go back to school—but of course they would pay for that. Matthew is a senior, not sure what he'll do after college. Everyone seems much calmer these days.

"I'm thinking of going to Africa," I tell my mother over the phone.

"Well, where else?" she says ironically.

"I've got the money saved," I tell her, as if she has accused me of sponging.

"Naturally you do, honey." She pauses. "Your father's going to worry, you know."

"I'll be okay, Mom. I can take care of myself."

"I suppose you can, after all this time." She sounds sad. "Africa," she says. "I suppose you're going alone?"

"I suppose I am."

I wait: Will there be one of those highly charged remarks about grandchildren? About how there aren't going to be any at this rate, ever? But all she says is, "Africa."

"I've never been," I say.

"Well, neither have I, Michele," she says, with some sharpness. "But you don't see me dropping everything and running off there, do you?"

I don't say: What exactly do you have to drop? And she doesn't say it to me. As I said, everyone seems calmer these days.

"Well," I say, "maybe you will someday. Go to Africa, I mean."

"Who knows?" says my mother.

"Who knows?" I repeat.

The Anatomy
of the Brain

Alex goes to get the brain while Carla finds the right page in the lab manual and arranges the dissecting tools neatly on the lab bench. Alex comes back with the square white plastic container and carefully sets it down. The large number 17, in black magic marker on the side of the container, tells them it is indeed their brain; all around them other white containers are being opened by other pairs of students and the afternoon's work is beginning. Carla and Alex each put on four disposable plastic gloves, dusted lightly on the inside with powder which is supposed to keep their hands from sweating, and will, for fifteen minutes or so. Two pairs apiece because medical students are highly paranoid. There is a rumor that there is a certain kind of virus, "slow virus," which can live on in these brains through any amount of pickling in formaldehyde, that you can get infected with this virus just by handling an infected brain, and that it will then remain completely symptomless for twenty or thirty years, after which it will kill you, slowly and horribly. That is the rumor, and none of these first-year students knows enough medicine to be sure whether it is true or not, so they wear two and three pairs of gloves, wash their hands nervously for five minutes or more after every lab, and make awkward little frightened jokes about how twenty years from now they'll all end up in the same hospital ward, dying together. A reunion.

Carla, gloved and ready, opens up the plastic container, for all the world like a big piece of Tupperware, and looks down at the brain, sunk in its bath of formaldehyde. In past weeks they have studied the surface anatomy of the brain and dissected the spinal cord and the brainstem. But the cerebral hemispheres, those two joined half-melons, gray and wrinkled, are still basically intact. Today, according to the lab manual, it is time to separate the two hemispheres and dissect the left one.

Carla is sleepy and a little bit disoriented; she had very little sleep and much passion and confusion the night before. Now it takes a great deal of concentration for her to handle the dissection, and even more for her to handle the meaningful looks which Alex is giving her. She looks at Alex and thinks, perhaps unfairly, I am in no mood for children.

Make your first cut so as to divide the two cerebral hemispheres and expose the medial surface of the brain. Try to find the following twenty-five structures:

Carla points to each structure with a metal probe from her dissecting kit, looking from the brain to the diagram in the lab manual. Alex shakes his head dubiously; he lacks any confidence in her identifications and would like to get their teaching assistant to confirm each one. But Alex is not the only one in the lab who feels this way, and the teaching assistant is three tables away, pointing out structure after structure to two intent students, while two other students wait patiently at his elbow to reserve his attention.

Carla puts extra authority into her voice. "And that's the hypothalamus, right there."

Alex looks. "You really think so?"

"Yes, of course. What else could it be?" Actually she doesn't care; she wants to get on with the dissection and not wait half an hour for the teaching assistant. By her tone she shames Alex, makes him wonder if he is missing something obvious.

"How about the calcarine fissure?" He is willing to accept the hypothalamus.

Carla is ashamed of herself for pushing Alex around, but one advantage of making the dissection move quickly is that there is less time for him to look at her mournfully or even say difficult little personal things. But as she searches for the calcarine fissure (will these words ever start to sound familiar?) Alex says softly, "I was hoping we could spend some time together after this lab."

"Here it is!" Carla says triumphantly, indicating a fold in the brain in approximately the right place. She does not look at Alex, and what she thinks is: Oh, God, I should never have done it.

She should never have done it, she knew it even while she was doing it. What she has done is this: A week ago she went to bed with Alex. He had come over to her apartment one evening to study; like good lab partners, they quizzed each other extensively on the endless new terminology of neuro-anatomy, and then they sat and talked for a while about good lecturers and stupid problem sets, and she made him tea. And after he finished his tea, he took her hand and kissed her, somewhat awkwardly, and so, because she had been feeling sorry for herself, feeling lonely and old, as well as a little bit horny, Carla went to bed with him. For all the wrong reasons, she knew it at the time.

*　　*　　*

Make your first coronal cut at the place indicated on the diagram,
cutting through the most rostral part of the cingulate gyrus.

Some of this vocabulary is already familiar to Carla; a coronal cut, for example, means that they will be slicing the
brain in the plane perpendicular to its horizontal axis—that
is, if it were still inside a head, the face would come off the
first slice and then slice after slice would follow toward the
back of the head. She pushes that thought out of her mind
and picks up a big knife and begins. The brain, as she slices
into it, seems ridiculously easy to cut; there is no resistance,
just this sliding of the knife through smooth glistening substance. She keeps her hand as steady as she can, and she doesn't
look at Alex.

Alex's performance in bed was about what you would
expect from a twenty-one-year-old who has spent the last
four years getting straight A's in college science courses.
Very very serious. No skill, but a great deal of sincerity
and energy. And he woke up the next morning ready to
be Carla's boyfriend. He wants a girlfriend, someone to
sit with in lectures and study with at night, and Carla,
who is ten years older than he is, and all tangled up, and
very easily irritated, is so obviously the wrong choice
that she almost expected him to understand without being
told.

Alex is examining the slice of brain with that familiar anxious look on his face. Medical students can get very anxious
about what they are learning; it is so clearly important to
understand how the brain is put together, and yet is is so hard
to look at this slice, with its patterns of white and off-white
and tan, and see anything at all.

"I'm never going to understand this stuff," Alex says, not
quite seriously. Alex is a champion studier, of course, and

what he really believes, Carla knows, is that he is going to have to do some heavy studying before the exam—but by exam time he will know it all perfectly.

"It seems to me that there is an inherent paradox in our studying this," Carla says suddenly, as a thought comes forcefully into her sleepy mind. "I mean, we are trying to use our own brains to understand the brain, and since by definition our brains are limited by the very structures we're studying— well, don't you think this may be at the outer limits of complexity for what our brains can understand?"

Alex is staring at her, about to smile, unsure whether smiling is the right thing to do. Carla wishes desperately that she had never gone to bed with him. She could say to him, casually, I'm a little spaced today because my lover from California was in town last night, and you know how it is, we didn't get much sleep. And then that would kill any incipient romantic thoughts Alex might have about her, and they could go on being lab partners and reasonably good friends. But instead she has put herself in a position where she cannot say that, where it would be cruel.

"I'd really like to talk to you later," Alex is saying to her softly. "I feel like I haven't seen you in a while."

That, Carla thinks, is because I have been avoiding you. But all she says is, "We better try to get some of these structures straight, don't you think?" and Alex, recalled to his duty as a student, picks up the knife to make the next cut.

Like a loaf of bread, Carla thinks, we're slicing this brain like a loaf of bread. The lab is hot and stuffy and the smell of formaldehyde is oppressive. There is a rumor among the medical students that breathing too much formaldehyde can cause cancer, but then there is another rumor that breathing formaldehyde actually preserves you, and anatomists always look younger than their real ages, and anyway what can you do to keep from breathing the formaldehyde? Wear a rubber glove over your head?

Deliberately, Carla takes a deep breath and then turns all her concentration to the slices of brain, trying to arrange the internal structures in her mind so she can appreciate their three-dimensional shapes. She is tired and a little confused, but her powers of concentration are strong; this is not, after all, the first time in medical school that she has been sleepy. She can make herself learn the material. Alex follows her lead, ready, like all medical students, to feel guilty about not taking these important subjects seriously enough.

Carla's lover from California is a married man. When Carla was taking the science courses she needed to apply to medical school, she also lived in California, in Berkeley, and she and this married man had a torrid affair, snatching their moments together when his wife, who is a very high-powered bank executive, was busy at work or away on business. Carla's lover, a somewhat less high-powered urban planner, never once suggested that he might leave his wife for Carla, which she knew was just as well, since she would not have had the strength of mind to refuse him, even though the two of them would never make it as a full-time couple. What they have in common, as was demonstrated once again the night before, is sex, incredible fantastic sex, and all the things which contribute to fantastic sex—a shared sense of humor, a shared capacity for cuddling and hugging, a shared fondness for the romantically sordid. Carla pictures the disheveled bed in her apartment, sees herself going home after the lab and making the bed, then making herself a grilled cheese and tomato sandwich and eating it at her kitchen table while she reads a biochemistry text, while her lover is flying back to California and his wife. It is not such a very unappealing picture, really. If only his business trip could have been three days instead of one, she thinks. She knows that after three days of him, she would have been sated and happy and ready for him to go. Instead, of course, they had to try and cram it all into one night, and here she is, heavy-lidded and a little shaky.

Alex has finally succeeded in attracting the attention of the teaching assistant. This man, a rather insectlike creature whose blue jeans are much too big for him and are bunched up under his wide leather cowboy belt, is bending over their slice of brain with a commendable degree of interest, considering that he has just looked at five or six identical preparations.

"I'm not sure I can see the fibers of the corpus callosum," Alex says.

"Sure you can," says the teaching assistant, a confident insect. He grabs a probe. "Look there—and there. You've done a good job here," he adds approvingly.

"I don't see what you're pointing to," Carla says, her voice sounding rather unexpectedly loud. Where he is pointing looks just like the rest of the brain to her, shiny, not fibrous, like something wet and gelatinous which has been poured into a mold and is going to dry and set.

"Look here." He points again. Now she thinks she can see some faint white fibers, but she could easily be kidding herself. "You know what those fibers do, don't you?"

Carla is surprised by the question. She has not been allowing herself to consider function; this is a course in structure. Anyway, it is impossible to look at this object she is slicing and think about thinking.

"They connect the two hemispheres," says the insect. "They're very important for transferring things between the right and left sides of the brain."

"What kinds of things?" Alex asks, ever the good student.

"Oh, you know, sensory experience, memory, that kind of stuff."

Two other students have appeared, hovering around the teaching assistant, politely asking him for help, leading him away.

"Those TAs can be a little weird," Alex says.

Carla nods, looking at those almost invisible white fibers. So that's what sensory experience and memory are, she is thinking. And that kind of stuff. She smiles to herself.

"He knows a lot of neuroanatomy, though," Alex adds hastily.

Carla looks at Alex, so bland and blond, so distinctly not an insect, a reasonably handsome boy from the Midwest whose family is desperately proud of him. It occurs to her suddenly that he's probably highly malleable; if she wanted to, she could train him, sexually as well as any other way. She doesn't really want to, though.

This fourth coronal cut will reveal a number of new fiber tracts. Note the optic nerve and chiasm on the inferior surface of the brain.

Carla herself is thin and tense and dark-haired, tightly wound personality, tightly wound short spirals of black hair. Fairly pretty, but also easy to overlook. It took her a long time to decide she wanted to be a doctor; eight years out of college, working as a journalist and part-time short-order cook, she decided to take all the prerequisite science courses and apply to medical school. In the process she got to be a pretty good studier herself, but she has never lost the sense that she is very far away from her fellow medical students fresh out of four hardworking years in college.

"Can't we even talk about it?" Alex whispers, not looking at her.

"About what?" Carla says, too irritated to stop herself. She has been breathing formaldehyde and dissecting a brain for almost two hours, and she is in no mood for Alex.

"You know what I mean."

"Listen," Carla says, very softly, and Alex leans hopefully toward her. Is he expecting an invitation, an endearment? "Look, we're good friends who went to bed together once—that's all." She whispers this gently, under the busy noises of talking and cutting and questioning which fill the lab.

"But why does that have to be all?" Alex is not soothed by her formulation. He does not have the sense to quit. Idly Carla thinks that maybe if he hadn't gotten into medical school he would now understand something about rejection. And of course, if he hadn't gotten into medical school, he wouldn't be here dissecting with her.

"Can we finish the lab, okay?" she says.

"Sure," Alex says, hurt, proud, hoping she'll feel guilty and repent and be kind to him.

Instead she makes the next cut; the remaining intact piece of brain is now fairly small, for all the world like the heel end of a loaf of old pumpernickel. Carla and Alex bend over the cut surfaces, checking them against the diagrams in the lab manual. Thalamic nuclei, hippocampus, mammillary body. It's hard to tell whether they're actually getting better at identifying things or whether they're just getting tired and are willing to accept dubious identifications.

Carla finds herself thinking again about what the teaching assistant said. Memory, sight, thought—and this used to be inside someone's head. But that way lies heaven only knows what, and she stops herself. Dissecting a brain is, let's face it, quite weird enough without thinking that kind of thing. And no point in putting your hand up to touch your own head, to remind you of what's inside it—and anyway, if you bring the gloved hand anywhere near your mouth, you'll probably give yourself slow virus. Carla's hands are hot and sweaty inside the gloves.

*   *   *

Arrange your sections of brain in series, identifying each structure on all possible sections. Make sure you appreciate the three-dimensional aspects of the following forty structures:

Outside the windows it is already getting dark; the October days are shorter than Carla expects them to be. Were they actually longer in California? She wants the lab to be over so she can escape the smell of formaldehyde and the reproachful presence of Alex and go back to her little apartment. A freshly made bed, a grilled cheese and tomato sandwich. At the same time, the lab is finally beginning to make some sense to her, as she carefully examines one slice of brain after another. It is all coming together into some sort of picture, she thinks, some understanding of the way all these strange names are packed together into a brain. Not that this understanding has anything to do with how the brain actually works, but maybe it's a start. Medical school involves only occasional moments of intellectual satisfaction, and Carla hugs to herself this sense that she is actually learning something important.

"See that?" Alex points to one of the slices of brain. "Know what it is?"

She assumes he is quizzing her, and she looks carefully. "The hippocampus?" She is not at all sure.

"Right. That's very important in emotion, you know. That's where feelings are." Alex's tone is hurt and challenging.

"Oh, for heaven's sake!" Carla, without thinking, picks up her scalpel, meaning to make some symbolic slash across that piece of brain, and Alex, guessing her intention, protects it with his hand. Before either of them realizes what is happening, she has slashed his finger, right through the two pairs of gloves.

They stand there, looking at the cut gloves and the small line of blood. They look at one another in horror. It is not a deep cut or a serious one, but they both do believe that there is a very remote possibility that twenty or thirty years from now Alex will die because Carla has contaminated his blood with the mysterious virus. How seriously do they both believe it? Is there really any chance that she has killed him?

"I should go wash this," Alex says.

He goes off to wash and Band-Aid his finger, and Carla stands staring after him. Like any medical student in a situation like this, what she thinks is, will I ever be a doctor? Will I always be making mistakes, hurting people, killing people? Mechanically, Carla begins to pack their brain back into its plastic container, the intact right hemisphere, the slices of left hemisphere. She can picture herself and Alex reviewing for the exam, standing over the pieces of dissected brain and trying to recall the important structures. She feels guilty and sorry; she knows that she is only trying to survive herself, to survive a period of loneliness and uncertainty, but she knows that though she is surviving, she has damaged Alex—and she is not really thinking of the cut finger and the slow virus.

And so, because she feels guilty for various things, she accepts when as they are leaving the lab together he asks her to come have coffee, just coffee.

"I feel so lonely," he tells her, as they come out of the building into the agreeably cold air. "You're the only one here I feel connected to."

Carla is touched, in spite of her sureness that this is the most dangerous of all possible approaches. So when they are seated together in a corner of the horrible hospital coffee shop frequented by the medical students, she lets him take her hand in his and press it under the table. There are no other medical students in the coffee shop; most of them are probably still finishing the lab. Carla sighs, trying not to think about sliced brains. The brain is treacherous, Carla thinks, and not only at the outer limits of complexity.

The Secret Lives
of Dieters

Donald loves to cook, even now, when he and Louisa are dieting. He has bought red snapper, leeks, mushrooms, and strawberries for dessert. "How will you make the fish?" asks Polly, who is in love with Donald.

"I'll broil it," he tells her, "with the vegetables and a little white wine and some spices."

"Herbs," Polly suggests.

"And lots of pepper. Dry mustard, coriander." Polly sees that in his mind he is picking jar after jar off a kitchen shelf, shaking each judiciously over the fish, arranged ready for broiling, garlanded with leeks and mushrooms.

Donald has also brought groceries for Polly, who has been home sick with mononucleosis for six weeks. For a while she was very sick, she had her sister taking care of her and there was talk of the hospital, but now she is just weak, recovering, and her sister has gone back to Pasadena. For Polly, Donald has brought canned broth, cottage cheese, fresh bread for her to toast, all suitable for invalids and incidentally dietetic as well, which is not true of the Sara Lee cheesecake. Donald keeps telling her how much he envies her the cheesecake. Polly is small and wiry or now, after the illness, small and a little wasted. She wants to offer Donald a piece of the cheesecake, but she is afraid to rupture what she thinks of as his Louisa-Diet; suppose he hated her for it later?

Donald puts his briefcase on the table next to the bag of groceries. He takes out a folder of papers, work for Polly to do at home over the next few days. Donald and Polly both work for Ground Zero Graphics, and Donald and his girl-friend, Louisa, live in the building across the street from Pol-ly's, on the western slope of Nob Hill in San Francisco. It is during these weeks of her recuperation, with Donald bringing her food and work, that Polly has fallen in love with Donald. After he leaves she goes to the window and pushes the bamboo shade to one side, watching him cross the street with his bag of groceries.

Donald is always willing to talk, to stay awhile; he can probably sense Polly's need for company and conversation, though he doesn't realize how specifically it is *his* company and conversation she desires. He tells her what he is going to make for dinner, what went on at GZG, how he and Louisa are doing on their diet. Before Polly got sick, she and Donald were not particularly close, but these half-therapeutic talks have given them such extensive (if superficial) knowledge of each other that when things turn bad between Donald and Louisa, he does not hesitate to tell Polly all the details. Perhaps he has come to see Polly as a remote spectator, safe in her apartment from any contact with other lives, able to listen and judge and advise. And Polly works the details of Donald's trouble with Louisa into her evening stories; for weeks now, Polly has told herself each evening the story of Donald and Louisa. What they are having for dinner. What they are talking about. Whether they go running, and if so, how far (she sees them set out sometimes, matching their paces, Donald in navy blue sweatpants and a red teeshirt, Louisa in a green warm-up suit). What they watch on television. Whether they make love.

It is the night of the red snapper broiled with leeks, mushrooms, and spices. Louisa is eating with concentration; all she has had all day is a blueberry yogurt and a bagel. Louisa is fifteen pounds overweight by her own reckoning, and she does not look bad, just a little soft around the hips and thighs. Donald is only ten pounds overweight, by his reckoning as well as by the height-and-weight table in the calorie-counting handbook; Louisa wants to be five pounds lighter than the table says she should be.

Donald divides the last little piece of fish between the two of them. He thinks wistfully about sugar and cream for the strawberries, decides not to mention it, just to serve the berries plain.

"There's something I think we should talk about," Louisa says. It is not a casual statement.

"Yes?"

"I think . . ." She pauses, picks up her knife, puts it down neatly across her plate. "Donald, I think we're getting to be too much of a couple."

He tries to get her to explain. They are eating strawberries, without cream and sugar. They spend all their time together, she says, they never do anything with other people, they take for granted that they will eat dinner with each other, go to the movies with each other, sleep with each other.

"You want to go to the movies with someone else," Donald says.

"Well, after all," Louisa says, "it isn't like we're married. Even like we want to be married. I don't want to be married."

"You want to have an affair with someone else," Donald

says. He is staring at the last strawberry, noticing a small mushy place on one shoulder under the collar of little green leaves. "Do you want to have an affair with someone else in particular," he asks, "or just with the next guy who follows you home from the bus stop?"

Louisa takes the last strawberry, mushy place and all, into her mouth, her fingers neatly extracting the stem and leaves as her teeth close on the fruit.

"Someone in particular, huh?" Donald says.

"Yes," Louisa says, "but even if there wasn't someone, I'd still think we were getting to be too much of a couple. I'd still think it would be a good idea for us to see other people."

"Well, but just tell me, who is this other person who just happens to be around, who you just happen to want to sleep with?"

"Someone at work," Louisa says.

Louisa teaches English at a small private high school.

"Michael, the math teacher? I thought he was gay."

"He *is* gay. It isn't Michael." Louisa's tone is patient.

"Well, who is it then?"

"A French teacher," she says.

"Named?"

"Philippe." Louisa leaves the table, goes into the bedroom, closes the door. If she went to the window, she could look across the street and see Polly's bamboo blinds. Behind the blinds, Polly is eating the cheesecake Donald brought her, small square piece after small square piece.

Louisa examines herself in the mirror. The diet is working, she believes it is working, but it doesn't really show yet. She takes out the bobby pins that hold her pale brown hair in a bun, shakes the hair loose over her shoulders. (Is Louisa a cruel and heartless woman? Polly is sure of it.)

Louisa leaves the bedroom, wrapped in a long quilted bathrobe. She sits on the couch, and Donald comes and sits beside her. Finally he says, "Louisa?"

"What?" Her response is too quick; she was unnerved by the sitting in silence.

"Will you promise not to have an affair if I promise to submit my application and my portfolio?"

She has been telling him and telling him to apply for a Master of Fine Arts program; he can study at night and become an illustrator, what he has always wanted to be, and leave Ground Zero Graphics, where he designs restaurant logos and business stationery. Donald has been unwilling to fill out the application, even more unwilling to assemble the portfolio.

"Will you?" he asks again. "Will you promise?"

"Okay, then," Louisa says. "I'll promise if you promise."

Donald takes a deep breath, lets it out. "What do you say I go out and get us some sweets," he says, "just to celebrate?"

"We shouldn't," says Louisa, but she is giggling. Donald is putting on his jacket. "What are you going to have?" she asks.

"Cheesecake," says Donald.

"I'll have the same," says Louisa.

Donald leaves the building, but Polly is no longer sitting behind her blinds watching the street. She is working on the assignments he brought her and is already feeling tired; she is not nearly recovered yet.

Polly thinks of herself as a small dark animal, though since she's been sick, her skin has turned cheesecake white; her hair, though, is very dark and bushy. She braids it into twenty-three tiny braids one day, waiting for Donald. She is no longer a small furry animal, she is a spider. Her apartment is her lair, or her web, it is always dark, and there are mysterious things piled in the corners and complicated woven rope sculptures on the walls. She imagines that her furniture is part of the web; she imagines that if Donald touches the furniture, he will stick to it.

How can she be in love with someone who can be in love with Louisa? Polly's last (and only other) great love was a tall, impossibly thin man with soft blond hair, who programmed computers in very esoteric, very advanced computer languages and ate frozen food while it was still frozen. His favorite food was frozen burritos. He printed out long poems about Polly on his computers and she drew strange spiky sketches of him, one he especially liked on the inside of a frozen burrito box, and finally he accepted a job in Boston and moved East; he still calls her in the middle of the night to tell her he hates his job, he hates Boston, he should never have left San Francisco, he has become a Red Sox fan, he is drinking too much. But that relationship did not surprise Polly; it made sense to her. Since he left, she has been waiting to fall for another sick personality, and instead here she is in love with Donald of Donald-and-Louisa.

"So did you put the portfolio together?" Polly asks.

"Yes. I even hand-carried the whole thing over to the school. I guess I'll have Louisa to thank if I get into this program."

"And her French teacher," Polly says.

Donald has brought canned salmon for Polly, cucumber and tomatoes, heavenly hash ice cream. For himself and Louisa, chicken breasts, string beans, Bing cherries.

"You don't think she pulled all that just to get me to send in my portfolio, do you?" Donald asks, transparently, hopefully.

"No." Polly wonders why he doesn't make some remark about all her little braids. She is a spider, she would like to suck him dry, all the good cooking and gentle self-doubt about his drawing and late-night expeditions for dessert.

Donald replaces the light bulb in Polly's bathroom; earlier, when she got on a chair to fix it herself she felt suddenly vertiginous, the grimy inside of the bathtub tilted up at her, and she grabbed at the medicine chest, carefully stepping down to the floor. It must be the aftereffects of the mono, since she has never had trouble with heights before. She is ashamed of the bathtub, she realizes after Donald has gone to change the bulb. She should have scrubbed out the bathtub. After he leaves she thinks again about scouring powder and sponges, but the thought of bending over the tub makes her nauseous, and it is some time before she feels well enough to eat her salmon salad.

Polly has begun to illustrate the stories she tells herself about Donald and Louisa. In a fresh clean sketchbook, saved in a dresser drawer for some day when she would want it, she has made a series of drawings. Donald cooking. Louisa and Donald eating. Louisa telling Donald about the French teacher. Louisa examining her body in the bedroom mirror (perhaps a little heavier in the picture than she is in life). Louisa and Donald running. The drawings are meticulously detailed, carefully shaded. Polly considers a new illustration: Donald and Louisa making love. Instead she draws Louisa and Philippe, the French teacher, wrapped in a hasty stolen kiss in a supply closet.

The diet is working. Two weeks after Louisa agreed not to have an affair with Philippe, she stands in front of the bedroom mirror again and knows the diet is working. She is only four pounds over the weight given on the chart, nine pounds over what she wants to be.

Donald comes into the bedroom and stands behind her.

"Still too fat," she says.

"Yes, I am," he agrees.

"I meant me."

He pulls a piece of paper out of his back pocket and hands

it to Louisa. It is a letter telling him that though official no-
tification will not be for another month, he has definitely been
approved for his Master of Fine Arts program.

Louisa hugs him.

"And I owe it all to you," he says. "You and your French
teacher." It is the first time either of them has referred to her
promise. Donald draws Louisa back onto the bed. They kiss.

Donald stops kissing Louisa. "You're doing it anyway, aren't
you?" he asks. When she doesn't answer, he says, "You're
having an affair with him anyway, aren't you?"

"Yes," Louisa says, and gets off the bed. She puts on her
bathrobe.

"But I sent in the application and the portfolio." He knows
he sounds silly.

"Was it such a bad thing to make you do that?" Louisa asks
angrily. She leaves the room and he can hear the water running
in the kitchen; she is doing the dishes. Donald lies on the bed,
wondering what Philippe looks like, whether Philippe says
things in French when he is making love to Louisa. Polly
would bet that he does. In her illustrations, Philippe is tall
and dark, his legs are good but his shoulders are too narrow.
Donald has nice broad shoulders. But of course he doesn't
know about Polly's drawings.

What can he do? What does it mean, getting to be too much
of a couple? Is it just an excuse to sleep with Philippe? Donald
could write to the M.F.A. program and withdraw his application, but he knows he won't. He could sneak calories into
the dinners he cooks so Louisa will get fat again, so Philippe
won't want her. Polly draws a fat Louisa, a Louisa crouched
over an enormous pile of French fries. But Donald doesn't
know about Polly's drawings, and he goes on cooking dietetic
dinners and he and Louisa both lose more weight. And Louisa
goes on washing the dishes, doing the laundry, buying toilet

paper and soap. And they do not discuss Philippe. What is there to say? Donald does not get home from Ground Zero Graphics until well after six, even later if he stays at Polly's to talk, and Louisa finishes teaching school at three every day. She can do whatever she likes all afternoon; she is always home when Donald gets there. Donald is hoping, perhaps, that Louisa will begin to feel that she wants them to be more of a couple. They are not at all a couple now, Donald thinks; they do not make love, they do not discuss how she spends her afternoons; they eat the dinners he cooks and watch television. At least he will eventually start that M.F.A. program so he will be busy in the evenings. He is willing to wait Louisa out.

A small steak. Salad. Green peas. For Polly, hot Italian sausages, macaroni salad from the delicatessen, three eclairs. Polly will be coming back to work in two days. It has been a long convalescence, and her muscles are still weak.

"You really have lost weight," she tells Donald.

"Yeah," he says. "The diet's just about over. Louisa is where she wants to be too."

They both hear a double meaning in that sentence (Where, after all, is Louisa; or at least, where has she been all afternoon?), and they do not look at each other. Polly is wondering whether she will still be in love with Donald after she has gone back to work. Is loving him some kind of artificial healthiness to balance out her illness? Why doesn't she have the nerve to tell him that if he wants to get even with Louisa, she, Polly, is ready for an affair? She is afraid he would be ready too, but only because he would be eager to get even with Louisa. Not that he doesn't like Polly, look how kind he has been during her mononucleosis, and look how he confides in her, but Polly knows that he does not think of her as a sexual being. Perhaps she should not have let him come into her apartment; he will associate her forever with sickness and cluttered smells.

The sketchbook of illustrations is almost full. Louisa and Philippe, Louisa and Donald, Donald alone. Louisa alone. But not Polly. She does not belong in those careful drawings.

"What kinds of things will you illustrate when you have the M.F.A.?" Polly asks.

"Children's books, I hope," says Donald, and Polly is pleased and yet annoyed by the ordinariness of his desires and the sincerity with which he expresses them. She has never wanted to illustrate children's books, she would rather make obscene animated films, not that she ever has.

Donald spends a long time in Polly's apartment; she knows he does not want to go home and begin another evening of not being too much of a couple. But finally he leaves, after checking to see that Polly's eclairs were not crushed during his journey from the bakery. She wants to offer him one, but she doesn't; she is angry with him because he is going home to Louisa, because in two days he will no longer be bringing Polly food.

Polly fills the sketchbook. She has a complete set of drawings now: the dissolution of a promising relationship (Donald and Louisa). She does the last few drawings even before Donald tells her the last installment, which in fact takes place that steak-and-salad night. But Polly is as sure of the ending as she was of Donald's ambition. He would want to illustrate children's books. And Louisa will move out. Polly draws Louisa packing. Louisa in the drawing is thin, but graceless.

"I want to move out," Louisa says.

"You're moving in with Philippe."

"Yes. But things weren't working out anyway. I think you really know that."

"Sure. We were getting to be too much of a couple, right?"

"A lot of things," Louisa says. "Listen, if you don't want to understand, then you don't want to understand."

Ridiculously, after dinner she does the dishes. She doesn't begin to throw things into a suitcase like a departing wife in the movies, she doesn't look around the apartment and begin to cry, she doesn't even telephone Philippe and ask him to come get her. She does the dishes.

Donald considers himself in the mirror. He is thin. He will be starting a Master of Fine Arts program. It is as if Louisa has whipped him into shape before leaving him. He is left much the better for her presence in his life, better looking, with new career prospects. He wants to go into the kitchen and smash the dishes and push her head under the faucet. Or maybe make love to her one last time, one unbelievably fabulous and passionate last time, on the kitchen floor perhaps.

He goes to the bedroom window and looks out: Polly's bamboo blinds, though that is not really what he is looking at. She is behind them, drawing the scene he has not yet described to her, but of course he doesn't know that. All he knows is that the unillustrated story is ending, leaving him thin, leaving him about to enter an M.F.A. program, leaving him alone.

Trivia

"Uncle Jack hates me," I said to my mother one morning: an experiment.

"Don't be silly." She leaned over my shoulder, checking my cereal bowl. "Finish up, he'll be here in five minutes."

"Uncle Jack hates me," I said to my Cocoa Puffs, stirring them gently around in their pool of milk.

My mother looked at me sharply and repeated, "Don't be silly." Behind her words I could hear her voice saying: Uncle Jack is a grown-up.

"Name eight different breakfast cereals," Uncle Jack said.

"Cocoa Puffs, Cocoa Krispies, Sugar Smacks, Rice Krispies, Frosted Flakes, Trix, Lucky Charms, Special K," I said, without pausing once.

"Froot Loops!" yelled my sister from the back seat. Uncle Jack and I rarely asked a question she could understand. She was only seven and she was very shy. She admired me, I thought in the beginning, for sitting up in the front seat next to Uncle Jack and answering his questions, not to mention asking my own. The question about the cereals was near the beginning of the summer, when I thought my sister admired me and before Uncle Jack started to hate me.

"Name eight different kinds of cigarettes," I said, and he did. The only ones he smoked were Kents.

During the school year, "Uncle" Jack taught English in a high school two towns over from ours. During the summer, he was head sports counselor for the Hiawatha Day Camp. Every morning that summer he had to pick up my sister Cindy and me and drive us to day camp because he lived only two towns away and there weren't any other children coming from our area so it wasn't worth sending a bus. Some of the girls I had met in the first few days at camp, before I stopped talking to anyone, had said I was really lucky to have Uncle Jack driving me to and from camp every day. They thought he was cute. I tried to think he was cute too for a little while, but it was hopeless. During the day at camp he wore only shorts, and a whistle around his neck. He had a slight potbelly and curly brown hair which was beginning to fall out on the very top of his head.

I was ten years old that summer and my attitude toward day camp had been poor from the beginning. If we let you stay home all summer, you'll do nothing but read and watch television, my mother said. You should be outside. I'll hate it, I said. You'll love it, if you'll only give it a fair chance. Ha.

I knew the real reason they were eager to send me to Hiawatha. They thought it would be good for Cindy to go to day camp, good for her shyness. Also, they didn't want her home over the summer because they were going to paint the house and she would be in the way all the time. But they were afraid to send her alone because she was so shy. I had occasional fantasies about beating up kids who picked on her. Fortunately for us both, it never came up.

"Name five state capitals," Uncle Jack said.

"Trenton," I said. "Albany. Sacramento. Boston. And Bismarck."

"Bismarck?" he asked.

"That's the capital of North Dakota," I said. That was near the beginning of the summer, when I still thought Uncle Jack would like me better if I told him things like that.

He taught me to play "Trivia" the very first day, hoping perhaps that it would enliven the summer-long series of forty-five-minute drives beside a ten-year-old girl. At first we took turns asking questions according to a rigid system; if you answered correctly you got to ask the next question. And at first he asked mostly questions about television or spelling questions or questions like the one about the cereals.

"Spell 'catastrophe,' " I remember he said once, on the fifth day or so. I spelled it. "Where'd you learn to spell like that?" he asked, and I shrugged.

I didn't bring a book to camp for the first few days because I wasn't sure there would be a place to put it. After that I always brought a book and I never put it anywhere. I don't think I have ever again refused so completely to cooperate as I did that summer. I would find a place to read as soon as we got to Hiawatha (the bench behind the rowing pond, the big supply closet in the arts and crafts cabin, or sometimes the picnic tables at which we ate lunch) and I would read until lunch. I would eat lunch with my age group. They didn't bother me; I think none of them was sure who I was. Then, as soon as they went off for their afternoon activities, I would read again until it was time to go home.

My counselor would come and try to reason with me every couple of days. Her name was Bonnie and she tied her ponytails with colored yarn, always the same color on both ponytails. Do you think this is why your parents are paying for you to come here, she asked me, so you can sit and read? If they're paying for me to be here I have a right to read, I said. It doesn't cost Camp Hiawatha any more for me to sit here and read. If you want to call my parents and complain, go ahead. She never did.

The camp director, Uncle Ray, came to reason with me one day early in the summer. He suggested I should just give the camp activities a try. Maybe I would find out that they were more fun than always reading. I had considered telling him that I had a severe heart condition and might drop dead any minute, especially if I had to do activities, but instead I just told him that I was having a great deal of fun, and if he wouldn't let me enjoy myself I would tell my parents and they would take me *and* Cindy out of the camp instead of having us stay for all four two-week sessions. He said he hoped I would think about his suggestion, and I promised I would.

My parents would really have been on Bonnie and Uncle Ray's side, of course. If I could have gotten out of going to Hiawatha by complaining, I would have gotten out. I didn't need poison ivy plants and bugs and screaming kids and lousy lunches to help me read. It was a very new feeling of power for me to be able to fool those grown-ups into thinking my parents were on my side. It was a little scary. It was much scarier, though, when I began to realize that Uncle Jack hated me. No grown-up had ever hated me before, and I wondered if it had something to do with my having fooled Bonnie and Uncle Ray.

Cindy did fine at Hiawatha. In her group of little girls there were three who wouldn't even go in the shallow end of the swimming pool, and two who wouldn't go on nature walks because of snakes, and almost no one would play dodgeball because of getting hit by the ball. All this did a lot to alleviate

Cindy's shyness, and her group spent most of the day on arts and crafts. Cindy was neat and good with her fingers, and almost every day as we started home she showed Uncle Jack something new made of popsicle sticks or papier-mâché or beads or little colored tiles. She also got very good at making lanyards; she made me one of red, blue, and black strips of plastic, and I put a key on it and wore it every day. The key didn't open anything.

In the beginning of the summer she was a little awed by my running game of "Trivia" with Uncle Jack. It seems likely that she sensed the developing tension. By the end of the first week or so she would get into the back seat of the car, press the side of her face against the window, and begin to sing to herself. She would sing steadily until we got to Hiawatha. And she certainly didn't need my protection when we got there.

Uncle Jack was not really threatened, I think, by my skill with brand names, or even with current movies ("Name three movies with Dustin Hoffman in them"). But in those areas I stumped him as often as he stumped me, and he resolved, I suppose, to show me that he had regions of expertise. I had just asked him to name the two main characters in *West Side Story*. He had a little trouble with Tony (he got Maria right away, of course, because of the song), but he finally remembered.

"Okay," he said, "if you're so smart, what are Romeo and Juliet's last names?"

"Montague and Capulet," I said, without much interest. "What are the two gangs called in *West Side Story*?"

I did not realize that I had shaken him; I thought at first he was just annoyed because he could not remember the names of the gangs (Jets and Sharks, I finally had to tell him), but then I began to wonder if he was getting tired of the game, because he didn't seem to want to ask any more questions. But the next day he started right in with Shakespeare. And although within a very few days I had realized that he did not want me to be able to answer his questions, it was not until years later that I began to understand in retrospect how precious his high-school-teacher intellectualism was to him, and how tenuous.

His Shakespeare questions, of course, were babyish. In what play does someone say, "Beware the ides of March"? What country was Hamlet prince of? What does Caesar say just before he dies? I was a little surprised by how easy the questions were; Uncle Jack had been as erudite as I on such subjects as brands of shampoo, but most of his questions on Shakespeare were about lines I had known before I had ever read or seen the plays. When I finally got around to studying Shakespeare in high school, of course, those same questions turned up on every quiz, and as I accumulated that set of perfect scores, I grew to understand a little more of Uncle Jack's frustration with me. He had no other way to understand Shakespeare, but for some reason, I sensed even then, Shakespeare *mattered* to him.

He tried me on the rest of high school English.

"Who wrote *Wuthering Heights*?"

"Emily Brontë. Her sister Charlotte wrote *Jane Eyre*." I had begun to elaborate unnecessarily, though I no longer thought it would please him.

"What book is Mr. Micawber in?"

"*David Copperfield* by Charles Dickens." I had seen the movie on television. I had actually been considering reading the book later on in the summer, but I decided against it because I felt that if Uncle Jack saw me carrying it he would know I hadn't read it before, which would somehow be a victory for him.

*   *   *

He did win one very distinct victory, but I spoiled it. He had the bright idea of starting in on me one day with sports trivia: Who holds the record for most scoreless innings pitched? What's the most famous double-play combination in the history of baseball? Name the positions on a football team. I couldn't get a single one, so I didn't win the right to ask any questions of my own. For almost the whole ride he reeled off question after question, and finally I said,

"I don't know anything about sports. I'm a girl."

He did not ask me any more questions about sports. I was pleased that I had said that instead of (my contingency plan) going to the library on Sunday and getting out some books on sports records. I hadn't realized yet that he hated me. I thought he would be impressed if I suddenly knew all about sports. Secretly, though, I think I knew that he was not enjoying the game. I was teasing him with my answers, but I was relying on my right as a child to tease an adult with impunity, or at worst, with no stronger penalty than momentary irritation.

But I was beginning to feel that each time I got into the car Uncle Jack welcomed me with something more than the avuncular good counselorship he was paid to manifest. He was too eager to begin the new round of "Trivia," and I had the impression he was studying at home. He would go back to plays he had asked me about days ago and ask slightly more obscure questions. Who says, "This above all: to thine own self be true"? Whom is he talking to? They weren't questions I had to study for. And he was altogether too pleased when he managed to stump me. There is a strict etiquette by which grown-ups have to be good sports when they compete with children. They aren't supposed to say, "Guess you're not so smart." And with those words, used once too often by Uncle

Jack, came the first truly dazzling revelation for me, one morning as I stared out at the highway. No, *I* guess *you're* not so
smart. I didn't say anything, of course. But I knew it beyond
all possible doubt.

About some things, of course, I wasn't all that smart. I was
still reluctant to believe that a grown-up could hate me. I
thought Uncle Jack should admire me. As time went on, I
realized that he was just going to hate me more and more, but
though this terrified me, it also made getting the right answers
even more important to me. One morning in the car I actually
broke down and cried when I couldn't remember the name of
the woods that came to Dunsinane. Uncle Jack was very kind;
he gave me a clean handkerchief, and I could feel Cindy staring
at me from the back seat.

I discovered a truly wonderful place to read at Camp Hiawatha. I could row the rowboat out into the middle of the
lake and sit in it for hours. When I wanted to, I could put
my book down and imagine I was an Indian in a canoe (Who
wrote the poem "Hiawatha"? What are the first two lines?),
or a survivor of the *Titanic* adrift in a lifeboat, or a refugee
from the Nazis. No one else at the day camp used the rowboat
because no one else at the camp ever did anything unless a
whole age group could do it together. There was only one
rowboat. It wasn't in very good shape, but it didn't leak. The
rowing pond was small and stagnant. I was somewhat con-
spicuous, sitting in the boat in the middle of the pond, but
people got used to me. Uncle Ray never even checked to see
whether I could swim. I wondered whether he was hoping I
would drown; I was beginning to wonder whether all sorts of
grown-ups hated me.

I have never been able to refuse to cooperate without alien-
ating people. That summer was my first experience of the

process: I was certainly strong enough, I was stubborn as a mule, I got sharp pleasure from my victories, I scared overtly stronger opponents, but I also made them all hate me. I had no doubts then that it was worth it, though I felt some bewilderment about the hatred. The lack of doubts and the vague bewilderment persist in me, though I am not sure I would enjoy the hours in the rowboat quite so much today; I would probably be too conscious of people going by on the shore.

The summer did not come to an end; it was a very long summer. It was tense rides in Uncle Jack's car and books in the rowboat. My parents were pleased by how tan I was getting, clear evidence of outdoor exercise. I was becoming frightened of Uncle Jack, not just of his hatred. I could not stop answering his questions correctly almost every time. I wondered whether he might hit me someday. I would never get in his car again if he hit me. But I wasn't sure I could ever go home again either if Cindy saw him hit me; I felt the shame would be too great. He didn't hit me, of course.

He could have stopped the game. He knew I would get most of his questions, but masochistically he kept laying his puny literary expertise before me.

"Who wrote 'The Rime of the Ancient Mariner'?"

"I can tell you the first verse too."

We were in many ways oddly well matched. I went at plays and poems much the way he did, memorizing odd lines and authors' names. But I was better at it. Most of the questions I asked him were about TV shows and commercials or comic-book heroes. He answered about as many of my questions as I did of his. I knew that I could ask questions he wouldn't be able to answer; he had never heard of many of the books I was bringing to camp, and since they were almost all off my parents' shelves, I knew they would "count." But at the same time that I could not stop giving him one correct answer after another, I could not start asking that type of question.

In a way I did not really want the summer to end. I knew the rules of my day very thoroughly: There was the stubborn fear with which I answered each one of Uncle Jack's questions, there was the pleasant fear when I managed to convince myself the rowboat was adrift on an icy ocean, and there was the bored blankness with which I answered my mother each evening when she asked whether I'd had a nice day at camp. The rhythm of the summer had become familiar, but behind it was some change waiting. I could feel it especially when I had answered a string of Uncle Jack's questions and knew that he was hating me; for the summer it was enough to know that he hated me and yet to continue answering his questions, but soon, I sensed, I would be expected to acknowledge hatred from a grown-up and do something about it. This idea frightened me more than Uncle Jack's hatred, and I comforted myself with the words my mother had not said: You're a child, he's a grown-up, don't be silly.

I was not completely relieved when my parents decided to take us to Virginia for the last two weeks of the summer because they had finished painting the house ahead of schedule. My mother asked whether I was sorry to stop going to camp and I said no. She was a little disappointed. Cindy was effusively sorry. She didn't see why we had to go to Virginia. She didn't want to see Williamsburg. Or the Luray Caverns. Or stay in a motel. I was eager to stay in a motel, though the rest of the program left me pretty cold too. But I was worried about the changes which might happen in my family once my parents realized that I was someone a grown-up could hate.

But all my fear and foreboding did not keep me from feeling that it was a victory for me over Uncle Jack that I should be leaving Hiawatha while he still had two weeks to go there.

He would drive there alone every morning, perhaps thinking of questions he could have asked me. The whole last week I barely missed a single question. And they had gotten a lot harder—I was sure he was studying.

The very last day, though, they were suddenly movie questions again, and I wondered whether he was somehow trying to tell me that he didn't hate me after all. We had long ago dropped our strict system of trading questions, and I let him ask one after another that day.

"What's the name of the actress on *Green Acres*?"

"Eva Gabor."

"What's her sister's name?"

"Which one?"

"The famous one."

"Zsa Zsa."

It took me a while to pick up the pattern.

"Name two movies with Raquel Welch in them."

"Who played Barbarella?" (I didn't know that one.)

"What color hair did Marilyn Monroe have?"

His questions got harder. I couldn't answer a lot of them.

"Two Jayne Mansfield movies?"

"Who was 'The Sweater Girl'?"

Guess you're not so smart, he said, every time I admitted I didn't know. I thought of the day he had tried sports; how could I say I wasn't supposed to know about beautiful actresses? Then I suddenly got one he wasn't expecting me to get: Name two of Marilyn Monroe's husbands.

"Joe DiMaggio and Arthur Miller," I said; I had been almost ready to cry at my long string of ignorances. He had been all ready to say, Guess you're not so smart, I could feel it. I looked out the window. We were almost home, and then I would never have to see him again, and I was suddenly delighted to be going to Virginia.

"Guess you think you're pretty smart," he said then, and I

was frightened because he never said that. "Well," he said, sounding good-natured, "I guess you better work on being smart, because you sure are never going to be anything else. Suppose that's why you aren't too good on movie stars? Maybe an ugly little girl who's going to grow up an ugly woman just isn't too interested in watching the pretty ones."

I wanted to look around and see if Cindy was listening. I knew we were getting near my house. If she told my parents what Uncle Jack had said, I would run right out of the house.

"I guess," Uncle Jack went on, breathing harder now, "I guess that maybe you won't have to feel too sorry for yourself. You'll feel better because you're sort of smart." He was slowing down to turn the corner onto our street. I looked at him. He was still breathing a little more loudly than usual, but he was smiling.

"The people I feel sorry for are the ones who are stupid and ugly both!" I said loudly. Breaking rules I had learned before I could remember learning them, I pulled open the car door while the car was still moving. "Like you!" I said, and jumped out of the car. It had been moving very slowly indeed, but I still skinned both my knees. I ran home, easily beating the car. Locked in the bathroom, I could hear Cindy come in and the car drive away.

I avoided the bathroom mirror as I washed my knees in cold water. Then I washed my face. I was almost giddy with the spiteful triumph of having said *that* to Uncle Jack, as well as with the stored-up triumph of all my right answers all through the summer. But even while I giggled to myself at the thought of my leap from the car, the memory of what Uncle Jack had said was behind my pleasure, as if I knew, even then, that I would need all my spite if I wanted to keep winning.

In Africa

"There's something I need you to tell me honestly," Frances says, and Marc is immediately sure she is going to ask about his love life while she was away in Africa. Frances takes a breath and continues, "How do I come off—how do I *seem* to other people?"

Marc pictures her as she was a week before at a party they went to, a party given by a famous old professor in his department. Frances sat in a circle of younger faculty and graduate students, and she told stories about Africa, and once when Marc looked over from his own conversation with the famous professor's wife, who likes him very much, he saw Frances, talking fast and flushed with the momentum of her own story, looking as if she was about to break into loud laughter. He could not really hear her voice over the general hum, but he imagined that it was loud and maybe a little bit shrill. From where he stood she was easily the most vivid person in her circle, but also somehow coarse, her features red and fleshy, a mist of warm excitement surrounding her like a not entirely kind floodlight. He stared at her for those few seconds, reminding himself that she was Frances, his own love, come home to him after a year in Africa, and then he turned back to the wife of the famous professor.

"You seem fine, just like always," Marc tells Frances, a little heartily, remembering that party.

Frances shakes her head. "I don't know, I feel like ever since I came back . . ." Her voice trails off and they let the conversation end. Together, they go into their kitchen and begin making dinner, hamburgers with melted Gorgonzola cheese on top, and salad. They do not usually cook elaborate meals, but everything they make tastes very good; friends have remarked on this. As she crumbles the cheese onto the sizzling hamburgers, Frances says, "This is what I missed most, you know, just domestic pleasures, like cooking together."

Yes, Marc thinks, with sudden savagery, but what kinds of pleasures did you have to console yourself with?

Without any reason or right (considering his own record, that is) Marc has become fiercely jealous of the lovers he has imagined for Frances, lovers she might have had during that year she was in Africa. She has told him nothing at all about any lovers, she has scrupulously dropped no hints at all, while he has been somewhat less meticulous. (Of course, she was all the way across the world while he was still here in this same apartment in Boston, so is he really to blame if she comes across some sign of a woman who visited him?) But Frances has said nothing about Marc and any signs she may have seen, and nothing about herself, so Marc has been left to invent her lovers, and he has done a thorough job of it, including a fitting and horrible death for each of them.

The do-good white man (Peace Corps, maybe) who ends up put against a wall and shot by the villagers he thought were his friends.

The Oxford-educated African who returns to help his peo-

ple and is caught by some fatal tropical disease to which he
has lost all his resistance during his years in England.

The happy-go-lucky tourist boy, ambling across Africa by
bus, robbed and murdered in some dirt-cheap hotel (where,
the day before, on the flea-infested bed, he and Frances, et
cetera, et cetera).

Marc rehearses these deaths in his mind, secure that if a
new possibility occurs to him, a new possible lover for Frances,
he will be able to invent the appropriate death.

While Frances was in Africa, Marc did very well indeed,
at least professionally. His dissertation was published as a
book, years earlier than most people expected, earlier in fact
than he had really let himself expect, and it got some very
nice reviews, and he has begun to wonder whether there might
be some very slim chance for tenure, even in these times, even
in this notorious department which never tenures junior faculty members. Also, he was given a course to teach on comparative European governments, and thanks to his reputation
as a lecturer, the course swelled from its usual fifty students
to almost a hundred. He was unable to keep from writing
about this to Frances in Africa, confessing that he found himself looking down from the podium and gleefully counting
heads.

So things went well for Marc. The apartment seemed empty
to him sometimes, and he often lay awake at night (and not
only when he was alone, either) and tried to picture Frances,
converting the time change in his head to calculate what she
might be doing. Frances in a small African village, sampling
the wells. Frances inspecting a large dam. Frances in a government office. But he could never picture it properly, he
could never really imagine what Africa looked like and felt
like, and he waited for Frances to write: Come meet me for a

couple of weeks at Christmas. But she never wrote it and for some reason he didn't suggest it either; he went home to see his family in Connecticut for a week and then, guiltily, met the woman he was having an affair with for a week of skiing in Vermont. (Frances doesn't ski and has said she has no desire to learn. What did she do at Christmas, and with whom?)

The invitation to spend the year in Africa, consulting on a series of water purification projects which were all connected to one particular international agency, came about naturally enough, considering the other work Frances had done, the articles she had published, the connections she had made. But Marc believes Frances would never have considered leaving him for a whole year if not for the miscarriage. He has, however, never asked her point-blank about this, perhaps because he is afraid that she will tell him, no, I would have gone anyway, I have always been waiting for an opportunity like this.

As they eat their hamburgers with Gorgonzola, Marc is tempted to ask this question which he has never asked. He thinks of saying something about perspective, how her question about how she comes off reflects an uncertainty in her own perspective. And that will lead with a kind of fake free-association into a remark about whether she would have gone to Africa if not for the miscarriage and how that reflects his perspective on their whole relationship.

He takes more salad, considers the structure of conversation he has created inside his head, and rejects it as tortured, ridiculous. Instead he says, "Speaking of domestic pleasures, what we could do this evening is open that fancy bottle of wine my parents gave us and get a little high."

He knows that Frances will interpret this (correctly) as an invitation to spend part of the evening making love, and so he is momentarily reassured (about everything) when she smiles across the table at him and says, "I think that would be lovely. Speaking of domestic pleasures."

Marc had any number of affairs while Frances was away, more than in any other year of his life (his life before Frances, that is, when he was a single man who had affairs of varying intensities and was not part of a long-term couple). By anybody's standards, in fact, he behaved rather badly while Frances was in Africa, taking up almost any woman who showed the slightest bit of interest. A couple of graduate students, even an undergraduate in his lecture course who called him up after the final exam. Several women he met at parties, one he met in a bar, one he met on an airplane. There were even moments when he thought the wife of that famous professor who gave the party was interested (twenty years older than Marc, devoted to her famous husband—Marc dismissed the thought). One-night stands and two-night stands and several fairly serious involvements and a multitude of friendly casual call-me-and-we'll-spend-the-night-together arrangements.

He was a bit amazed that it all happened so easily, came to take for granted that it was because he had Frances, who was thousands of miles away but would eventually be coming back; that's why he could relax and let it happen. Maybe some of the women liked him better because they knew about Frances too, because it meant they could dally with him and then move on. Of course, right before Frances came home he had to end what had become a very intense affair with a woman he sometimes thought he had fallen in love with, Lisa Ann. He even wondered if he would ultimately break up with Frances and live happily ever after with the other woman, but then Frances arrived and he found he hardly even thought about Lisa Ann, and three weeks later when he called her to see how she was doing, a man answered the phone, so Marc hung up. So maybe even that relationship was not as serious as he thought.

Lately though—now that Frances has been home for almost two months—Marc finds himself thinking occasionally about Lisa Ann, thinking he should really call her again, even thinking maybe they could steal an afternoon together, especially if she now also has someone she would be deceiving.

The miscarriage was a very sad thing, though in some ways all for the best. Frances did not want a child, was not ready for a baby as she said, suggesting of course that sooner or later she would be. She might never even have known she was pregnant, except for scrupulous record-keeping; they got the positive pregnancy-test results when she was six weeks pregnant, and the miscarriage happened two weeks later, just like a heavy menstrual period. Marc was ready for a baby and had been delighted to find that Frances, not ready, was still willing to go through the pregnancy, have the baby. I can't really see aborting our child, she had said to him, so they had two weeks of believing they were going to be parents. They decided to get married, they made love a lot. And then the miscarriage, and a month after that she said yes to this sudden invitation and began getting ready to go to Africa.

After the miscarriage, before she left, they were very gentle with each other, and they never said, for example (Marc to Frances), you never wanted it, you rejected it from your body, or (Frances to Marc), oh well, it's all for the best really, and now I can go to Africa.

It really is true, Marc thinks, as he uncorks the fancy bottle of wine, that since her return Frances is different in public. It is as if during that year, when she did heaven only knows what (and with heaven only knows whom) in strange circumstances which he cannot even picture, Frances lost the ability to behave normally in what ought to be her own natural surroundings. Alone with him, she is very much as he remembers her, but when she is with other people there is something a little off about her. You watch her and you are sure that everyone else in the room will remember her, will carry away a picture of her, vivid and loud and emphatic and warm, steaming in the temperate air of a New England autumn as if she were in an equatorial country.

Marc and Frances drink the wine, sitting together on the rug, leaning against the couch, listening to Mozart. They finish the bottle and make love, and all the time Marc cannot stop picturing her as she was at that party. Frances, however, seems to enjoy the evening without any further doubts about herself—but would he know if she had them? Finally they sit wrapped together in a quilt and she says, dreamily, "I remember once last year, I was visiting this Peace Corps volunteer in this tiny village in the middle of nowhere, and I had brought out a package for him that someone had sent from the States. And when he opened it, guess what it was? His mother had sent him these canned Mexican foods. So we ate them, he insisted on my sharing them because he said they wouldn't mean anything to anyone else in the village. In fact, they tasted pretty terrible, but I sort of knew what he meant anyway. So we had canned enchiladas, canned refried beans with chili sauce, you know. Can you imagine? In the middle of Africa, we're sitting there eating canned enchiladas!"

It is the first story she has told about Africa which fits in with any of Marc's suspicious imaginings; immediately he is sure that she has thought of the story because after the enchiladas she and the Peace Corps volunteer ended up naked, wrapped in a blanket, as he and Frances are now.

"Why were you visiting him?" Marc asks, his voice light.

"Oh, because he was working on this local water purification system I needed to see. He was sort of silly, but he meant well. But can you imagine, that desperation for a little treat, the way he licked the sauce out of the cans?"

Marc thinks he understands now that she has in fact told the story because it is the exact antithesis of the evening the two of them have just spent; it is the story of a hopeless searching for domestic comfort in an alien environment. But how did that other evening end?

This particular evening ends with the two of them taking a long shower together and getting into bed, without either of them veering off, as they are sometimes inclined to do, to work for an hour or two into the night. Frances falls asleep immediately, Marc is awake only long enough to think: Killed by the villagers he thought were his friends.

The next day, for no reason he quite understands, Marc calls Lisa Ann, and this time she herself answers the phone, not a man.

"I was thinking we could have coffee or something," he tells her.

"I don't know," she says hesitantly, and Marc realizes sharply that Frances would certainly have said, "*Or something* indeed, is that what they call it nowadays?" Or something like that. He is filled with a remarkable longing for Lisa Ann, a thin well-dressed woman who edits a medical magazine, who lives in a bright immaculate apartment which he knows very well, who hates to cook and likes to eat in fancy restaurants where she always orders the most expensive thing on the menu, which she then pays for herself, scrupulously fair. (But where does she get all her money? Her editing job cannot pay all that well, can it? Lisa Ann too may have complicated corners of her life where Marc cannot follow her, he supposes gloomily.)

"Please," Marc urges her, over the phone. "I miss you, I need to talk to you." He imagines how they will go to her apartment together after their drink, how he will emerge later, triumphant in his own secrets, to go home to Frances.

"No," Lisa Ann says, "I just don't think it's a good idea." And then when he presses again, "No, Marc, no way. I am not here for your emotional convenience." And she hangs up on him.

So it is Frances whom Marc meets that evening for a drink and for dinner, Frances looking cheerful and a little tired at the end of a long day, wearing a red corduroy dress that she has had, Marc thinks fondly, almost as long as he has known her. Frances is not delicate and beautifully dressed like Lisa Ann, but as she greets him in the bar of the restaurant there is a strength and health and comfort about her that he finds welcoming and warming. What does it matter what she did while she was away, he almost certainly did worse.

And then they are joined by two graduate students Marc knows. In fact, embarrassingly enough, the woman is someone he went to bed with a couple of times while Frances was in Africa. And here she is out with another graduate student, looking very much a couple in this rather pricey restaurant. And here he is with Frances, and for a few minutes, as the four of them order drinks, Marc feels exceedingly content, as if all is working out smoothly, couples forming with no ragged edges, everyone provided for, love and drink and food enough to go around. He wants to put an arm around Frances, but then wonders if that would somehow (how, exactly?) be in bad taste.

He watches the graduate student, Myra, a rather wispy young woman with blond permed curls and a pleasant giggle, and it dawns on him that she is in fact extremely ill at ease, whether because she is embarrassed to see Marc or because she is embarrassed to be seen by him with her current companion. She is telling a story, talking too fast, about an undergraduate who offered her five hundred dollars to change his grade. Marc remembers her giggling in bed and says, teasing, they never offer me money, only their bodies. And then immediately he thinks, talk about bad taste, but he does not stop watching Myra, who will not meet his eyes. So he looks away, into the mirror over the bar, and in the mirror he inspects Frances. He thinks of the story she will surely tell now, her story about bribing a corrupt official somewhere in Africa, and how the story will end with Frances waving her arms, almost yelling, imitating an outraged bureaucrat. She will tell her story and her features will coarsen, and she will no longer look attractive and welcoming, she will look like a neon sign blinking a little desperately in the smoky light of the bar. And she won't know what she looks like any more than Marc knows what she did that year in Africa. She may suspect, as he suspects, but she can't know.

He watches her carefully in the mirror, waiting for the story to begin, and finally he does put his arm around her after all, and she looks directly into his eyes, and he wonders whether she knows he is waiting for her to tell that story. She will tell it anyway, though, he thinks, and he tightens his arm on her shoulders, and Frances smiles at him, almost gratefully, as if she does indeed, right at that moment, suspect.

Clytemnestra
in the Suburbs

Clytemnestra Bernstein is hiding in the closet. Her handsome but no-good boyfriend, Guy, is prowling around the basement of their comfortable suburban home, probably taking pictures of the wood-grain washer-dryer. Clytemnestra is hiding because she wants to relish her stolen goods.

She was in the ShopRite, comparison-shopping for marshmallow cookies covered with pink coconut (believe it or not, there were three brands), when it occurred to her that she could put little things into the big front pocket of her smock, bigger things into her big straw basket purse. She stood in line for the computerized cash register with raspberry Jell-O, capers, maraschino cherries, and macadamia nuts in her smock pocket, with cheddar cheese soup, sugar-frosted bran cereal, and ketchup in her purse. She paid for the marshmallow cookies, and in fact she bought the most-expensive-per-cookie brand; they looked a little pinker and a little fluffier.

In the closet, Clytemnestra eats capers, cereal, cherries, and macadamia nuts. She likes the way the nuts mingle with the aftertaste of the cherries. Tonight she will make cheddar cheese soup for Guy and herself, raspberry Jell-O for dessert. Let him photograph that if he wants to.

In fact, he wants to, he photographs the Jell-O. There will be a PTA meeting tomorrow night, he tells Clytemnestra, breaststroking around the table to get the angles for interesting light effects on the surface of the Jell-O. You want to go to a PTA meeting, Clytemnestra says. Shall we invent a name for our child?

Iphigenia, if it's a girl, Guy says, of course. He gets carried away. Iphigenia if. If only Iphigenia. And, of course, if you want a son—

Yes, I know, she says. Orestes. He killed his mother, didn't he?

Okay, says Guy. Iphigenia it is. He has found an angle on the Jell-O that really pleases him. Clytemnestra imagines his close-up lens falling plop into the shimmering raspberry. I stole that Jell-O, she thinks happily. What do you wear to a PTA meeting?

At the PTA meeting Guy asks permission to take pictures. He tells the PTA people that he is making a collection of photos of the new life he and Clytemnestra are discovering together in this lovely town, he wants to send the pictures to his parents to show them that he and Clytemnestra have truly left the city and found the good life. Clytemnestra can't believe the PTA people will accept this. But she hasn't reckoned on the contempt they feel for the city, their anxiousness to hear that newcomers agree, the perfect way to live is here. The PTA people pose and pose but finally get down to business, and Guy is able to move quietly along the wall and take the pictures he wants.

"So, Temmie," says the president of the PTA, "you will have a child in our school next year?" They are eating cookies (oatmeal cookies, not a trace of pink coconut) and drinking coffee.

"Yes," says Clytemnestra. "Jenny." But in her mind it is

Genie. "She stayed with my parents to finish out the term."
How did she ever come up with a statement like that? Look
how the PTA president is nodding, smiling, agreeing that it's
better not to move children in the middle of the school year.

I got great pictures, Guy tells Clytemnestra that night. Did
you see some of those people? Jesus, no one's going to believe
they're real. He reaches out for Clytemnestra. Come on, Temmie. Let's have a hot New York screw. Let's show them how
it's done in the city.

Clytemnestra slings her big straw purse over her shoulder.
This time it will be premeditated theft. Is there a distinction:
second-degree shoplifting versus first-degree? And this time
she makes two stops. First the card shop (card shoppe, actually). Matching paper cups and paper plates, all decorated
in red, white, and blue (July Fourth is only three months
away). A stuffed Snoopy doll (for Genie, of course). She pays
for a birthday card (it is not going to be anyone's birthday
soon). Then she moves along the street, rejecting the liquor
store as too risky, and goes into the little dress shop. A long
consultation with the saleslady: Do they have a somewhat
longer skirt (Clytemnestra is tall) in that same shade of turquoise, that same coarse cotton? The saleslady doubts it, goes
back to look. Into Clytemnestra's purse goes a red velour shirt.
The saleslady returns, dejected. No, there is no such skirt.
But try again, the saleslady suggests, as if it might suddenly
materialize.

Guy has been out at the golf course taking pictures. He is
excited about an invitation he has obtained to an American
Legion meeting. What could be better? This book, he tells
Clytemnestra, is going to be fabulous. That probably means
more big-city screwing; when his work is going well he gives
generously of himself, when his work is going badly, he needs
all his energies for his artistic anguish. Well, good. Screwing

is one of Guy's talents. Photography, to be fair, is another.

They are living, Guy and Clytemnestra, partially on Guy's advance. A publisher is eager to put out the book that will show once and for all the amazing insipidity and emptiness of life in the American suburbs. The photographs will evince a wry wit, an eye for the black humor of everyday life, and all the other qualities people find in Guy's work. And what about the wry wit of placing Clytemnestra Bernstein in a little suburban town for four months? What a sense of humor Guy has.

Guy rarely takes pictures of Clytemnestra. For his models he usually likes heavy-fleshed women, and Clytemnestra is thin. He likes women who sink into round poses, and Clytemnestra folds herself into angles. In his pictures of the heavy women there is always a mocking shade, as if Guy's handsome face and body were visible in the corner: Contrast the photographer with his models.

Why is Guy living with Clytemnestra? She does not torment herself with the question anymore. Before she knew how deep-down no-good Guy is, she wondered constantly: Was there something wonderful about herself that she had missed? Was she really a muse? But now she does not wonder about such things; she wonders only when Guy will leave her, will try to hurt her, and plots her own response (but notice please that she does not plan to leave him first).

They are becoming more and more caught up in the life of the suburb. A Recreation Commission fair. The senior class play at the high school. Two open houses and a housewarming. Life in the fast lane, says Guy. Life in the nine-items-or-less lane, says Clytemnestra, but he doesn't get it so he ignores it. Guy is known as a camera nut, always taking pictures. Candid shots of everyone. Frequently people ask him for copies. He makes prints for them of the posed pictures, which do not interest him.

Clytemnestra shoplifts. She has never done this before. She has always been law-abiding, unless you count marijuana or double-parking (well, once she lied on her income tax). She loves coming back to her comfortable suburban home with her pockets and pocketbook full. She investigates new stores: books (easy), records (hard), shoes (impossible, but she does get away with a pair of silver socks).

At the end of May the town pool opens. Guy and Clytemnestra go down and she lies on her towel in her blue two-piece bathing suit ("How *do* you stay so skinny?" asks a woman from the PTA, settling down beside her) while he takes photographs in his tight black bikini bathing suit, cameras swinging against his naked chest. Women squeal, but they pose. Hey, watch it, a man calls, what are you going to do with a picture of my wife in a bathing suit? Everyone laughs. Everyone seems to like Guy. They can't see he's no good, apparently.

The sun is unexpectedly hot. Roasting to death, Clytemnestra thinks. Then she thinks of Iphigenia, her daugher Genie. Genie will enjoy the pool when she comes. The woman from the PTA is very sympathetic; how Temmie must miss her daughter! Yes, Clytemnestra thinks, I do miss her. I have to get her some new clothes.

In the clothing store, Clytemnestra gets almost an entire wardrobe for a girl of seven into her straw bag. She pays for only a little teeshirt with a frog on it. She agrees with the saleslady that the teeshirt is absolutely precious. Back home, Clytemnestra stores the clothing in the dresser in the second bedroom. The walls look a little dingy to her, and she makes up her mind to buy paint (it would be impossible to steal enough paint, all of the same color).

Clytemnestra paints the little bedroom a nice pale blue. As she paints, she thinks about curtains and bedspreads. Guy wanders in and takes pictures of Clytemnestra painting. I don't know, Temmie, he says, I hope the landlord isn't going to be pissed. He doesn't ask her why she is painting; it is part of Guy's credo to accept eccentric actions. After all, he is an artist. Clytemnestra feels like an artist herself as the walls dry smooth and perfectly blue. A pink spread on the bed with white tassels that hang down to the floor. The Snoopy doll perched on the pillow.

One day Clytemnestra sees a picture that includes her own figure. It is one of the pictures Guy took the day the swimming pool opened. There she is, Clytemnestra Bernstein, stretched out next to the PTA lady, thin suburban wife next to fat suburban wife, both of them baking down at the pool. Then there is a picture of Clytemnestra painting the bedroom, hair up under a kerchief, view past her out the window showing the house next door.

Clytemnestra is slowly but surely filling the bookcase in Genie's room, accumulating stuffed animals for the bed. Guy doesn't go into that room, because there is no reason for him to go into an empty bedroom. Getting daring, Clytemnestra steals a big Raggedy Ann doll; it is too big for her to stuff it conveniently into her straw bag, so she drapes her towel (she is on her way back from the pool) over it and moves quickly out the door, keeping her back to the saleslady who is, in any case, busy harassing two small boys: Are they going to buy anything?

Guy spreads out some of the prints he likes best. Proud homeowners in their gardens. American Legion members around a table. The flag over the Recreation Commission. Mothers with babies in the park, the mothers wearing culottes, the babies crying in their strollers. The cheerleaders at the high school. And all done with that quality of mockery that will make this book so definitely not the photograph album of the good life that all their neighbors think Guy is assembling.

Some people are confused when Guy and Clytemnestra show up at the high school graduation ceremonies. Do they have a relative graduating? Guy, handsome and smooth, manages to give everyone the impression that he is there doing someone a favor, photographing the big event for close friends with a graduating child. Clytemnestra, watching the rows of slightly cynical students in the late afternoon sun, can see that these will be good photographs for Guy's book: the robes, the mortarboards, the acne, the parents in pantsuits. All of Guy's pictures, it seems to Clytemnestra, have this effect: They make you ashamed of the pictures you might want to save. They mock graduations or nice days down at the pool so that when you look through your album you can no longer take pleasure in your own memories.

Clytemnestra steals a purse that someone has left on a folding chair. All the parents are pressing up to the front to take pictures of the procession (Guy is, naturally, taking pictures of the parents taking their pictures), and no one sees Clytemnestra slip the little purse into her big bag. Back in her own folding chair, she opens the little purse. She takes out two twenty-dollar bills. When the ceremony is over, she decides, she will pick a likely-looking graduate and give him or her the money. And so she does. In fact, she presses the money into the palm of the valedictorian, a short girl with frizzy blond hair, who is so rattled by her own successfully delivered speech that she does not even really notice Clytemnestra; mechanically the valedictorian smiles and says thank you, then goes on accepting the congratulations of her classmates, their parents, and the high school teachers. Clytemnestra offers the money as apology for the picture of the valedictorian that will surely appear in Guy's book. He may even have noted down a fragment of her speech to use as a caption, "We cannot wait to see what the future will hold for us because it is we who will determine the future," perhaps. As she is leaving the grounds of the high school, Clytemnestra lets the little stolen purse drop behind a bush.

That night, after the graduation, Guy devotes himself to Clytemnestra's ecstasy. Is that good, Temmie, he keeps asking, and it is. And it gets better and better. He must have been really pleased with the pictures of the graduation. Clytemnestra lies there, wondering again how she deserves Guy, how she deserves such a handsome skilled man, even if he is no good. Even if he is going to hurt her someday, probably someday soon. Through the open window Clytemnestra can hear the sounds of the graduation block party. Probably Guy wishes he were at the party (it amuses Clytemnestra to imagine Guy wandering around the party, through the miasma of adolescent hormones, snapping clever pictures).

The next day he begins to talk about having a barbecue. They could repay all the invitations, all the open houses and cocktail parties. There is a grill in the backyard, they can buy charcoal and steaks and corn on the cob. Clytemnestra listens to him planning it. That's not fair, she wants to say, now you're posing the pictures. She can just imagine herself in the photos he will take: the hostess of the barbecue. She sits for a while in Genie's room, thinking that the children will probably prefer hot dogs to steaks.

Then Clytemnestra goes out for a walk. It is just getting dark. She walks around the famously safe streets, smelling the neatly planted trees. It is time for me to go back to the city, she is thinking. She is still thinking it as she turns up a strange driveway and goes back behind a house she does not know. The house is completely dark. The back door is open and no dog comes to meet her. Tiptoeing around in the dark, Clytemnestra helps herself to a small silver bowl, a cassette tape player, a necklace from the jewel box on the dresser in the master bedroom. In the night-table drawer, she finds a pile of cash and happily tucks it into her pocket. Just doing my bit to make suburbs unsafe, thinks Clytemnestra. That will teach them to leave their door unlocked.

She slips quietly out the back door, Clytemnestra Bernstein getting away with her loot, grinning to herself at the thought of this photograph with that caption. Black humor indeed.

Gingerbread
Men

"What really bothers me," John confides, "is that she can't handle it on an emotional level." That's how John talks. He is sitting at my kitchen table, helping himself to the oatmeal cookies I have just baked for my daughter, Deirdre. Deirdre is playing with some of the children who live up the street; I can hear distant shrieks as they dare one another to jump off the low sloping roof of the garage into the leaf pile. They do this constantly, and no one has yet been injured, so finally we parents have given up forbidding it. But the afternoon is already beginning to get dark and soon I will call Deirdre in and give her milk and still-warm oatmeal cookies. That is, if John hasn't eaten all of them. I regard him with patient suspicion, waiting for him to notice. He takes another cookie.

"I mean," he tells me through the crumbs, "she's how old, twenty-seven?"

I don't answer; the person we are discussing is my old college roommate, true, but she is also his wife, so I don't see why *I* should have to verify her age for *him*.

"She's twenty-seven," he goes on, "and she's acting like some kind of adolescent. I mean, she just can't handle being in school. She keeps telling me she's going to flunk out. She gets so tense about studying that if I move in the next room it hassles her. I mean, I just can't relate to it. No music, I can't talk on the phone if she's studying. . . . I mean, wouldn't it bother *you?*"

"She was always a little bit like that," I say. "At least she was when we were in college. Look, she's probably been very scared about going back to school. Give her a little time and she'll relax."

He takes another cookie. I decide there is no point in subtlety and gather up the rest of the cooling cookies and put them in a hideous widemouthed ceramic cookie jar made in the shape of a grinning frog, a gift to Deirdre from her father, my ex-husband. I keep it around because it reminds me of him. John looks hurt to see the cookies disappear.

"She's up there right now studying," he tells me, nodding to the ceiling, indicating the second floor of my house, which I have rented to him and his wife, Trina, my old college roommate.

"Well," I tell him, "maybe you should go up and make supper for her. I have to make something for me and Deirdre now anyway."

He looks disappointed, even betrayed. Perhaps he expected an invitation, maybe the cookies were so good that he is hoping for a whole dinner cooked by my capable maternal hands.

"I should call Deirdre in," I say, getting up. "It's already dark out."

He takes the hint, and when I come back inside, towing a somewhat recalcitrant child, tempting her with talk of fresh cookies, John has gone up to Trina, and the atmosphere in the kitchen is distinctly less oppressive.

I live my life on a fairly tight schedule; even the periods of aimlessness are planned for and budgeted. I get home from work at four-thirty, picking up Deirdre from the day-care center on the way, and then, if it's nice, she goes out to play and I usually bake something to make our milk-and-cookies together more of a treat. We don't eat dinner until seven, or even eight. That half hour or so of milk-and-cookies with my daughter is important to me, as you might imagine. I think it is to her too; she takes the fresh cookies as an expression of love for her, which of course they are. The problem is that the timing coincides with John's return from work. He and Trina, by agreement, use the back door and the back stairs up to their floor, which gives them a reasonable degree of privacy, since Deirdre and I use the front door. The second floor is quite self-contained; it has a small kitchen and a bathroom. I mean, I rented them the second floor on the understanding that it would function more or less as a separate apartment. But John has taken to interrupting his journey from the back door to the back stairs to veer into my kitchen on his way home from work. The first couple of times he did this I didn't mind at all; I was glad to have company while I waited for Deirdre to come in from playing and I suppose I was proud to be seen in my role as supermother: She comes home from a hard day of being a computer whiz to bake homemade cookies for her daughter. At first I didn't even mind letting him have a few cookies.

But when John started trying to stay in the kitchen after Deirdre came in, I was annoyed, and I finally had a little talk with him, explaining that it was important to me to spend that time with Deirdre. I didn't add that he is an especially bad third, since he talks right through her, over her, and around her. So now he comes and eats my cookies and then leaves, always a little resentfully, like an older sibling making way for the spoiled baby.

The other problem I am having with these visits from John

is that lately all he wants to do is complain about Trina, and my loyalty to Trina is strong. I tend to have very strong loyalties; once I have decided to accept a person as *mine*, I can forgive just about anything. John, of course, I have never fully accepted; this loyalty of mine does not extend to the boy-friends, lovers, and other encumbrances of the people I love. Also, the objects of my loyalty rarely tend to be male. Once or twice, but rarely; not my ex-husband, for example. I don't think I ever accepted him fully; there was always an element of sufferance there. And how right I was. Didn't keep me from marrying the bozo, though. And my current "man," lover, whatever, I have no deep sense of loyalty to him either, though perhaps one is growing, in gratitude for his perfect predictability. Anyway, what I am saying is that I have very little patience for listening to John complain about Trina. I suppose I continue to allow him to come and do it out of some sense that I am acting as her spy; I can let her know how things look to him. So far, though, I haven't said a word about it to her. Trina and I, it seems, have other things to talk about. We haven't discussed John much at all.

Trina, in fact, comes down to visit me that very same night. She waits until after ten o'clock, when she knows Deirdre will be in bed. Is ten too late for a five-year-old? Who knows? I tend to be very unsure about things like that, but it seems to me that Deirdre gets plenty of sleep. So she is in bed and I am sitting in my living room reading when the phone rings. Trina is scrupulous about calling to see if she is welcome, even though she can hear my phone ringing after she dials my number. Even though in college the two of us lived in one room for three years.

I tell her, sure, come on down, and I put the kettle on the stove. All the oatmeal cookies are gone, but for Trina there is a slice of the devil's food cake I made two days ago. It was not offered to John. Trina curls up on my couch. Her hair is up in the same tight bun that I remember from college; when she studied, she pulled her hair back as severely as possible. I imagine that she doesn't like it shading the paper as she bends over her work; by pulling back her hair, she is exposing her face, her brain, as well as her books and papers, to the merciless light of her bright high-tech desk lamp. Sitting on my couch, she reaches up and takes out the bobby pins and her hair slowly uncoils, then opens out around her face.

Trina is beautiful. I have always thought so, and I am not the only one. Not that everyone thinks so. She is small and light and her features are sharp. Her eyes are dark but her lashes and brows are pale, matching the cloud of hair. Trina has a sort of pale curly hair which has been, on occasion, called either Botticellian or Pre-Raphaelite, usually by the besotted and pretentious. In fact it is neither; there are no ripples visible, no curls or ringlets or waves, nothing but a dense pale mass. It has never seemed to me the sort of hair to suggest innocence or dewy romance, but the besotted see what they want to see.

I also like the way Trina is aging, if you can call it that, going from twenty-two to twenty-seven. I hadn't seen her for almost three years when she and John moved in. They were out in Seattle, which is where they met and married. I hadn't even met John. When I saw Trina for the first time in three years, I thought, good, she is becoming elegant. That is the right thing for her to become. By elegant I only mean that there is now never anything even remotely accidental about her clothes, the way there so often is about mine. This evening, for instance. She is curled up on my couch in a long dark-blue corduroy skirt and a white button-down shirt, and around her neck is a string of carnelian beads. Nothing wildly elaborate or expensive, just so very deliberate. While I am still wearing the blue turtleneck I wore to work, because it is comfortable, but I have replaced my wear-to-work pants, which are reasonably respectable, with a pair of green sweatpants, which are coming to pieces. But I don't just mean that Trina keeps her good clothes on in the evenings. I didn't look the way she does when I was dressed for work either.

It gives me pleasure to watch her eat the devil's food cake. I wonder what John thinks of her coming downstairs to visit me. I don't ask.

"So how is medical school?" I finally do ask.

Trina shrugs. "I just wish I had more of a talent for science," she says.

Back in college, I was a math major. Trina majored in English. Out in Seattle, she decided to go to medical school and took all the prerequisite science courses. She did fine, but she continues to feel that she is a stranger to anything scientific. This is probably contributing a great deal to her anxieties about being back in school.

"You don't need a talent," I tell her. "Science is ninety-nine percent trivial memorization, especially medical school."

She smiles at me, patiently, to let me know that I am the computer genius, I can hardly understand her problem.

"I have a lot of trouble reading the stuff," she tells me. "It takes me a long time. I just wish I could develop a sort of feel for it."

"You will," I say. "Give it a little time."

If I close my eyes then eight or nine years are lifted. Trina and I are sitting in a room late at night and I am telling her not to worry about her schoolwork. She was always a compulsive worker and worrier, a perfectionist up until the night before the exam, when her concern for perfection turned to a certainty that she would fail. That was the context in which I knew Trina; it does not feel the least unnatural to be sitting here, after all these years, our combined two husbands, one child, multitude of apartments, jobs, lovers, friends, and all the rest, listening to Trina talk about studying.

I was the other sort of student in college. To be female and a math major was sufficiently strange that I found it necessary to develop a certain amount of distance from my classes. I was a haphazard student, fortunately a fairly talented one. I also did well on tests, much better than I deserved to. Pressure brings out the best in me. Trina, on the other hand, tended to freeze on tests. She needed to have all the material under control, well digested and assimilated, or she was hopeless. In college, I took it as a challenge to go out drinking the night before one of my own exams, but the night before one of Trina's, I would coddle her and bring her tea and cookies, and urge her to stop studying after a certain point and go to sleep so she would be well rested. You see how well I remember all this. You see why it doesn't bother me in the least that Trina is twenty-seven and tense about her studying.

But it is not, after all, the night before an exam, so we eventually leave the subject of studying and begin discussing men, a progression again very reminiscent of college. Back then, our sexual habits were the opposite of our study habits; Trina was somewhat reckless and promiscuous, quick hot affairs and long slow relationships mingling in her wake, and I was cautious and anxious, serious and sincere. Now, of course, she is married to John, and we accept her love and fidelity more or less as a given. When she talks about other men, she talks about the ones who came before John; she fills me in on those years when we didn't see much of one another because she was out West and I was here in Cambridge. I, on the other hand, am free and single, and my affair with my current love interest counts as gossip. She wants to meet him. I explain again that I don't see him all that often. She finds this a little titillating, married woman that she is. She asks:

"So are you faithful to him, then?"

"Not by design," I say. "But you know, with working, and with Deirdre, and with trying to keep life from getting too frantic, I don't really feel like there's a lot of time left to fill."

"Well, Joan," she says, giggling, "as long as you're getting enough."

That is not said seriously, to mean getting enough out of life; it is said lewdly. Again, a reminder of college, of the way roommates talk to one another.

Eventually Trina goes back upstairs to her studying, to her husband. I like having her in my house, but I am also used to living just with Deirdre, and I am happy to pick up my book again.

Clayton, my boyfriend, calls to ask me if I want to see a show on Saturday. Clayton and I usually go out together when we see each other. We see most of the shows that come through Boston on their way to Broadway and the Broadway road companies that come through on tour, and we eat out, and then we come back to my house for the night. So that is another reason Trina has not met him; we are usually out or else in bed. John has been asking me a lot of questions about Clayton lately, and *that* I find disturbing.

In fact, lately John has taken to mooning around my kitchen and making lonely little remarks which suggest that he is developing unhealthy interests having to do with me. Not that anything has been said, but I have a very definite hunch. And of course, I find myself wondering, have I deserved his prurience by allowing myself to listen to the stories of his tribulations with Trina? Why haven't I told John to shut up?

Actually, it is a relief to let John ask me about *my* love life, rather than complain about his own. I can imagine him imagining a man for me, perhaps a man who is hedonistic and profoundly easygoing, who lets the world go by while he and

I do creative things to one another . . . is this my fantasy or John's? Someone who is a little crazy, a little brilliant, not at all respectable.

In fact, Clayton is *Mayflower* respectable. The most unrespectable thing about him is me, his Cambridge hippie girlfriend, as I'm sure he thinks of me. And even there he needs an underpinning of respectability: I am a systems analyst. If we meet friends of his at the theater or in a restaurant, as we do often enough, I can feel him waiting for the moment when I will be asked what I do. I doubt he would be able to handle it if I worked in a holistic health clinic or made patchwork quilts for a living.

I find this very endearing in Clayton. I do not find it so endearing that John may want me for *his* Cambridge hippie girlfriend. Trina, he keeps telling me, is really getting too into being a medical student. That's how John talks. The implication is that he and I are the free spirits, the ones untainted by professionalism. For John, it is more convenient to ignore what I do; my selling point with Clayton is a minus with John. But not a big enough minus, which is a pity.

Anyway, I find I am looking forward to seeing Clayton. We go to see the show, meant to be sentimental and tearjerking, which is on its way to Broadway for the Christmas crowds, and it is very terrible. If it were a movie, I would laugh, but I think of the actors' feelings. Somehow, this terrible show puts me in a very good mood, and I go back to Cambridge with Clayton, send the baby-sitter home, and practically rip Clayton's clothes off.

Clayton is a businessman. He "does consulting." He keeps his body in beautiful shape, he makes love like a dream, and he is essentially sweet. We don't discuss his work or my work. I make him feel that his life has something a little bit daring and exotic in it, and he makes me feel very nice.

That night when we are lying in my bed glowing at one another and laughing a little about the terrible play, the phone rings. Trina, in tears, asks if she can come down and stay the night with me. I tell her that of course she can, and I put on my bathrobe. Clayton is a little embarrassed; I, of course, am not. This is not the sort of thing that embarrasses a person in front of her old college roommate. I make a bed on the couch for Trina, and she cries and tells me how she has been fighting with John and John has stomped out of the house and she doesn't want to be there when he comes back, or know whether he comes back at all. It occurs to me that I didn't hear any of this, the fight or the stomping out, and I realize that Clayton and I must have been even more absorbed than I thought, since I am usually at least a little alert for noises in case anything is wrong with Deirdre.

Clayton himself comes out after a while, dressed in the beautiful wool bathrobe which he keeps in my closet. His presence seems to cheer Trina up, and I think that it reminds her of college days, the presence of a boy in a bathrobe who belongs to one or the other of us. She says something to that effect, and Clayton smiles a little sheepishly, and then I make us all hot rum.

Trina is not looking well tonight. I suppose she is genuinely too tense all the time. John says that she studies until late at night every night. He also says that she is doing fine in all her courses and the tension is completely unnecessary. She does look a little haggard, though it is hard to tell whether that is from medical school or the fight with John. I assume that she will not tell me about the fight because Clayton is there, but she tells us both.

"I was on the phone with someone I know from school. We were going over some stuff—there's a midterm next Wednesday in biochemistry. So after a while, John was just standing there watching me talk on the phone and looking really angry, so I hung up. And he just exploded."

"Well," I say, "it *is* Saturday night. Maybe you should go a little easier on yourself."

Trina shakes her head. "I really don't know if I can pass this exam," she tells me.

"Trina," I say, "you're going to pass."

"Probably I am," she says. "But it's scary. You don't understand." She turns to Clayton, pleading her case. "I uprooted us, I made us move cross-country so I could go here. I changed my whole life, I quit my job, I'm going into debt up to my neck. And I'm just not used to being in school. All these kids, they know how to study, they know how to take exams. They know they'll pass. They can even afford to fail a test or two. But I can't."

Clayton nods. Trina seems to be close to tears again, but the tension is broken by the arrival of Deirdre, who has heard us talking, and who anyway never sleeps well when she is put to bed by a baby-sitter. I often have to put her to bed all over again when I get home. She comes and sits in my lap, and wrinkles her nose at the smell of the hot rum, and Clayton and Trina look at the two of us tenderly. I look at the three of them and feel an enormous tenderness myself. Deirdre I will carry to her bed and tuck in, maybe sit with her for a while. Trina I will wish good night, offer a few last bits of comfort and reassurance. And Clayton I will take back to bed with me.

Trina does not fail any of her tests, but neither does she relax. John continues to come and complain to me, and I wonder a lot about what their relationship was like before Trina started school. Is John really upset about the way she is handling school, I wonder, or is he always dissatisfied about something? I continue to sense that he is making tiny little figurative advances in my direction, but so far I have fore-stalled any outright declarations. I have also made it clear that he is not welcome to visit me every day, but he continues to come a couple of times a week, and he continues to complain.

"And I don't even have to tell you what our sex life is like," he says to me.

"No, you certainly don't," I tell him, but he misses the point. He assumes that I am agreeing with him. Actually, I am beginning to wonder how Trina can possibly stand to be touched by him.

"I mean," he tells me, "you can just imagine it."

"Right," I say.

This talk about their sex life is, of course, meant as a desperately subtle appeal to me. I don't mean to say that I think John would be ready to ravish me then and there on the kitchen table if I just said the word. I doubt that even in his fantasies he goes much further than a guilty kiss or two. I think it's the betrayal of Trina that he craves, both mine and his own. He is out to punish her.

Interestingly enough, that very night John and Trina have a grand sexual reconciliation. I am in Deirdre's bedroom, reading her a chapter of *The Lion, the Witch and the Wardrobe*, when we begin to hear the noises from upstairs. Moans and groans. I am a little embarrassed; when Clayton is here, I am always careful to keep my bedroom door closed and not make too much noise. What Deirdre and I are hearing is mostly John, who is gasping and moaning so loudly that I refuse to believe he doesn't mean for me to hear. Also, there is a rhythmic thumping on the ceiling which suggests that he is making the bed rock upstairs.

Deirdre looks up at the ceiling. Then she begins to giggle. I close the book. I am still embarrassed, but after a minute I am giggling too. Deirdre and I look at each other and laugh even harder.

I do find myself hoping that this noisy reconciliation means that from now on John will be a little less eager to complain to me about Trina. But of course it doesn't mean any such thing. I cannot figure out whether I am actually watching their relationship fall apart, or whether this is just their normal pattern. I know from my own marriage that people can go on for long periods of time in patterns which, to an outsider, would surely appear to be the last lingering agonies of a disastrous relationship.

Trina brings her books downstairs one night and studies in my living room. John is entertaining an old friend who is passing through Boston. The two of them are upstairs drinking beer and talking about women, or at least that is Trina's impression. She spreads out her work on my coffee table, sitting on the floor, her hair pulled back, her neck exposed. I watch her steady underlining, moving from her own notes to the book and then to a printed sheet of diagrams. I am happy to have her there, and I feel an unpleasant furor in my stomach when I wonder: Shall I tell them they have to move out at Christmas, during her semester break? Shall I tell her that John is always complaining to me about her? Shall I tell her that on some level he is after me?

I hear Deirdre calling me from her room, and I go to her before she can come in and disturb Trina.

"Do you like having other people living in the house?" I ask Deirdre.

She considers. Like all children perhaps, she has a tendency to accept things like that. They are decreed by the adult world, and as such are part of the natural order.

"I guess so," she says.

"Do you like John?" I ask.

"Sure," she says. "He's going to make me a basketball hoop on the side of the garage."

That's the first I've heard of it. It suggests to me that John is cozying up to Deirdre behind my back, and I am instantly suspicious.

"That's nice," I say, hoping that he will never do it and that she will hold it against him.

When I go back to the living room, Trina looks up from her books and papers. I am ready for a statement about how she will fail whatever exam she is studying for. Instead I get a bewildered smile.

"Joan," she says to me, "I'm going to be a doctor. Can you believe it?"

And the two of us grin at each other, and I sit down on the couch, thinking that I will not turn them out at Christmas. Trina shakes her head, her tight bun, and returns to her underlining.

The next day when I come home from work there is a distinct feeling of snow in the air. Deirdre insists on going out to play in a large game of tag down the street. I make her put on an extra sweater, then, after she is gone, begin to make gingerbread men. It is a pleasure to be handling this rich brown dough; after my day among the computers and the computer people, I think I need this more than Deirdre does.

John comes in as I am arranging the raisin buttons. I don't hear him come in; he is standing in the kitchen doorway when I turn around.

"Gingerbread men," he says, as I try not to show that I am startled. I have told him to knock or ring the doorbell, but of course he comes in and out to go to his own apartment and it is so easy for him to drift into mine.

"Gingerbread men," he says again, shaking his head as if in wonder. "Imagine making gingerbread men for someone you love."

"Deirdre is really into gingerbread men," I say, to make it clear who it is that I love, just in case there is any doubt.

"You're just so amazing," he tells me. "You have time for all the important things."

"And some of the unimportant ones," I say, looking at him meaningfully.

"Oh Joan," he says, collapsing into one of my chairs, "I just don't know what to do."

"Maybe you should get help," I suggest.

He ignores me. "I just can't handle this business with Trina," he confides.

I press in a raisin eye with more force than is necessary.

"She has to do what she has to do," he tells me. "But why can't she handle it like a grown-up?"

"No one can handle school like a grown-up," I pronounce firmly. "School is designed for children and it makes people into children."

He is still ignoring me. He is, as he himself would say, too deeply into his own feelings to notice what I am saying.

"It's like living with a zombie. All she does is study and worry."

"John, I have heard all this before," I say loudly. I put the pan of gingerbread men into the oven and close the oven door emphatically. "You and Trina will just have to work it out between you. It doesn't do any good to tell me about it over and over again, and it's boring for me."

I wait for him to take offense and leave. Instead he gets up and comes over to me and takes me in his arms.

"Oh Joan," he whispers, "I need you so much."

I pull away, but I am being backed into my kitchen sink.

"John, let go of me," I say, in the tone I use to Deirdre when I am really furious but holding it in.

He lets go of me but continues to stand much closer than I want him. "Joan," he says, in that same whisper, "please, don't push me away."

I cross to the other side of the kitchen. "You know, John," I say, trying to keep my voice reasonable, "there *is* such a thing as loyalty." *Does* he know?

He glares at me. Would he rather hear that he just doesn't turn me on?

"Loyalty," he says sarcastically.

"Trina is one of my closest friends," I say, trying to pompous him out of the ring. I don't add: And she's *your* wife, because I trust that is obvious, even to him.

He stands there, trying to think of a cuttingly sarcastic retort, and Deirdre comes running in, the front door banging distantly behind her, a white sugar dusting on her hair.

"It's snowing!" she announces, jubilant. She is not completely sure that she can remember last winter; for her, this first snow of the season is a proof of all the laws of nature. "If it keeps on snowing, can we build a snowman?" she asks me, as I smooth the melting snow off her hair.

"Sure," I say, "and if it doesn't snow enough this time, then next time."

She nods, trying to absorb the promise of not just one snow but a winter full of them.

"Hi, Deirdre," John says.

"Oh, hi," she says. She looks at him for a minute. "I guess I don't need that basketball hoop now," she tells him. "It's snowing."

Poor old John. He takes his leave then, as well he might, giving me a mournful rejected look. Deirdre wants to go back out to the snow.

"But there's something special in the oven," I say.

"What is it?"

"Can't you smell it?"

She sits at the table and waits to be shown. I bargain with her: First take off your coat and your mittens and your sweater.

By the time all that is done, the gingerbread men are ready. I pour us two glasses of milk and we each take a gingerbread man, slightly too hot to touch.

Should I throw them out, John and Trina? Should I tell them to start looking for another place? Should I take their troubles seriously?

I put aside a particularly attractive gingerbread man, hoping Trina will come down to visit me later.

Nineteen
Lists

FIVE GOOD REASONS FOR NICOLE AND MATTHEW TO BREAK UP

1. Whenever they treat themselves to dinner in a nice restaurant, they have a fight right there in the restaurant.
2. After eight months of living together, he is tired of always being the one to scrub the bathtub.
3. She has lost her job in San Francisco and is thinking of moving to Boston.
4. They never like each other's friends.
5. She no longer feels the least bit tender when she sees him sleeping.

(When did all this start? When did she stop feeling tender? When did scrubbing out the tub really begin to bother him? Who knows. But she lost her job two weeks ago and she hasn't really been looking hard for a new one.)

THREE REASONS WHICH ARE NOT ACTUALLY IMPORTANT TO THEM BUT MIGHT SEEM SO TO OTHER PEOPLE

1. They are of different religious backgrounds; her family is Presbyterian and his is Jewish.

2. She has gained almost thirty pounds over the last year.

3. His parents are wealthy and hers are not.

(All these things are important to their parents, particularly to his. His friends have been known to be snide about her gaining all that weight while hers blame it on him or at least on her living with him.)

FOUR REASONS THEY NEVER REALLY TALKED ABOUT GETTING MARRIED

1. Matthew has been married before and it didn't work out.

2. Nicole has always said she'll never get married.

3. Living together was never really smooth or comfortable even though at times it was a great deal of fun, like for example all those evenings they went out for Chinese food, which is why it is so disturbing that they can no longer eat out together without fighting.

4. Matthew wants to have children eventually and Nicole doesn't.

(Or does she just say she doesn't want children, the way she says she doesn't want to get married? Matthew believes both, but maybe that's just because it makes breaking up more comfortable for him.)

FIVE REASONS THEIR SEX LIFE HAS BEEN LESS THAN SATISFACTORY RECENTLY

1. She likes it rough and he doesn't.

2. Since she gained all the weight she's become self-conscious and she needs to have the light out and maybe even wear a nightgown.

3. He has begun to fantasize about having sex with men and so he has become self-conscious about that, a little wary of all his sexual impulses.

4. He gets nervous when she doesn't have an orgasm before he does.

5. She has had a vaginal infection.

(But is all this only recently? Well, things have been getting worse and worse. Their sex life really was pretty good once upon a time.)

THREE THINGS IN SAN FRANCISCO NICOLE WILL REALLY MISS IF SHE GOES EAST

1. Walking back from Chinatown after dim sum on Sunday morning, pausing as she climbs the hill, and turning around to look down the breathtakingly sharp slope past the Transamerica pyramid, out to the blue of the bay.

2 Those improbable buffalo in Golden Gate Park.

3. Halloween on Castro Street with all the gay men in fabulous costumes.

(No mention of Matthew? He isn't one of those things she will miss? Oh well, she has to give up those dim sum brunches anyway if she's ever going to lose weight.)

THREE HABITS OF NICOLE'S MATTHEW WILL BE GLAD TO SEE THE LAST OF

1. She never scrubs out the bathtub or even seems to notice when it needs scrubbing, which he finds truly disgusting.

2. She makes long-distance phone calls without waiting for the rates to go down at 11:00 P.M.

3. She eats leftover take-out Chinese food without heating it up again.

(Yes, the bathtub really is important. And even though Nicole doesn't ask him to scrub it, even though she pays for her own phone calls, even though she doesn't try to make him eat cold

Chinese food, still the thought of never seeing any of this again fills him with relief.)

FOUR THINGS WHICH HAVE GONE WELL WHILE
THEY LIVED TOGETHER

1. She has cut his hair for him and it looks much better than the barber ever made it look.
2. He has finally gotten his notes organized and begun to write his book about the movies of the 1950s.
3. She has learned Spanish and started reading South American writers.
4. He has been offered two more night school courses to teach.
(How much of this is due to their living together? Well, the hair of course, and she did encourage him to start the book, and he did encourage her to learn Spanish. So they *have* done each other *some* good.)

TWO MAJOR CHANGES IN HER CLOTHING HABITS NICOLE HAS
MADE, PROBABLY BECAUSE OF HER WEIGHT GAIN

1. She has stopped wearing pants altogether and relies on skirts a little bit too long for fashion with either elastic or wraparound waistbands.
2. She borrows his blazers, which are a little too big for her even now.
(In other words, above the waist she looks vaguely professorial, since his blazers are all tweedy and respectable, and below the waist is the full shapeless skirt. Did the change in her appearance contribute to her losing her job? Probably not; she was working in a learning skills center tutoring backward children and the whole center closed because of budget cuts.)

FIVE PIECES OF EVIDENCE THAT AFTER THEY BREAK UP
MATTHEW WILL HAVE NO TROUBLE FINDING NEW LOVERS

1. One of the women in the night course he teaches on the history of the American cinema has invited him to a party and another has offered to show him a Brazilian restaurant she knows, out in the avenues near the ocean.
2. An old friend of his has recently broken up with his girlfriend and the girlfriend has been calling Matthew on the phone to talk about it.
3. When he went into a gay bar to have a drink and to prove to himself that he wasn't really interested in sleeping with men, two men tried to cruise him in the space of half an hour.
4. He gave directions to a tourist girl on the cable car one day and she asked if he wanted to come along and show her Fisherman's Wharf.
5. When he went to buy new Levi's the salesman propositioned him.

(Is he *that* gorgeous? No, but good-looking enough, what with the new haircut and all. Tall, thin, dark hair, dark eyes, projects a general impression of sincerity and sensitivity mingled with competence, a very sweet smile, fits lots of fantasies.)

FOUR REASONS NICOLE MAY FIND IT MUCH HARDER
TO REPLACE MATTHEW

1. She is significantly overweight.
2. She is harder to get along with.
3. A good man is hard to find.
4. She is rarely sexually attracted to women, so her field is probably narrower than his will be, provided, of course, that he decides to give men a try.

(Of course she will be the one moving to a new city, which might give her some sort of edge, and perhaps the percentage of heterosexual men is a little higher in Boston, but even so, unless she loses some of that weight things may be tough for her.)

FOUR SIGNIFICANT STEPS IN THEIR AGREEING TO BREAK UP

1. One afternoon when they are sitting in their living room looking out at the fog, Nicole announces that she is thinking of moving to Boston.
2. Two days later Matthew comes home from teaching his night course and says that since she wants to move to Boston and things aren't working out too well between them anyway, perhaps it's all for the best.
3. The two of them spend a beautifully sunny Saturday walking together out by the ocean, crying a little over the idea that they're breaking up, pausing every now and then to kiss and hug, ending up in a Chinese restaurant where they get through dinner without a fight.
4. The very next day they have a terrible fight and both feel relieved that the relationship is almost over.

(They are both aware of how intelligent and adult they are being about all this. And they know they will always remember that day out by the ocean with romantic tenderness.)

THREE CHANGES IN HER EATING HABITS WHICH NICOLE
INTENDS TO MAKE WHEN SHE IS LIVING ALONE IN BOSTON

1. Obviously, she wants to eat less.
2. Cold Chinese food for breakfast every so often.
3. More soups, more bakery bread, less salad, no sprouts ever.

(Does she really like cold leftover Chinese take-out? It isn't just that she's too lazy to heat it up? Yes, well, she is a strange creature in some ways. And of course the anti–sprout-and-salad stand is probably just a rejection of California—and thereby Matthew—and not a good idea for someone who needs to diet.)

TWO POSSIBILITIES WHICH BOTHER MATTHEW WHEN HE CONTEMPLATES THE APPROACHING BREAKUP

1. Nicole will move East, lose all the extra weight, get an adequate job, find a wonderful lover, and learn Portuguese so she can also read Brazilian writers.
2. Nicole will move East, lose none of the weight, get an adequate but not exciting job, have a succession of bizarre lovers, and somehow feel triumphant.

THREE REASONS NICOLE DOES NOT GO EAST IMMEDIATELY

1. Her rent is paid up till the end of the month and she is collecting unemployment.
2. She has an old friend in Boston she can stay with for the first few days, but the old friend is in law school and has exams for the next week so she doesn't want Nicole to arrive till her exams are over.
3. She feels sad whenever she thinks about packing.

(Why does Matthew picture her as so sure of herself when she is really as frightened as he is? She has no idea that he pictures her that way.)

FIVE COMMUNALLY OWNED OBJECTS WHICH COULD POTENTIALLY BE SOURCES OF CONFLICT

1. The big wok with the cover and the little ring stand which fits over the burner of the stove and holds the wok steady.
2. The four-record set of the Brandenburg Concertos they

bought to make love by on the four-month anniversary of their living together.

3. The Bette Davis Film Festival poster Nicole talked the man at the theater into giving her and Matthew then had framed.
4. The electric yogurt maker.
5. *The Joy of Cooking*.

(And who will get what in the end? Nicole will let him keep the wok, the poster, and the yogurt maker, all of which would be difficult to take cross-country with her. Anyway, her feelings about sprouts and salads extend a little to yogurt as well, and the poster was really meant to be a present for Matthew when she got the man to give it to her, and she can always buy a new wok. The records and the cookbook she'll take with her.)

THREE VISIONS NICOLE HAS OF THE FUTURE MATTHEW

1. Book finished and published, full-time teaching job somewhere or other, wife and precocious child, clean bathtub.
2. Living with a somewhat younger man, always about to finish the book, putting on a little weight.
3. Divorced again, this time with three children to worry about, handsomer than ever, a well-paid movie critic.

(So Nicole knows that Matthew is attracted to men? Well, he hasn't told her but she suspects as much. Nicole is very perceptive.)

THREE SUGGESTIONS MATTHEW MAKES TO NICOLE

1. Why doesn't she stay in San Francisco since that's where all her contacts are to help her get a new job?
2. Why doesn't she go back to school when she gets to Boston and get a degree in education?

3. Why doesn't she get her hair cut short and maybe get a permanent?

(Naturally he is trying to help when he makes these suggestions, but really he is also trying, whether he knows it or not, to make her into a less interesting person, or a person who will seem less interesting, or at least a person who in his fantasies will have a less interesting and less triumphant future without him.)

FOUR SIGNS THAT NICOLE IS REALLY GOING AT LAST

1. She makes a plane reservation.
2. She buys two suitcases and a big duffel bag.
3. She calls her friend in Boston one day, before the rates go down, and she says she's coming in a week.
4. Her San Francisco friends begin to call up or stop by to say good-bye.

(The friends that Matthew doesn't like? Exactly. And he likes them even less now when they seem to be regarding him with hostility as the man who is driving their dear Nicole to go three thousand miles away from them. He considers this extremely unfair; after all, didn't he suggest to her that she stay in San Francisco? Also, this procession of friends reminds him of the new life she will put together for herself without him.)

FOUR POSSIBLE FUTURES FOR THE SEPARATED NICOLE AND MATTHEW

1. A successful Matthew, published, handsome, and sensitive; a successful Nicole, thin, employed; the two of them happy on their separate coasts, complete recovery.
2. Nicole never loses the weight, Matthew never feels comfortable about sex with men, their jobs are less than thrill-

ing, they both wish they had tried it together a little longer.

3. Nicole triumphant, Matthew miserable.

4. Matthew triumphant, Nicole forgotten.

(Of course, probably most likely is that they will lose track of one another completely and the triumphs or miseries of each will have no resonance in the life of the other. Three thousand miles is more than enough for that.)

I Am Having an Adventure

Pammy went to Egypt with a man she hardly knew because it sounded like an adventure and anyway she seemed to have dropped out of her French Civilization course in Paris. The other girls in her program had been concerned about her, always inviting her to come with them to museums to do the homework assignments, always offering her their lecture notes to copy. But Pammy went to no museums, no lectures, and finally the other girls began to give up on her. After all, they reminded one another, no one ever failed this course anyway. Perhaps, they speculated, Pammy had a lover in Paris, and that was how she filled her days.

In fact she had no lover and she had trouble filling her days. She slept a great deal and wandered through the parks watching the French children and sat in hotel lobbies and sometimes ordered a drink in a hotel bar. And it was in a hotel bar that she met the man who took her to Egypt. Another reason she went with him: She was flattered that he saw her as the sort of girl who could be picked up in a hotel bar and invited along on a business trip. He had bought her a couple of drinks, she had told him about the junior-year-abroad program, the French

Civilization course, she had admitted that she wasn't really interested in the course anymore, and he just suggested that perhaps she would like to come along with him to Cairo for a week, his company would pay. Men did not usually see Pammy as that sort of girl. She was tall and robust and a little bit awkward and she had short brown hair which, before she came to Paris, her mother had persuaded her to have made ridiculous in a permanent which sat like a little fuzzy cap on her large squarish head. She had no particular skill with makeup and she was ill at ease in any but the most unobtrusive clothing. The other girls in her program, most of whom she knew from college, a few of whom she knew from high school, all said that Pammy would look wonderful in her forties when the rest of them were fading. She had the kind of classic presence that gets better as it ages, they assured her. What they meant, and what Pammy understood, was that they couldn't quite picture her as a college girl. They already saw her as a matron.

But anyway, there was this businessman from Los Angeles, involved in some kind of business which Pammy never exactly got clear, good-looking, dark, and well-groomed, somewhere in his early thirties, suggesting that she come to Cairo with him for a week.

"Well . . ." she said, tempted.

"Why not?" he said. "It's only for a week."

He had his taxi stop for her at the hotel where her program was housed. The other girls were already off at lecture. Pammy left a note for her roommate saying she'd be back in a week and not to worry, and took with her her smallest suitcase and fifty dollars in traveler's checks. Sitting in the taxi on the way to the airport with this man she had never even kissed, Pammy thought, well at last I am having an adventure.

He kissed her for the first time in the cab that took them from the Cairo airport to the Cairo Hilton. Pammy had found the airport almost too much of an adventure; it had been crowded and the people had been pushing and shoving and out front where the taxis waited there had been a mad scene of people screaming and fighting to get into cabs ahead of other people. It seemed to Pammy that they were all shouting at *her*, and she shrank back and watched with awe as Joe, her companion, gave some money to the man who was carrying their bags and the man promptly secured them a taxi, loading all the bags into the trunk and gesturing to hurry up and get in, while another man who had been waiting for a taxi began to carry on shouted negotiations with the driver. But at last Pammy and Joe were speeding away from the airport and Pammy had time to notice the hot dry feeling of the air and to think with wonder that she was actually in Egypt, which, she was ashamed to remember, she had had to look up in an atlas the evening she agreed to go with Joe. It wasn't that she didn't have a fairly good idea of where it was located (Middle East and all), but she was actually a little surprised to find that it was, number one, right on the Mediterranean, which she thought of as being a European sea, and, number two, part of Africa. But she had looked it up and now no one would ever know how ignorant she had been up until just a few days ago. "Yes, to Egypt," she imagined herself saying to one of the girls in her program, upon her return. "Well, it isn't really so far away after all, practically just across the Mediterranean from Italy, even if it is in Africa."

She was sitting in the taxi imagining this conversation ("But who did you go with, Pammy? A *man?*"), when Joe put his arm around her shoulders and kissed her. It was a long kiss, and she was a little embarrassed, because of the driver who might be watching in his rearview mirror.

"We'll be at the hotel soon," Joe said, releasing her, and Pammy nodded. She was disturbed because she had not really liked kissing him. He kissed with his teeth and also with a strange sort of suction which she found unpleasant.

The Hilton was reassuring. Pammy looked around the lobby, promising herself that she would come down later and explore the hotel shops, perhaps sit for a while in one of the armchairs, a cup of coffee resting on a little brass table beside her. Their room had a balcony and after the bellboy left, Pammy started to open the glass door that led out onto it, but Joe grabbed her arm and said, "Don't do that, you'll let out all the air conditioning." Then he pulled her over to the bed and began to unbutton her shirt. While he undressed her he warned her about Cairo, telling her, in an angry and threatening tone of voice, that it was a dangerous city, a filthy dirty city, a city full of diseases. She could not eat or drink anything outside the hotel. Of course she could not go walking outside the hotel by herself, or did she not know what would happen to her if she did? He undressed himself, pushed her onto the bed, and climbed on top of her.

Only when he had finished, dressed himself, and left, abruptly, telling her that he would be going out for the rest of the afternoon, only then did Pammy allow herself to roll over on her stomach and give way to depression. How had she gotten into this? She had hated the way he had been, he had hurt her, there were clear bruise marks forming on her shoulders. She didn't want him to come back, and she was afraid to leave the hotel even for a short walk. She sat up and decided to take a shower, since showers usually helped when she was depressed. She took a long one with the water turned on hard, and when she came out and dried herself she was in fact feeling much better about everything. The bruise marks were perhaps not there at all. Joe was a little rough, no denying it, but after all, the first time with any particular man wasn't supposed to be the best, that she could judge from her own limited experience and also the stories of all the girls she had gone to high school and college with, and next time she would make it clearer to Joe that she needed him to be gentle. In the meantime, here she was in a Hilton hotel in a strange city in a country across the Mediterranean, actually in *Africa,* and she had the afternoon to go down and explore the shops and drink coffee in the lobby and send postcards to the girls in France. And when Joe came back she would be glad to see him, and after all, she thought, it wasn't like he was someone she would ever see again after this trip.

Comforted, Pammy dressed herself in fresh clothing and took the elevator down to the lobby. She spent a long time in the dress shop, trying on caftans, and wished she had brought more money with her. She would have liked to go back to Paris with a long midnight-blue caftan, slit up the sides, with golden embroidery on the front. Or did she only look ridiculous, her graceless body draping the slinky fabric into strange and unattractive angles? She stared at herself once more in the three-way mirror. It was so hard to tell. She wished there were other women standing beside her so she could have a point of reference, this is clumsy, this is beautiful. She shrugged and turned away from the mirror, already eager to be back in her own normal clothes, her denim skirt, her light blue cotton blouse, reminding herself that, after all, she had come to Cairo with a man, he had picked her up in a hotel bar and invited her to come with him, she couldn't be all *that* unattractive. She put on her skirt and blouse and told the salesgirl that perhaps she would be back later, and walked on to the jewelry shop, where she stared for a while at the gold-and-bead necklaces and the pins shaped like the profiled head of a woman wearing a tall slanting headdress. It was a familiar profile. She asked the salesgirl, who told her it was the head of Nefertiti, a familiar name. The only thing she tried on was a ring, which didn't fit on her finger, and she wouldn't let the girl look for a bigger one; feeling outsize and foolish, Pammy went on to the souvenir shop. Eventually she did indeed end up in an armchair in the lobby with a cup of coffee on the table beside her. She had bought some postcards of the pyramids to send to the girls in her French Civilization program. She thought about the messages she could send ("Came rushing off to Egypt on impulse with the most *attractive* man!" "Well, girls, here I am in Egypt! Will wonders never cease?" "I've simply been *carried off*, but you'll have to wait till I get back to hear the details!"). She sipped her coffee. None of them was a message Pammy could send. They were messages she could receive, scrawled on postcards from other girls. A dark woman wearing a long caftan came and sat in the next armchair and smiled at Pammy. Pammy thought enviously that the other woman, though she was also large and in fact more than a little overweight, still somehow managed to move gracefully, authoritatively. When Pammy finished her coffee and went upstairs to her room, she left the postcards she had bought stuffed into the crack between the bottom cushion and the arm of the chair. When Joe came back, she was glad to see him.

They had dinner that night in the Hilton, and again the next night. Pammy had spent the whole day in the hotel, lying in bed for most of the morning and then treating herself to a long and luxurious lunch in the restaurant, as opposed to the coffee shop. She wasn't actually treating herself in the sense of paying for herself, of course, since she just put it on the bill. She was feeling lazy and pleased; Joe had not wanted to have sex again the evening before, when he got back, and he had promised her that one of these days he would arrange a tour that would take her to the pyramids, a safe tour, he assured her, with a clean bus and a trained guide to protect her from the natives. She couldn't help wondering why Joe came on business trips to Cairo if he thought it was so dirty and dangerous. No wonder he wanted company, though, if he was spending his whole day in a city he hated; naturally he wanted a friendly face to come back to at the end of the day. When he came back the second day, she greeted him with a deliberately friendly face, she smiled and hung on his arm, to make up for the day of dirt and danger he had just passed. She was afraid that such girlish behavior did not exactly suit her, but Joe seemed to like it. On their way to the restaurant for dinner, he steered her into the dress shop and insisted that she choose a dress. She took the midnight-blue caftan, because at least she had tried that one on, and she had wondered if it might not after all look nice on her. So they had dinner, and after dinner Joe suggested that they go to the Hilton nightclub, and they went up to the room so Pammy could change into her new caftan. They didn't get to the nightclub though, because Joe interrupted her changing clothes to push her down on the bed. At first it was all right, but then it got to be even worse than the other time, and Pammy pulled away from him and told him to be careful, he was hurting her. When this had no effect, she got angry and told him more sharply that she didn't like being bitten and mauled.

And then, very suddenly, he got angry, much angrier than she had been, and began to twist the skin on her arms and hiss horrible things into her ear.

"Cut it *out*," Pammy said, pulling one of her arms free and jamming her open hand right into his face, pushing him away from her.

He jumped off the bed and started screaming at her. "Filthy spoiled brat!" he screamed, and "Frigid bitch!" Then he got calmer, though his voice was more full of hatred than before, and told her, "I'm going to take a shower. When I come out you better be ready to cooperate. I didn't bring you along for your brilliant conversation, you know."

He went into the bathroom and shut the door. Pammy

waited until she heard the shower running, then got up and dressed, hastily, putting on slacks and a shirt. She packed her suitcase, hesitating for a second over the new caftan. She decided to take it, since after all, what use would he have for it if she left it behind? On her way out the door, trembling, thinking every minute that she heard the shower being turned off, Pammy thought of something. She went to Joe's pants, which he had discarded on the rug by the bed, and found his wallet. The Egyptian money looked strange and foreign; she took it all. She had felt briefly guilty about taking the caftan, but she felt no guilt at all over the money. She went out of the room and closed the door quietly behind her. All the way down in the elevator she was terrified that she would find him waiting for her in the lobby, and when in fact there was no sign of him the sudden rush of jubilation carried her right out of the hotel, past the taxis and the drivers, and out into the city.

Her suitcase did not feel heavy. She struck out across the large parking lot, passing parked buses taking on passengers and crowds of people waiting for buses. The air was warm and had a strange smell, the smell of a strange city. She came to the street and stopped, watching pedestrians dodging their way across, among cars which did not slow down. She waited until a large group of Egyptians came up beside her and then she crossed with them, not looking at the cars, but only at her guides.

She wandered for a block or two on the other side of that busy street, and then she came to a halt, slowing down bit by bit until she was standing still on the sidewalk. The streets were full of people, the cars went by honking furiously. She looked at the Arabic writing on the store signs and thought with sudden longing of Paris, where at least the alphabet was familiar. A battered placard on the building behind her proclaimed in English: DR. THEODOSIUS, PARIS-TRAINED. She thought crazily of ringing his bell and asking for his help. As she watched the people hurrying by, young men arm in arm, families walking five and six abreast, she was overwhelmed by the thought: They are all speaking this strange language, none of them will understand me. She put down her suitcase and stood quietly.

When the two young men came along and asked if she needed help, it did not occur to her to notice that they were a little bit ragged. She noticed only that they were clearly not Egyptian. They spoke English. She told them that she needed to find a hotel that didn't cost too much, and they took her to the place where they were staying. One of them insisted on carrying her suitcase the whole way.

The hotel in which Pammy now found herself staying was not very much like the Hilton. It seemed, in fact, to be completely unrelated to the Hilton, they had nothing in common. In this new place, which was called the Lotus Hotel, Pammy paid an astonishingly small sum of money and was entitled to sleep on one of a number of mattresses spread on the floor of a big square room. And on the other mattresses, of course, there were other people sleeping. There was a bathroom down the hall which was also used by the people who were sleeping in two or three other large rooms. There were sheets, though they were too small to cover the mattresses and there were not enough to go around. But several of the people preferred to spread their sleeping bags on the mattresses; they claimed it reduced the chance of bugs.

The people staying at the Lotus were all young and all from Europe, America, or Australia. The two young men who had originally guided Pammy to the hotel, for example, were Australian. It was very comforting, Pammy decided, that first night, lying down on the sheet which she had tucked around

her mattress as well as she could, it was comforting to know
there were other people around her, sympathetic people, people her own age who knew how to survive without much
money. Perhaps they would be able to advise her about getting
back to Paris. Perhaps there was some cheap way, as far from
normal airplane travel as this room was from a normal hotel.
Pammy stayed awake thinking about this and also listening to
the sounds of two couples making love. This is an adventure,
she told herself firmly.

For a day or two she was almost afraid to go outside the
hotel; she was sure she would find Joe waiting for her, demanding the money she had stolen. She went out only with
groups of people, and they showed her places to eat, places
to get kebabs cheap and big bowls of beans which were cheaper
still. She had a strong feeling that if she waited at the hotel
for just a little while, she would meet someone who would
want to go places just with her alone, and in fact, she had
only been there two nights before an American boy named
Brad had more or less joined up with her. He had just come
from Turkey and Israel and Greece, and he was planning to
go south from Egypt, farther into Africa. He was tall, a good
five inches taller than Pammy, and very thin, and he had curly
red hair. He took her with him to see the pyramids. They got
a bus in the big square near the Hilton, and standing squashed
in the crowded bus, Pammy thought briefly of the tour to the
pyramids that Joe had promised to arrange for her. An air-
conditioned tour bus, a guide. She smiled to herself. Already
she had picked up the sense of extreme superiority that everyone staying in the Lotus Hotel felt toward everyone staying
in the Hilton, toward the takers of taxis and guided tours.
Pammy was really impressed with the survival ability of the
people at the Lotus, even with herself. Even something small
like using the toilet: A month ago, if you had shown her the

toilet at the Lotus Hotel, she would have sworn she would never in a million years have been able to use it, it would have made her sick, and now here she was, surviving. She knew she was not exactly very clean these days; it was astonishing how quickly she had gotten used to the idea that clothes, even underwear, need not be washed after every wearing. She wondered if she now had the grubby, ragged look of the other people at the Lotus, and she supposed she did. It was exciting to be riding on a crowded Cairo city bus, out to see the pyramids. She wondered if that night Brad would want to make love, and if she would be embarrassed because of the other people in the room.

When the bus finally dropped them off at the pyramids, Pammy had a strange sense of familiarity. She knew she had seen this scene before, in a movie probably. She grabbed hold of Brad's arm and let him lead her through the crowd of Arabs selling camel rides and horseback rides and bead necklaces, and she looked at the camels, all decked out with brightly colored saddles, and it just made it all seem more and more like a movie. She followed Brad right up into a pyramid, into an entranceway a little distance up on one side. There was an Arab waiting there who wanted to guide them, but Brad told him they didn't need a guide. They had to crouch down for a lot of the climb inside the pyramid, but finally they came into a central room which was empty except for a big stone box, open at the top.

"The sarcophagus chamber," Brad said. "I wonder if that's the bottom of the original sarcophagus."

Pammy nodded. She found the room disappointing, small and dark and not mysterious.

"What we have to do here is just stop and meditate for a while," Brad said.

"Meditate?"

"You know, feel what's going on. This is a pretty amazing place, when you think about it. I mean, think how long it's been here. And think about all that stone on top of us. Just open your mind to the pyramid." He smiled at her to reassure her that it would be easy, and then he went and sat down next to the stone box, the sarcophagus.

Pammy felt a little silly. Brad was staring down at his crossed legs. She wasn't about to sit down on the floor and join him; she was sure there was a faint smell of urine coming from that floor. She walked away and stared into the hole in the wall that led back out of the pyramid. She hoped some other tourists would come along and interrupt Brad's meditating. And then, very suddenly, she *was* aware of the enormous weight of stone above her. The air in the chamber felt compressed and burdened, she imagined the hundreds of years of those blocks of stone pressing down unceasingly. She felt a little bit sick.

Before she had quite thought about it, she found herself crouching her way back along the passage, leaving Brad in the sarcophagus chamber, hurrying down the long, narrow down-sloping hall, climbing back out of the pyramid. The sun and the hot dry air and the space of the desert revived her. She waited at the base of the pyramid until Brad came climbing out.

"Why did you run away?" he asked her, and then, without waiting for an answer, he went on, "You have to open your mind to these messages, even the really heavy intense ones."

That night in the room at the Lotus Hotel, he reached for her hand. She rolled over slightly, moving a little closer to his mattress to make it easier for him if he wanted to maneuver her, but not actually bringing herself into contact with his body, since after all if it were up to her, they wouldn't do any more than hold hands. All the other people in the room made her feel self-conscious, even if two of them *were* already having a noisy sexual encounter. And besides, she was dirty, she didn't really want to be touched or tasted, she didn't want to touch or taste another dirty body. She was, however, willing to go along with it if Brad wanted to; it seemed to her to be something she owed both to him and to her adventure. Still, she was relieved when he whispered in her ear, "This is a little public for me, I think."

"Me too," she said, and squeezed his hand.

The next day he went off to another group of pyramids, and Pammy didn't go with him. She was thinking that perhaps it was time for her to think about calling her parents and getting her father to arrange for an airplane ticket or some money to be sent to her. She would tell him that she had had her purse stolen with all her money and traveler's checks and her return ticket. Still, her parents would be sure to ask about what she was doing in Egypt in the first place, about what had happened to her program in Paris. And she didn't know where to go to make the call. Perhaps she would wait another day or two, she thought. It was reassuring to know that she could get back to Paris anytime she wanted. She thought of the luxury of life in Paris, was amazed that she had never noticed it before. What would the girls in her program say if they could see her now? Oddly enough, she felt much less awkward in Cairo than she had felt in Paris; the people at the Lotus Hotel were so clearly aiming for survival, not decorative effect. I can do this, she thought happily, venturing out of the hotel for the first time on her own, finding a pastry shop where she had been before, eating a grainy honey-drenched cake; I can do this perfectly well, and I even found a boyfriend. She thought of her program in Paris, which she had not been able to do, which she had dropped out of. And she had not found a boyfriend in Paris, though lots of the other girls in her program had, mostly American boys on other study-abroad programs. What would happen when she went back to Paris, she wondered, would she pick up the program again, go neatly dressed to lectures and museums with a crowd of neatly dressed girls, clean hair waving around their clean faces?

She wandered around through the streets of Cairo, looking at herself in every shop window she passed. She was wearing dirty blue jeans and a red sleeveless shirt and nothing under it because none of the other girls staying in the Lotus wore bras. Anyway, her breasts weren't all that big. It made her nervous, though, when the Arab men looked at them. She felt like a lot of people were looking at her, and she stopped drifting and began to walk more purposefully. She had thought she had her bearings with respect to the Lotus, but she was surprised to come out into an open square and recognize the Hilton off on the other side of it.

She stood still for a minute, imagining herself in that midnight-blue caftan with the gold embroidery, which was tucked away in her suitcase back at the Lotus. She saw herself in that caftan, languidly emerging from the elevator in the Hilton lobby, gracefully resting her hand on the arm of a dark man in a tuxedo.

"Who is that?" the people in the Hilton lobby were asking each other, and one of the girls from her program was exclaiming to another, "Why, it's Pammy! And *where* did she get that *man?*"

Not Joe, of course, and not Brad either. Maybe someone part Arab. The son of an oil sheik. Omar Sharif.

Pammy floating across the Hilton lobby, her slim bare legs sliding in and out of the side slits in the caftan. Only she (and perhaps the dark man) knows the secret: Under her caftan she is completely naked, there is only her naked body, clean and perfumed and powdered.

"Pammy, Pammy," calls one of the girls from her program, timidly. "Oh, darn, she didn't see us."

Walking languidly, as if she were indeed wearing the blue caftan, Pammy crossed the square and went into the Hilton. She didn't even stop to calculate whether Joe would have left the country yet. She went into the lobby and found herself almost reeling from the air conditioning. How could she have forgotten what a glorious thing air conditioning was? She sank into an armchair. How could she have once felt she belonged in this lobby, belonged without even thinking about it? How could she once have taken all this so much for granted, how could she have been so silly as to imagine that she fit in here? Oh well, she thought, I've fallen away now and there's no climbing back.

And then she thought, how silly, I can go back anytime I want. But it was clear enough that she was out of place in the Hilton lobby, her clothes, her general grubbiness. She was a waif come in to absorb a little air conditioning.

A man came and sat in the armchair next to hers. A rather fat man in a sport shirt and khaki pants, a man in his forties. He was looking at Pammy.

She thought, so this is how I can earn my ticket back to Paris.

"Hello," the man said.

"A hundred dollars," said Pammy.

"I beg your pardon?"

"That's how much I cost. A hundred dollars for as long as you want." She was surprised to realize that her hands were trembling; it surprised her because she felt completely calm.

"Really, young lady, I don't think . . ." The man was getting up, looking a little flurried. He backed away from her, shaking his head.

Pammy shrugged and smiled at him as he retreated. The

air conditioning was so very pleasant. She could afford to wait in the coolness; there would be another one along. Or perhaps that one would come back, wasn't he hesitating over there by the elevators, looking furtively back over his shoulder? Pammy raised her arms over her head and stretched luxuriously.

The hem of the midnight-blue caftan sweeps gracefully along. A bracelet glitters on Pammy's arm, and the cuff links of the dark man return the sparkle.

"Did she see us?" asks the girl from the French Civilization program.

"She's only looking at *him*," the other girl answers. "And can you blame her?"

Pammy is laughing now at something the dark man has said, her clean soft curls bouncing, the gold embroidery, the glimpses of her bare legs, the secret that only she knows— and perhaps the dark man too.

"Maybe we should just go right up to her and say hello."

"I'd be too embarrassed. They're too elegant."

Pammy, the girl in the midnight-blue caftan, tosses her curls and tightens her grip on the arm of the dark man in the tuxedo.

A Gift of
Sweet Mustard

His wife's eating habits make it easy for Alan to bring her presents when he comes home from work. He stops in one of the gourmet food stores (there is one on the bottom floor of Macy's, one on the bottom floor of Liberty's, and another he walks past if he gets off the bus a stop early) and he buys her a jar of some fancy condiment. That's what she likes: chutney, chili sauce, Dijon mustard. She likes the exotic ones: harissa, which is Moroccan red-pepper paste, and Japanese dried-seaweed powders, but she also likes Worcestershire sauce, and Tabasco, and ketchup. Alan puts the little bag in his nice leather briefcase, imagining spices and oils soaking into his neat files of papers.

If Alan's wife, Joanna, had her way, she would eat only very plain food, spread with her various bottled sauces and preparations. Boiled potatoes, baked brisket, steamed cauliflower. Alan likes the seasoning of a meal to be cooked into the meal itself, and for his sake Joanna constructs what she calls "dishes": stews, curries, pot roasts, casseroles. But then she sits across from him and decorates her portion, sometimes with the proper accompaniment (chutney with curry), in which case Alan has some too, but often with some completely weird topping (chili sauce on lasagne).

In his briefcase is a jar of champagne honey mustard. He has bought it partly to celebrate his own goodness as a husband; at work the blond California Girl who works in the next office had dropped in on him for a chat and suggested they go somewhere after work for a drink. Alan said he couldn't, he had to be somewhere. Of course, he didn't say he had to get home to his wife, which is what a really good husband would surely have said. No one at work knows he is married. San Francisco being what it is, there is probably mild speculation about whether or not he is heterosexual, but Sandy, the California Girl, seems to have decided that he is. Alan has felt for some time that Sandy is interested, and even while he is patting himself on the back for not being at some hotel bar near Union Square, winding the ends of her long blond hair around his fingers, he is titillating himself with the knowledge that he made no real effort to discourage her and that there will be other opportunities.

In fact, Alan has decided that if Joanna should turn out to be having an affair, he will immediately take up with Sandy and tell Joanna about it, so it will seem that he too has had a lover all along. He doesn't really think Joanna is having an affair; there is no evidence whatever that she is having an affair. He just can't imagine what she does all day, so naturally he suspects the worst.

The bus is crowded, as it always is, and he stands staring down into the lap of an Oriental girl with short curly hair and a ceramic pin on her blazer lapel. The pin is a yellow kangaroo with a red-and-blue-striped stocking cap on its head. The pin warns Alan not to take her beautiful face too seriously. Alan is thinking about the champagne honey mustard, and how Joanna will try a little on the end of her finger and then spread it all over her share of whatever they are having for dinner.

She cooks "dishes" for him, but it is not really as if she is trying to win his approval. Joanna feels no need to apologize for her own eating habits. She is faintly patronizing toward his, as if she is indulgently preparing food for a picky child. It is Alan who is always trying to propitiate, bringing home his little jars. And this, it seems to him, is true of their whole relationship; Joanna is always eccentric, and he is always apologizing for his own normalcy. He tries to imagine the meal Sandy would cook for him; he would bring a bottle of white wine or perhaps, if she made red meat, a good California burgundy.

Joanna is particularly delighted with the mustard. She has never seen such a thing before, and she kisses Alan for bringing it to her. Her mouth tastes of strange sweet mustard. Alan accepts the kiss as a reward. She has made lamb chops for dinner and, sure enough, she coats the good meat with her new condiment. The little jar sits open next to her plate and she dips her knife into it again and again.

Alan is inhibited even about putting salt and pepper on his food. His mother taught him that hostesses would be offended if he adjusted too radically what they had cooked and from this he inferred, correctly, that she would be offended too. Sometimes he is almost offended on Joanna's behalf as he watches her dump bought flavors onto the food she has herself prepared.

He talks a little about his day, referring to coworkers who have become characters between the two of them. Not Sandy (though Joanna would appreciate the California Girl); he has never mentioned Sandy to Joanna, which would seem to prove that he has had wicked thoughts about Sandy right from the beginning.

"And what did you do today?" he asks. Joanna looks at him, surprised. She considers.

"Not much." Her knife dips again into the mustard. "Went

out for a while. It was nice today, but it looks like we're going to have rain again tomorrow."

Thinking of Sandy, of the reverent tones in which she talks about her career, Alan asks, "Joanna, do you ever think about getting a job?"

Now she really looks surprised. In a puzzled voice, as though he is being willfully incoherent and she is being patient, she asks, "Do you resent supporting me?" She does not sound defensive; it is perfectly clear to Alan that if he says he does, she will not go out and get a job, she will leave him. But won't she have to get a job then?

"No," he says, truthfully, "not at all. I just wonder if you don't feel some sort of a need . . ."

"If I do," Joanna says, "I'll look for a job." She says it to humor him, to reassure him: Yes, Mother, if the cold gets worse I promise I'll see a doctor. Said with perfect confidence that the cold will not get worse and there will be no need for the doctor.

For dessert there are store-bought cookies. Joanna does not put anything on top of sweets, nor does she put anything in her coffee. Alan, who likes cream and sugar, finds this perverse.

Alan is, of course, dazzled by Joanna's apparent freedom from the constraints under which most people (notably himself, notably Sandy) must operate. He has always been dazzled by this, especially since Joanna comes from a background almost identical to his own. They are both Jews from the middle-class New York suburbs, though they didn't meet until they were both undergraduates at Stanford. It was he who insisted they marry, two months after graduation, and now he sometimes wonders whether if they had done as Joanna suggested and just lived together, she would have gotten a job. He suspects not.

At Stanford they had both felt a little out of place. They had separately begun to wonder a little what they were doing there. They had been drawn together by their lack of interest in outdoor sports (though lately Alan has begun to think about running in the evenings) and by their mannerisms, which were described by the other students, sometimes admiringly, as "cynical" and "aggressive." Before meeting each other, they had both cultivated these mannerisms as sources of individuality; as a couple, they were constantly told how perfect they were for each other.

One advantage of meeting, marrying, and living in California: The whole thing went on far from the approving eyes of their parents. Each set has visited a couple of times, and of course they came out for the wedding, but basically Alan and Joanna have been allowed to discover the familiarity and the strangeness of one another without suggestive family illustrations of what they may someday become. Joanna's mother is actually quite upset that her daughter does not have a job. She herself has gone back to school and plans to become a real estate agent.

After dinner Alan and Joanna sit together in their living room. He goes through the files he has brought home, and she lies on the floor and reads. That's one thing she does during the day, he knows; the paperback books pile up very quickly. She was a comparative literature major in college (he was an economics major, and after a year or two of work experience, he plans to apply to business school). She must spend time in used book stores; very few of the paperbacks are new. He imagines her picking up a man in a used book store, going with him perhaps to some coffee house in North Beach. Alan doubts it; Joanna has never had much to do with literary types. The book she is reading now is in French. She reads a lot of experimental modern literature, which he doesn't like much.

When he wants to read one of her books, he asks her to recommend one, and she always recommends books with traditional prose and solid plots.

They go to bed early and make love, and Alan is reminded
of one reason why Sandy has only limited appeal for him.
From the very beginning of his relationship with Joanna, the
sex has been fabulous. He knew back then that she was as
overwhelmed as he; they were both fresh from other undergraduate affairs and they admitted to each other when intimacy
had overridden discretion that their former lovers could not
compare. So that is Alan's final protection against nameless
men in bookstores. It is also, he suspects, one of the main
reasons she married him.

As the winter goes on, Alan's flirtation with Sandy becomes
ritualized. They pay special attentions to one another, they
spend time in one another's offices, and on several occasions
they slip very close to a kiss. Sandy has gotten the message
that Alan has "someone," but she has also made it clear that
she doesn't much care. He finds her familiar, after people he
knew at Stanford, but still pleasantly exotic. All winter she
talks about skiing conditions. She knows someone with a cabin
at Tahoe. She is concerned that women are discriminated
against in the business world when it comes to promotion.
She is taking a course in French cooking, and there are many
jokes between them about how he must come over sometime
and she will try out her new skills on him.

And yet it is still Joanna whom he finds truly strange and
truly alluring. The sense of a secret in his own life has perhaps
helped him to be cool about the secret substance of hers. Or
is it really so secret? He still cannot imagine what she does
all day. Of course, his own mother had no job. But she had
children, and a big house which she kept in perfect order.
Joanna shows no particular interest in housekeeping, though

since they are both neat people the apartment is rarely very messy. Actually, in many ways the apartment does show Joanna's touch; it is full of odd things she has picked up somewhere or other: teapots with no lids, empty perfume bottles, plastic cartons meant to hold milk bottles and printed with warnings that to steal them is a punishable offense, sofa pillows that do not match the sofa, and, of course, all those books. There are also her familiar college possessions. Her electric typewriter, which she got from her parents when she graduated from high school, sits in its case against one wall. Alan wonders if she ever takes it out and types. Perhaps she writes letters sometimes during the day (his electric typewriter, which he got from his parents for the same occasion, is stored neatly in one of the closets along with his stereo—they use Joanna's stereo, which is better). He recognizes some of the books from college courses. Since she had those books when they moved into the apartment, they are on the shelves. It is the more recently acquired books which are piled precariously in the hall.

Alan imagines bringing Sandy into the apartment. The thought horrifies him, but it also pleases him. It confirms that it is Joanna, not Sandy, who is the incomprehensible factor in his life. Joanna, who does not have a job, not Sandy, who also plans to apply to business school someday. He continues to flirt with Sandy and to stop on the way home for lime pickle or grated cheese for Joanna, and he continues to make love to Joanna at night with a delight he knows he will never approach with anyone else.

One day near the end of winter he comes home and Joanna has gotten her hair cut; it is short and dark and curly. Joanna is average height, fairly thin, but with generous hips and breasts. Sandy is taller, her hips are narrow, and her breasts are very small. Alan feels dazzled sometimes by the promise of Sandy and the reality of Joanna. He likes Joanna's hair short, partly because it emphasizes the differences between her and Sandy. He no longer worries that she is having an affair; it is as if his own self-restraint guarantees that she is also faithful. An affair, he feels, would "solve" the puzzle of Joanna's days in much too obvious a manner. Her movements would make sense to anyone, instead of being a mystery even to him.

And yet, one night when he comes home and she says she has something to tell him, that is the conclusion he jumps to right away: She has been having an affair and she is about to confess. His almost forgotten plan about Sandy is suddenly clear in his mind. He says nothing; he hands her the jar of hot green chili sauce he has brought for her.

"Green!" Joanna exults. She knows only red chili sauces.

"I thought you'd like it," Alan says. There is a pause.

"Pot roast for dinner," Joanna says.

"But you had something to tell me?"

"It'll keep." She serves the pot roast, pouring the green chili sauce over her portion. Alan is suddenly reassured. Joanna is not having an affair, he is positive. And he will not have to sleep with Sandy, which makes him feel relieved, he doesn't stop to analyze why. Perhaps Joanna is going to tell him she has found a job? Or perhaps just that her parents are coming for a visit.

"Maybe I'll try some of that chili sauce," Alan says. Joanna passes it over to him, and he puts a delicate spoonful on the edge of his plate, away from the pot roast gravy. He dips a piece of meat into the chili sauce and burns his tongue so badly that he gulps down a bottle of warm beer, which Joanna assures him is the best thing. He stares at her as she eats pieces of meat slathered with the fiery sauce, and she smiles at him.

"Oh well," he says, "as long as you like it."

"I love it," she says.

"You must have a mouth of iron," Alan says, still feeling a faint pain on his tongue.

"No nerve endings," Joanna says.

After dinner Alan says again, "You had something to tell me?"

Joanna actually looks embarrassed. Then she goes out of the room and returns with an enormously fat folder.

"I've written something," she says.

"You've written something?"

"I've written a novel," she says, still looking embarrassed.

There is a small silence.

Alan asks formally, "May I read it?"

Joanna nods. She puts the folder in his lap. "I'll go in the bedroom," she says. "I couldn't bear to watch you read it."

Alone, Alan checks the last page: two hundred seventy-three. Joanna has never written anything that he knows of, except various papers when she was in college, which were all very well received. In fact, she did much better than he did. He feels the weight of the folder. So there is a solution, after all, to the puzzle.

Finding himself a little irritated (did it have to be such a state secret?), Alan starts to read. Quickly he is more irritated: The writing is "experimental," the sort of thing Joanna would never recommend to him out of her piles. There are too many characters in the first few pages and too many breaks; the writing is in fragments and they do not connect. Alan is soon skimming, aware that this is a terrible thing to do (skimming his own wife's novel, which she has been writing in secret for so long and has finally entrusted to him), but unable to concentrate on the scattered images.

Then he comes across a sex scene, which he reads carefully, though he cannot identify the two participants from the pages he has already read (perhaps the woman was the character in the back of the open truck, he remembers that scene). The sex scene is extremely graphic, and Alan is aroused. He tries to decide if the man is meant to be him; there is a detailed description of the man's penis but Alan is unable to decide whether it matches his own. The woman is surely not Joanna, at least not physically; she has long straight brown hair and she is a little overweight. The man in Joanna's novel finds the woman's body unexpectedly attractive when she is naked, and Alan agrees. He wants to put aside the manuscript (a glance at the subsequent pages shows him there will be only more fragments) and go into the bedroom to Joanna, but perhaps she will be offended.

He sits with an erection, the folder open on his knees. He is angry with Joanna because he cannot read her novel. And he is quite sure it will be published; it will be published and it will be a huge success. Joanna's existence will become public. Everyone will understand why his wife has no job; she is a writer. Alan is angry, but also very sad. He wonders about himself: Has he nothing to look forward to now except Sandy?

Bloomingdale's

The Paramus branch of Bloomingdale's is holding three after-noon lectures for local home economics classes. Each afternoon will cover one important subject for teenage girls: fashion, makeup, and diet and exercise. Since all the girls will have to miss school those afternoons, they must get their parents to sign permission slips.

The home economics teacher says to the home economics class: "And I hope you will remember that you are repre-senting our school and dress accordingly. No jeans, please."

"Are other pants okay?" a girl asks.

"I think we'll say double knit is fine, but corduroy is out," the teacher says, and the girls nod.

There is one girl in the room who looks different. Some are fatter, some have worse acne, but she is the only one who does not seem to have made an effort. Her name is Maggie. She is one of very few girls to wear no makeup, her jeans are baggy, her man's teeshirt is an ugly brown, and her hair looks a little dirty. The other fat girls wear clothes that the magazines say will distract attention from their waists, and they take special trouble with their hair. Just by looking, you could not tell that Maggie is the only overweight girl who isn't on a perpetual diet, but that's true too. She is sitting next to her best friend, who has also made little obvious effort, but manages to look quite all right in her jeans and shirt. Maggie's best friend is thin and her skin is clear. She sits hunched over, covertly doing French under the desk.

[It is so hard to give any dignity to high school. And I am afraid to tell you the truth. Because the truth would be I was the fattest, the ugliest, the one on whom a thousand full skirts, interesting necklines, and layers of Cover Girl makeup would have been useless. And my best friend was one of those people who cannot make a graceless move, and her blond hair swung around her face perfectly, and even her handwriting was beautiful . . . but the truth would make my story less convincing; you might write it off as the leftover self-hatred and jealousy of an unhappy teenager, so I will tone it down to where you will begin to believe me.]

The home economics room is full of sewing machines. They sit around the sides of the room and wait for the girls to sew. There is a bulletin board with a poster on it, released by the Simplicity Pattern Company, which shows six very pretty teenage girls in dresses made from Simplicity patterns. The writing on the bottom of the poster says these are the winners of Simplicity's "Sew It and Model It Contest" and copies of the poster, along with rules for next year's contest, are available from Simplicity for seventy-five cents.

There is another bulletin board with charts of the four basic food groups on it. That is for the advanced home economics class, in which girls learn about planning a family's meals. It is coordinated with the senior health class, in which girls learn about the other kind of family planning.

Maggie shifts down in her chair so her feet sprawl out. Her best friend, who is artistic, draws a very clever caricature of the teacher and shows it to Maggie, who grins. The bell rings and they all go off to gym.

Once, a year ago, Maggie dressed up for school. She wore jeans that the lady in Bamberger's said were just her size, and a flowered shirt with pearly buttons. The clothes felt very tight. She borrowed some of her mother's face powder and held her hair back with two matching barrettes. She was not comfortable that day, but she held a picture of her prettiness in her mind and moved with care and deliberate grace. Gym period came, and she faced the full-length mirror in the locker room, and she bulged out of the clothes and her face looked greasy. It has been so long since then that probably no one can remember her in anything but the baggy clothes she is wearing now. Home economics is required, and so is gym.

[In fact, everything we took was required that year, even music, where the teacher, who wore fake stick-on sideburns, had a special program called "Jukebox Jury," in which we rated the top ten songs every week, then discussed their musical qualities, and later had to identify lyrics on a test. So you see, I don't need to exaggerate.]

Maggie comes to school the day of the first trip to Bloomingdale's in a skirt and teeshirt, and all the girls get on the school bus. Maggie sits with her best friend, and everybody sings for a while, starting with "Found a Peanut" and going on to a football song. Maggie knows all the words (that was their first music lesson) and she lets herself sing softly until she catches her best friend's eye and feels obliged to giggle. She looks out her window at Paramus, New Jersey, shopping-center capital of the world. All over Paramus there are enormous shopping malls. Some are enclosed in superbuildings, with trees along the indoor promenades between the stores. Waterfalls tumble off the roofs of department stores onto Styrofoam rocks in lily ponds (the lilies are plastic, as are the frogs crouching on them), and one mall has a bunch of automated plastic cows (life-size) grazing on the Astroturf.

The Bloomingdale's mall is one of the classier ones. Maggie and most of her classmates are more familiar with some of the cheaper stores at the more plebeian malls. The bus parks, the girls climb out and follow the teacher into Bloomingdale's. As they move toward the escalator, they finger the scarves, stroke the tweed blazers, and a few of the daring try a spritz from one of the sample perfume bottles.

Maggie is at the back of the group; she sees the first girls rising into the quiet heights of Bloomingdale's on the escalator. She has always been slightly afraid of up escalators, but she gets on and off without hesitation. The girls are led around the handbag tables and into a small auditorium. It is almost full of other home economics classes; there are just enough seats left. They all sit down. The faces are young and pretty, colored with creams and powders, the bodies are dressed in pastels, the necks are circled by thin gold chains dangling crosses, stars, charms, and hearts onto shirts or into necklines.

[And yet they couldn't *all* have been pretty, could they? I could watch them in the hall at school and see individual flaws. Some of them were beautiful, some were pretty, and some fit in only by virtue of careful attention to detail. But all together, they blended into a pretty group, a group of pretty girls.]

It takes five minutes to quiet the girls down. A woman walks onto the stage and welcomes them all. She is handsome, wearing a dark red suit, and she handles herself easily. She comments on what a nice-looking group they are and how pleased Bloomingdale's is to welcome them. The first topic, she announces, will be fashion. Several Bloomingdale's people come on the stage and talk: the lady from the College Boutique, the man from Teen Sportswear, finally the lady from Lingerie.

The girls giggle. "Now," she says, "there is nothing funny about underwear. After all, we're all girls together here." They giggle again.

The Bloomingdale's people pick six pretty girls out of the audience, ask them to come up on the stage, and analyze their clothes. They tell one to put on a blue sweater ("See how it pulls your whole look together?") and another to put on a plastic belt painted to look as if it were made out of linked chewing-gum wrappers ("See how the right accessories highlight your outfit!"), and soon they are all festooned with Bloomingdale's merchandise.

"I bet everyone goes down and buys those things right after the lecture," Maggie whispers to her best friend.

"There'll be thirty people wearing that belt in school tomorrow," whispers her best friend, and they giggle.

The next week they pick six girls and have them take off all their own makeup with cold cream. Then a very effeminate man ("faggy," the girls whisper) with a tie printed to look like gum wrappers applies makeup to them while he explains what he is doing: "brings out" "conceals" "shadows" "plays up" "shapes" "highlights" "brightens" "plucks" and "covers." The six decorated girls then walk around the room so everyone can get a good look, while the man answers questions.

"What can I do about my freckles?"

"My brows never come out even."

"What liner goes well with green eye shadow?"

"Is it better to have your lipstick match your blush exactly?"

Maggie whispers to her best friend, "I dare you to ask how to cover serious birth defects." Maggie thinks makeup looks silly and has never been really tempted to use it, so she is able to laugh. Still, she sometimes imagines she is Cybill Shepherd posing for Cover Girl makeup ads. These are the kinds of fantasies she tries not to have, and she is ashamed of herself for having them. She feels that to daydream about being Cybill Shepherd is just the sort of silly irony she should avoid.

[In case you wonder, I can also still recognize Susie Blakely, and Lauren Hutton, and every other model who ever glowed on the cover of *Mademoiselle* in her autumn-russet cheek gloss and peach-coral lip paint, hair by Sassoon.]

The makeup man produces a little blue plastic thing; it looks like a tiny propeller. When he presses a switch it spins like a fan and he explains that it is a battery-operated eyeliner dryer. Maggie laughs aloud and everyone looks at her.

The third week is diet and exercise. The girls are told to eat fruit instead of candy and to get fresh air during their menstrual periods (giggles). It is suggested that they make a habit of chewing each mouthful of food thirty-two times ("Your jaws will get tired and you won't take so many mouthfuls!"), and that they spend twenty minutes a day doing some simple exercises. To demonstrate the exercises the Bloomingdale's people pick six overweight girls. Maggie sees the woman coming toward her and tries to look both hostile and invisible. The woman picks her, leads her to the stage, where she stands with the five other overweight girls, all embarrassed and fidgeting.

"Lie down on your backs," the woman says. "Now lift your legs off the floor." Maggie does not lift her legs. She lies on her back in the soft Bloomingdale's carpet. The woman says, "Now, we're not trying." She picks up Maggie's ankles, rather gingerly.

Maggie screams. The lady drops her ankles. All the other girls jump up. Maggie lies there. The lady touches her shoulder and Maggie screams again and kicks the carpet. Maggie's teacher hurries up to the stage, and Maggie is on her feet with bits of lint in her hair. She is so angry that her head burns. She is so angry she wants to spit. She spits at her home economics teacher, who shrieks.

Maggie is standing alone on the stage and crying, and everyone stares at her, and if there is understanding in the eyes of the other five fat girls she does not see it. Maggie wraps her arms around herself and shudders, wishing she were invisible, weightless. She has a sudden tearstained picture of herself flying above Bloomingdale's, holding on to a battery-operated blue plastic propeller.

Television
Will Betray
Us All

As you know, if you remember the late 1940s, my mother was at the center of a highly celebrated kidnapping and child custody suit. Her father, who was an immensely wealthy self-made man, had her kidnapped from her mother, the lower-class wife of his humble origins, long since deserted, long since sunk into drink and squalor. He had the best lawyer his money could buy, and she had the best lawyers that could be gotten for the money of a certain tabloid, which had negotiated the exclusive rights to her story. The whole thing made for quite a to-do. In the end, the court returned my mother to her mother and the tabloid had a field day, closely followed by most of the other newspapers in the country, even some of the respectable ones. My mother, who was fourteen by the time this was all over, settled down with her mother, who gave up liquor and took to lecture tours. Eventually my mother met and married my father and they moved out to the suburbs of San Francisco and had me, not to mention my brother and sister.

I tell you all this for two reasons. First of all, I do it to give myself the authority of the interesting person, the celebrity once removed. I expect you to recognize the story and say, Oh, so *that's* who her mother is. Second of all, to explain why the TV crew shows up at our house one day and I get my first look at Gorgeous Joe, and, for that matter, he gets his first look at me, though I doubt he remembers it.

So this TV crew shows up at the house and, lo and behold, someone is making a special TV movie about The Case of My Mother, or The Case of the Rich Little Poor Girl, or whatever it is they are calling it, and their idea is to film an interview with my mother and use bits of it to start and end the program. The part of my mother in the movie itself will be played by a singularly succulent little sex-bomb of a sixteen-year-old (I rather like that, though in fact she's only fifteen, which makes her closer to my mother's actual age at the time, even if it does ruin my phrase) who has become quite famous recently after a hot series of bra ads. My mother, it turns out, to my surprise, has known all about this project for some time, and has already been to see a lawyer and discovered she has little chance of stopping it or suing successfully. She has decided, with great reluctance, to cooperate with the interview, so that she can at least get some of her side of the story into the show.

I am surprised by this evidence of my mother's determination and toughness. I am also at least a little bit surprised by this new reminder that she is in fact who she is, or was. What can I say, she is so much my mother, so much the somewhat plump hospital-gift-shop volunteer, haphazard gardener, subscriber to the recipe-of-the-month club, that it is hard for me to remember that she is also the little girl, the young lady, in the newspaper clippings that fill a certain thick blue vinyl scrapbook. A scrapbook which was produced for her children only on very rare occasions, after much teasing and many promises, a scrapbook she always seemed half-ashamed to page through with us, though after a while her shame would fall away and she would be as fascinated as we. But that sweet young lady dressed in furs, muff and tippet, dressed by her father to show how much he wanted to give her, or that girl in the ribboned dress, supposedly homemade for her by her loving mother, though actually, she admitted to us, bought at a department store and hastily gussied up with extra frills and ribbons to make it look more homemade— was that my mother? I was a little surprised every time, just as I was more than a little surprised to see the TV crew arrive. My brother and my sister may have taken the scrapbook more in stride, I don't know. They certainly grew up to take other things in stride a lot better than I did. As witness the fact that when the TV crew shows up I am watching them out a third-floor window, resident mad-auntie-in-the-attic at the age of twenty-seven, while my brother and sister are both out in the world, living on their own, my sister in her college dormitory, my brother with his wife and children. Both of them perfectly functional, my brother and my sister. Only mad auntie left grinning out the attic window. Well, two out of three isn't so bad, I often think of saying to my mother.

My mother, because it is her immediate response to visitors before noon, is serving coffee and coffee cake when I come creep-creep-creeping downstairs. I hover just outside the kitchen, looking the three TV people over, a tall thin black man in a denim jacket and jeans lavishly decorated with metal studs, an earnest young woman with short curly brown hair, and Gorgeous Joe. No question which of these three is the one who actually gets to be on TV. There he sits, gracefully folded into one of my mother's cane-and-chrome kitchen chairs, there he sits, careless but not offensive display of crotch, thighs tight against his nice gray pants, the endearingly mussed blond hair, the unexpectedly dark eyes holding mine.

My mother introduces me, her daughter Barbara Ann, a

name he has no doubt forgotten by now. The Ann of course was originally intended to be a separate, freestanding middle name, not a pseudo-Southern downbeat at the end of the Barbara, and to be honest I can no longer remember the exact flight of youthful eccentricity in which I decided to add on the Ann. My mother introduces me, the other two nod, but Gorgeous Joe uncurls to stand and take my hand and look more deeply still into my eyes, telegraphing to me the message that if only all these people would go away, he and I could tear off all our clothes and get down to it. I try hard to telegraph back, I'll bet you tell that to all the girls, but part of me wants to ignore that and lead him right up to my bedroom. Men, picking them, has never been one of the few things at which I am either skillful or lucky, but I will say that the times I have taken on obvious and experienced womanizers, things have gone much better than I would have predicted. What I say is, so they've done all that practicing, why not take advantage of it?

Meantime I settle into another of my mother's chairs and watch her flutter around nervously, trying to cope with this intrusion of her past as sensational media figure by pouring on a liberal dose of her present as suburban California housewife. Coffee and coffee cake, but also organic bakery date-nut cookies, herbal tea for me and the black man in studs.

"You know," my mother says suddenly, leaning against her dishwasher, perhaps drawing strength from it, "I'm really not eager to do this interview. I regard this whole movie you're making as a violation of my privacy."

"Well, ma'am," Joe says, with a drawl which I can tell is completely fake, "I can certainly understand how you might feel that way. But you know, none of us here thought up this movie. In fact, we don't have very much to do with it, except to film this interview. Seems like your best option might be to do the interview and sort of set the record straight for the whole movie."

"Yes," my mother says, tightly, "that's what the lawyer said too, and the executives at your network. It doesn't seem to occur to any of you people that I don't care nearly as much about setting the record straight as I do about keeping the record quiet."

Joe spreads his hands to indicate helplessness and a hunky chest. I sit and sip my herbal tea. I was not offered coffee; it is considered too strong a stimulant for me. At the moment, I have all the stimulants I need. Before I can finish my tea, they have adjourned to the living room and are setting up lights and cameras. My mother goes upstairs to change her clothes and I follow, curious to see what she will make of herself.

It is amazing to watch, this transformation of my mother. I wonder whether she is remembering long-ago injunctions about how to dress for the cameras. She puts on a sharp black-and-white linen dress I have never seen before, and I am left to wonder, does she always, at all times, have at least one dress in her wardrobe that is suitable for meeting the press? She also has smoke-gray stockings and high-heeled black pumps. She brushes her hair fiercely and twists some of the front hair back into a knot, secures it with a bobby pin, muttering to herself the whole time. Cursing? Rehearsing? And then makeup, crimson lipstick and dark eyeliner, blush, shadow, pencil, all on my mother who usually wears a little powder and a pale pinkish lipstick. She looks herself over in the mirror.

We go downstairs, me trailing behind again, and I watch from the doorway as the man in studs and the woman arrange my mother on her own living room couch, shining lights into her eyes, setting her on edge in her own room, now treacherously metamorphosed into their stage. Joe drapes himself next to her, looks up to meet my eyes and wink at me, then turns his attention to my mother, his subject, his object. Out comes the voice, cough syrup, liquid Jell-O. He is pretending to put my mother at ease, while his accomplices fool around with their equipment.

From my position in the doorway, I feel a sudden urge to go to my mother's aid, to fling myself between my mother and the cameras. Normally, of course, I assume that my mother can take care of herself; I, after all, am the one who has proven unable to cope. My mother bakes perfect pies and raised at least two perfect children and after all these years of marriage it is obvious that my father loves her still, while in my life it is usually obvious after one night that any man on whom I have bestowed my favors is done for the time being. But I look at my mother up against Joe and the lights and the cameras, and it seems to me that here is something I could handle better than she. These people are not so far from my vision of the world. The cameras and the lights and the overdramatic makeup are with me always, in one way or another. She will try to deal with Gorgeous Joe by giving reasonable but guarded answers to his gelatinous questions, and I, on the other hand, understand that Jell-O dissolves promptly in acid.

The interview goes badly. My mother's answers are too guarded, and Joe is pushing things too fast. He wants, as I knew he would want, some evidence of scarring, and my mother wants only to show that it was a small episode in her past which left her unmarked. She had a drinking problem? Joe is asking, about my mother's mother, and primly my mother tells him it was a hard time for both her mother and her father. Joe's questions get sharper and meaner and my mother's answers get shorter and vaguer. Finally she stops, stares at him in complete silence, the sweat on her makeup shiny in the bright lights, and she says, I really don't care for that kind of question. What has he just asked, some intimate detail about her mother's post-trial sex life, some gossipy point about her father's mistresses?

Joe apologizes, never breaking stride. My mother is unwilling to continue with the interview, and they settle that the crew will come back tomorrow for some more filming. Watching the willingness with which they pack up, I understand quite clearly that this was all planned; tomorrow they will come and seem more familiar and Joe will ease up a little on the questions and my mother will open herself to the cameras. I wonder whether to tell her this, as I watch the TV people leave. Joe, on his way out, turns to wave to my mother and to smile past her at me. I understand you, you lizard, I think. And I'd be happy to put you through your paces. I'm a nervous person, practically an invalid, a perfect martyr to my own delicate emotions. I need fresh fruit and healthy outdoor activity, like maybe a TV interviewer or two. I grin knowingly at Joe. If he were a piece of fruit, he would be a plastic banana.

After they leave, my mother, tight-lipped and still bizarrely snazzy, announces that she's going out for a while. I know she needs comfort and encouragement, and I feel briefly sorry that she cannot come to me for it, but I know she will go to her very close friend Annette, and the two of them will knock back a few ladylike glasses of white wine (since it is after lunchtime now) and my mother will be able to tell her story and find comfort in Annette's messy Mexican-tiled kitchen, among the overgrown avocado plants. Annette is the only friend to whom my mother has confided the story of her past; Annette has seen that blue vinyl scrapbook and probably heard extra details that my mother never told her children, details that Gorgeous Joe would give his left ball to know.

My mother reminds me about the various things there are

for me to eat in the house and drives off to see Annette. I take a plate of grapes out back to the swimming pool and sit, spitting the pits into the water, thinking about Joe. First I think maybe I will let him seduce me mentally as well as physically; I will believe he loves me for myself and tell him all kinds of private things about my mother, and then when it turns out he was only using me, when the TV movie comes out with all those details prominently displayed, I will have a breakdown. I will betray my mother, Joe will betray me, television will betray us all. Perhaps I will attempt suicide, I think lazily, then have to laugh. Suicide over Gorgeous Joe? Then I think perhaps I will use him to betray my mother, but consciously and with full intent. I will invent the scandalous intimate details, invent the ones that will hurt her most, which will put some permanent wrinkles into her relationship with my father. And then afterward I will reveal that they were all false and ruin Joe's career. I have to laugh: ruin Gorgeous Joe's career? Finally I think maybe I will give him a really good scare, turn up in his home, announce I have moved in, I love him and only him. In a way that one is the funniest of them all.

I finish my grapes and go into the cabana to change into my bathing suit, drape myself by the side of the pool to await Joe. I know that in my bathing suit, lying on my side in the California sunshine, I can sometimes approximate the good looks of a cheerleader. I have long blond hair and reasonable curves and a pretty good suntan—why shouldn't I, I live at home and I don't have a job and I lie around the pool a lot. Of course, when I'm having one of my difficult spells, this shadow of the cheerleader only makes it more upsetting for anyone watching; nothing so unnerving as a healthy, pretty thing somehow twisted out of all predicting.

Joe arrives not very much later, pretends to be looking for my mother so he can apologize to her once more, accepts my offer of a swim. Ten minutes and we are doing it next to the pool. He isn't as good as he might be, but not so bad for a plastic banana. I think about my mother, afterward, as we lie in the sun. I make a rule for myself: I will not betray her. When Joe starts to ask me little questions, I make my answers blander than hers were; I play cheerleader then, and with a vengeance. I have figured something out about Joe. He is not just into it for the conquest, my blond hair, my curves, but neither is he in it for the tricky espionage of the TV movie. No, Gorgeous Joe is celebrity-struck. To him, the point is that I am the child of someone famous enough for him to interview. How enormously touching, I think, all those interviews, all those celebrities, and still so impressed by it. Poor baby, and he will never be interviewed himself; what could he ever hope to do that would interest anyone?

I am so touched by this realization that I feel a sudden urge to make him a present of the kind of information that would be so valuable for him: I am mad auntie in the attic. I am unstable; I have breakdowns. I go crazy every now and then. I am the California dream gone sour, the cheerleader madwoman. You have not just scored with the relative of a celebrity, you have made it with a sideshow exhibit. I want to tell him some of this, but I remember my rule. This would be a betrayal of my mother. Instead I put my bathing suit back on and demonstrate my perfect pool-in-the-backyard crawl for a while, back and forth through the chlorinated water in neat identical laps. Joe, sitting up to watch me, has maneuvered himself back into his clothes. Poor boy, he looks a little lost, a plastic banana far away from its friend the felt-covered pear. A character in search of a cue card. I pull myself out of the water, a deceptive picture of health and vitality. He stands up and opens his arms and I go to him for a hug which will leave him very wet.

Standing wrapped in his arms, I feel suddenly very very sad. I have to bite my lips not to cry. I want to cry and cry in the arms of Gorgeous Joe. But I don't; I will not betray my mother. And anyway, suppose he asked me what was wrong, what would I say? I am crying because no one would ever go to court for the right to keep me? I am crying because my father would never have me kidnapped rather than lose me? I am crying because my presence is no victory for my mother, or my father, only maybe, at this particular moment, a tiny little triumph for Gorgeous Joe?

I don't cry. I smile at him, as cheerleader to winner. What he doesn't know won't hurt anyone.

Cowboy Time

What Joyce and Edward had in common was their taste in men. They both liked what they called "cowboys," rough tough types with boots and not too much education. Actually, Joyce and Edward had quite a few other things in common as well, including their appearances: They were both tall and thin and dark. Attractive. For that matter, they dressed alike for work; they would meet sometimes on the bus coming from the financial district, both in sober suits, expensive button-down shirts.

They lived on the same block near Union Street in San Francisco, in a neighborhood full of single young professionals and small restaurants. They both had good incomes: Edward was a lawyer and Joyce an advertising consultant. And they had the same taste in men. They had been friends for almost two years, having met at a party of young professionals, where they agreed in a corner, over California white wine emphatically not of the cheapest variety, that the party held no sexual prospects for either of them.

Their backgrounds were different: Edward came from a small town in California; his father owned a hardware store.

Joyce's father was a lawyer and her mother taught music in a private high school in New York; her parents lived on the Upper East Side. Joyce herself had drifted around quite a bit after finishing college (Maine, Texas, Wisconsin, instead of Boston; waitress, artist's model, receptionist), and her parents had been immensely relieved when she finally settled in San Francisco and landed the advertising job. She was immediately good at it; her guesses consistently turned out to be correct, rather to her amazement at first, and her reputation and salary increased.

Edward, on the other hand, had been the best of all possible superachieving children from the word go. He had worked ferociously hard through college and law school, made his parents enduringly proud, and gotten himself to San Francisco, where he proceeded to loosen up as he discovered the opera, the symphony, and the bars, particularly the "western" bars.

All along, from the moment I first thought about moving back to New York, there were warning voices in my brain. Part of it, of course, was San Francisco; I would come to a street corner and look down a steep hill at the bay and Alcatraz, and wonder how I could even think of leaving a city where such beauty was available on my everyday walks. But the real problem about moving to New York was that my family was there. Three thousand miles away from them I had been able to put my life in order (I am even beginning to sound Californian, I see), and I was aware that if I reentered the parental orbit, so to speak, I might throw away my new "success" just for the mean pleasure of letting my parents watch, helpless. I like and respect my parents; the level of resentment I am expressing here is, I think, not at all atypical for a child of extremely successful intelligent Jewish parents. Edward is completely unable to understand it, his parents being neither Jewish nor extremely successful. As for intelligent, he tells me his mother is very bright in a stifled sort of way, and I am inclined to believe him because one way or another (heredity or environment, that is), there must be something in his background to explain his own mental abilities.

Anyway, I had doubts about moving back to New York. The main reason I was thinking about moving was somewhat crass and embarrassing: I had begun to believe that for better or worse I was genuinely talented and suited for the advertising world and might go very high. And of course you can't go as high anywhere else as you can in New York. And perhaps there is a general feeling which comes from my parents (after all, if they didn't want me blaming them for everything, they should never have paid for those three years of analysis when I was in high school) that no achievements really "count" except those achieved in New York. Why should I be proud of finding and maintaining a beautiful apartment, valuable friendships, a good job, when they were all in a city that wasn't really a city at all (there being only one City)? And there I was, ready to accept the challenge.

You may have noticed that I didn't include lovers or "sexual relationships" on that list of successful maintenance jobs. The omission was deliberate: My sexual encounters are not so much "maintained" as they are "pulled off." Even Edward has relationships that last longer than mine.

Joyce and Edward arrived by taxi from Kennedy Airport; Joyce's parents had been unable to meet them because the plane landed at the same time as a meeting they both had to attend, a neighborhood tenants' association meeting. Joyce's mother was president and her father was chairman of the legal committee. They were home from the meeting by the time the taxi delivered Joyce and Edward. After a flurry of hugs and introductions, Joyce's mother escorted them to the spare room, formerly Joyce's own bedroom, and now her father's study. Not until her parents had withdrawn, leaving Joyce and Edward among their luggage to freshen up, did Joyce fully realize that they were both meant to sleep in that room, on the brown corduroy sofa which unfolded into a double bed (her own bed, long since given to the Salvation Army, had had four posts and a canopy). She and Edward stood looking at one another for a minute, then collapsed onto the sofa.

"What exactly did you say in your letter?" Edward asked.

What had she said? She had asked if they could put up her good friend Edward, a lawyer who was also thinking of moving to New York and was interested, as was she herself, in investigating the job market there.

"You know," Joyce told him, "this is a big concession for my mother. She's never let me sleep with a boyfriend before, not under her roof. She always said it would upset my little sister."

Joyce had never been reticent with her mother about the sleeping arrangements on the occasions when she had brought home those other boyfriends. She had been perfectly willing to make scenes, to assure her parents loudly that they were hypocrites, that they knew perfectly well her little sister would not be the least bit disturbed, that they were playing stupid 1950s parental games. She had sneaked loudly around the house at night and screwed her boyfriends on the living room couch, daring her mother to come out and find them, which of course she never did, not with all that noise to warn her.

But Joyce found she could not do the opposite, she could not go after her mother and explain that when she called Edward a friend she meant a friend, and would her mother please make up a bed for him on that same living room couch.

Edward understood. Laughing somewhat sheepishly, they un-
packed. Edward made a joke about getting documentation to
send to *his* parents. Joyce told him that compared to the other
boys she had brought home, he was a real prize.

"My parents are going to love you," she said.

"I can just imagine the others," Edward said, leering.

"I'm sure you can."

Twice in my life I have made the mistake of having serious
sexual relationships with "appropriate" men, cultured, well-
behaved men, men of education and sensibility, men with
whom I knew I could be good friends (as I am with Edward,
who is all of those things). Sexually they were disastrous, those
relationships; I couldn't have been less interested. What can
I say: What I like is what Edward and I call "cowboys." They
are what turn me on. The term "cowboy" is not meant to
identify occupation or ethnic group; my cowboy career really
started with a Puerto Rican taxi driver with whom I spent a
series of afternoons while I was still in high school, much to
the admiration of the other girls in my class. The closest I
have come to a real cowboy was a weatherbeaten twenty-two-
year-old from Montana who was one of the buildings and
grounds staff at college and used to come by my room early
in the morning for quickies, much to the horror of the other
girls in my dormitory (no one will be surprised to hear that a
private girls' high school in New York is much more sophisticated in these matters than a college in Ohio).

So I have really known all along exactly what I wanted and
needed when it came to sex. Those two "appropriate" affairs
I mentioned were misguided attempts to go against my own
instincts and achieve sexual and romantic "success." Since
then, I have settled for my own kind of success, which consists
of demonstrating over and over that the world is full of cow-

boys with the reciprocal fantasy. Part of their fantasy is generally to mistreat me emotionally ("I don't need you, you spoiled bitch"), and while I in my turn luxuriate in the painful abuse, I also value the guarantee that nothing will be permanent. They will leave me, and quickly, because they need to, and I will not have any lovesick cowboys in my life. That, after all, *I* don't need. What I love most about Edward is that he understands all this so perfectly.

Joyce's little sister, Suzy, had become a punk. Her hair was cut short and tinted purple on one side. She was sixteen years old. Joyce recognized the punk phenomenon, but without knowing very much about it. She liked Suzy immediately. She did not particularly like the music that pounded constantly from Suzy's room, but she had been an adolescent in that house herself, and she understood the value of loud popular sounds in a home devoted to the classics.

Suzy had a boyfriend, an extremely punk character who did not succeed in looking lower class in his stained leopard-print teeshirt and too-short pants. Joyce watched the two of them go off with a distinct feeling of jealousy; she had to stay home and get dressed for a cocktail party. Her parents were giving the party in her honor and had invited a number of people they thought might be useful to her, or to Edward, as well as old friends and even a few celebrities. In San Francisco Joyce would have enjoyed such a party, but here in her parents' home, she felt an adolescent's supercilious boredom at the prospect.

She examined herself in the spare-room mirror: She was wearing a dark-red silk dress and a lapis lazuli pendant. She looked like an attractive woman dressed for a cocktail party. Edward came up to stand beside her. He was wearing a dark gray suit. She took his arm and they mugged for the mirror: Mr. and Mrs. Cocktail Party.

Joyce had enjoyed sharing the room with Edward. Their friendship had proved rather stronger than she had realized; it had stretched to include cozy nocturnal hugs. They could lie in bed and talk late into the night. They could laugh at one another's morning grooming routines, at Edward's push-ups ("Have to keep in shape for when you get back to the gym in San Francisco, huh, Edward?") and Joyce's thigh-tightening leg lifts ("Tighten those thighs, my girl; you never know when you might find something to tighten them around").

Joyce's mother knocked on the door to remind them that people would be arriving soon. On Edward's arm, Joyce made her entrance.

Someone in this story is going to fall in love. Consider the possibilities: Edward with my sister's boyfriend. Edward with my sister. My sister with Edward. Edward with me. Me with my sister's boyfriend. Me with Edward. My mother with my sister's boyfriend. My sister's boyfriend with Edward. But no. Edward fell in love with my parents. It really started at that cocktail party. My parents, I should explain, are not exactly nobodies in certain New York circles. Most particularly, they figure in liberal lawyer circles and wealthy music-lover circles. My father is a genuinely good man, as I have known all my life; he devotes a great deal of time to the ACLU, he helps the poor and deserving (or occasionally the poor and undeserving), and he works hard for political causes in which he believes. That he manages nonetheless to make a very good living is hardly a fault. And my mother had a brief career as a singer, during the course of which she apparently got to know everyone who is anyone today in the New York musical world. Needless to say, I don't mean punk. Or Broadway.

So poor Edward. They really got him from both sides. On the one hand, the party was full of successful lawyers who were also Good People and Doing Good. Worlds more interesting than the people Edward worked with in San Francisco, who were so much more consciously "professional." And on the other hand, Edward was a recent arrival in San Francisco, desperately in love with the opera, the symphony, the Mostly Mozart Festival (which is a pale shadow of the New York festival, as I could have told him), in love with all these things and also in awe of them. And at that party were people he had heard sing, someone he had once seen conduct. . . . It was enough to make his head spin. It did make his head spin.

I actually made a valuable contact at that party. One of my mother's old friends had brought along her sister, who was in my field. We hit it off, she and I, and spent much of the party getting drunk in a corner and telling scatological stories about our separate agencies. We were distinguished from the gathering at large by being neither committed to any art nor professional doers of good. She told me she was sure she could help me get a job.

Edward came out of that party aglow. As I said, he had fallen in love. With my parents, with their friends, with the "glitter" of that side of New York life. It has happened before, I suppose. Poor Edward. And he had thought San Francisco was the big time.

Joyce and Edward lay in their chaste double bed. He wore pajamas. She wore a nightgown. Her head rested on his outstretched arm. Joyce had begun to relax; at last, shut away from her parents, she could remind herself that she and Edward were a charade, she could enjoy the irony, and she could even be proud of her parents.

"Joyce," Edward said rather tentatively, "I've been thinking about something."

"What's that?"

"I've been thinking—I mean maybe this is really silly, but we could get married."

There was a short silence, during which Joyce rejected the response "To each other?" in favor of:

"You aren't serious?"

Edward laughed. "I realize this is rather sudden. But then again, here we are in bed together."

For a minute Joyce was relieved. But no, it turned out that Edward was perfectly serious, at least within the overtones of camp that always graced his manner. He saw the two of them married, living in New York, moving in her parents' circles. He wanted it badly.

He did not give up the idea over the next few days. Joyce's father took him around to some law offices. They all ate out. Every night Edward marshaled his arguments: They could sleep with anyone they wanted to. They got along so well; look how happily they had been living in just one room. Joyce also understood some things that Edward left unsaid: He didn't just want her family's help and contacts, he wanted to really fit in and be a family member. Old fantasies, given up but apparently regretted, were coming back, his parents visiting their successful son and his successful wife. And he was unable to follow the twists of Joyce's feelings about her parents.

She gave up arguing, she just shook her head, smiled and said no, told him not to be so silly. He could not believe that deep down she did not want to bring her parents the pleasure such a marriage would surely cause. Joyce's parents liked Edward. Joyce could not explain that everything she dreaded about returning to New York would be magnified a hundred times if she returned as Edward's wife. He persisted in thinking it was the irregularity beneath the surface that put her off; he could not understand that it was the surface itself.

I have noticed that it is not an uncommon thing for gay men to believe that their straight female friends want to sleep with them. It is probable that this is sometimes true, and it also seems likely to me that for some of the men in question it is a necessary assurance. I had never really given much thought to whether Edward might believe this, and I was rather taken aback when, as part of his matrimonial crusade, he began to make sexual overtures to me. And he did it in a manner that implied that he felt that it was a concession to me. Living in one room, sleeping in one bed, it was a little awkward to be rejecting him. But he got the message and returned to his descriptions of a marriage involving separate rooms and lots of cowboys for us both. He was driving me crazy.

In the meantime, while all this ridiculous disputation was going on morning and evening, I had looked up the woman I had met at the cocktail party, she had set up some interviews for me, and I was well on my way to landing myself a very good job. And my father, of course, was dangling all sorts of tempting things in front of Edward.

The only person who knew the truth about what was going on was my sister Suzy. I had told her how things stood between Edward and me early in the visit, partly to amuse her but mostly to prove to her that I was not the staid half of a cocktail-party couple I seemed to be. When he developed his bad case of wedding bells, I confided in Suzy, who of course understood exactly why I was not interested in the marriage.

And it was Suzy, in the end, who got me out of that insane situation, or at least provided me with the opportunity to get myself out of it.

Joyce's parents had two tickets for *The Bartered Bride* at the Met. They had been able to obtain a third, but not a fourth. Joyce insisted that they take Edward, not her. She was glad there was no fourth ticket; difficult as it had become for her to spend time with Edward, she was still more uncomfortable on a double date with her parents. She knew that they liked

Edward not just because he was neat and polite and a lawyer; they liked him because he was clever and kind and deeply enthusiastic about the things that meant most to them. Joyce was not able to be so completely enthusiastic about anything to her parents, and Suzy, of course, was sophisticated, cynical, and bored to a degree which left Joyce far behind. Edward deserved the opera ticket.

Suzy took her sister to a party while the other three were at the opera. Most of the people at the party (and all of the music) were punk, though Joyce wore blue jeans and a sweater. No one else at the party was over twenty years old. It was held in a large apartment on Central Park West, belonging to a girl whose parents were out of town for the weekend. There was a great deal of quality marijuana, which Joyce smoked, some Quaaludes, which she did not take, and some cocaine, which was all gone before she got to it. Everyone danced, many of them not in couples. Suzy and her boyfriend disappeared; Joyce saw them under the kitchen table when she went looking for a drink of water. It all made her feel rather old, but in a sweetly nostalgic way.

She had come back from the kitchen, she was crowded into one corner of the couch, watching the angular movements of some of the punkier dancers, when she noticed a boy leaning against the wall. He was not dressed punk. He wore a denim jacket and white carpenter's pants and he had long blond hair, that is, it reached his shoulders, which seemed long compared to the hair on the people around him.

Joyce was delighted, after she began talking to him, to discover that he was not a high school student; he worked in a bar and had been invited by one of the boys who played in a band that occasionally appeared in the bar. He was from Arkansas. He was a nineteen-year-old high school dropout of a cowboy.

*   *   *

I considered the living room couch, just for old time's sake, you might say, but I didn't have the nerve. I took him into the spare room where we deflowered the fold-out bed that Edward and I had been sharing for the past week. His name was Ray and I liked him for not seeming the least bit taken aback by me, or my parents' apartment, or the story I told him about how they would be coming home from the opera any minute along with this guy who was gay but wanted me to marry him for complicated reasons having to do with his being in love with my parents.

"You want me to fuck him too?" Ray asked, in his leisurely Arkansas tones.

I heard them come in, I heard them in the living room wondering whether I was home, whether I was asleep. I strolled out to welcome them, holding my bathrobe closed around me, my nerve no doubt bolstered by the dope I had smoked, not to mention the aftereffects of the first sex I had had in a while.

Edward looked at me, and I think he knew immediately what was going on. I adored him for the way he accepted defeat. When Ray followed me out, wrapped in Edward's bathrobe, Edward actually managed a grin and a cool remark.

"Cowboy time, I see," he said. At that moment, seeing my parents' faces, I could almost have married Edward.

Gringo City

People who are moving forward, pursuing some goal, no matter how elusive or unlikely, frequently go off to the famous places of the world. To paint in Paris. To climb mountains in Nepal. To pile up fortunes in the great cities of South America. To make it big in Hollywood. But people who have somehow fallen out of their own patterns can often be found in the less celebrated corners of human habitation, quietly watching their lives go by, unable to fit those lives into any fantasies they can recognize. And of course, I place myself in the second category, since I retreated to a small town in Guatemala with my friend Martha after we were both deserted by our husbands.

Martha and I had been only casual friends before our common bereavement, if I may call it that. But it took only a few days for us to move from casual friendliness to certainty that the next part of our lives would be spent together. We had both been left in the same situation, Jenny and Martha, two leftover-hippie women in Cambridge, Massachusetts, each with a kitchen full of whole-grain pasta, bean curd, and carob. Me with my job in the overpriced yarn store and my halfhearted attempts at fabric sculpture. And Martha with her two children, Adam and Tara, ages three and five respectively. As for what had happened to our husbands, all we knew at that point was that both had disappeared within the same week, each leaving a short and extremely apologetic note: I'm sorry, I just can't handle this scene anymore. If you had condensed their two notes, that's what you would have gotten. Martha and I speculated extensively about whether there had been collusion between the two of them, or whether it was one of those coincidences which really reflect not astounding chance, but merely the convergence of lives cast in the same molds. We had all of us been a little lost and leftover for the past few years, our husbands similarly unhappy in their supposedly cool jobs (one working in a plant nursery, the other in a bookstore), and Martha and I had taken refuge in our version of domesticity, which would have been anachronistic anywhere but in Cambridge. Our husbands, denied this outlet, had moved confusedly along and had finally moved on.

It became clear to Martha and to me that we would also have to move on. We had been by turns tearful and cynical about our situations, we had shared all our bad memories, all our instances of the irritating habits of the dear departed (as we had taken to calling them), we had treated ourselves to some riotous nights out together, and yet there we still were, in lives that had been created to include our husbands. We began to discuss where we should go. There were a number of fairly obvious possibilities: Seattle. Portland. Santa Fe. Berkeley. Half as a joke, we went to a travel agent one day and picked up a collection of brochures. Hawaii. Bali. Japan. And then I looked at the Guatemala brochure ("Mayan Adventure Holiday"). There was a picture of dark green jungle, a picture of a white church with people on the steps waving incense burners, and a picture of a group of Indians dressed in bright multicolored fabrics. And I remembered a story that an old friend, long since moved to Seattle, had told me about traveling in Mexico and Guatemala. Mexico, he said, was all tourists and anti-tourist hostility. Americanization was rampant, and also anti-Americanism. In Guatemala he had found Indians who were still truly Indians, he had studied weaving in an Indian village, he had gotten away from gringos and tourists. The country was beautiful, the people were beautiful.

And then it turned out that Martha had associations with Guatemala too. Way back in college (which she never finished) she had had a course on the archaeology of the Indians of Central and South America. She had seen slides of ruins in Guatemala, surrounded by that same green jungle. And she remembered the slides, just as I remembered my friend's stories. Another one of those coincidences. Perhaps not very astounding, but we took it as a sign. I don't know exactly when it stopped being a joke, perhaps after we checked some guidebooks in the bookstore (former workplace of one of the dear departed, mine, to be specific) and realized that all the prices quoted for food and lodging in Guatemala were exceedingly cheap, perhaps after I had found a special night-flight airfare deal which would take us by way of Miami. We did have some money, Martha and I; both our husbands had left without touching the money in our bank accounts. My little family group had been saving up to buy a van, and Martha's to buy a good stereo system and pay for summer camp for Adam and Tara.

And so we found ourselves at the airport, our worldly goods in a variety of duffel bags, backpacks, and shoulder bags, Adam and Tara demanding over and over again to be taken on the airplane immediately, Martha and me checking the little leather pouches around our necks every few minutes: tickets, passports, traveler's checks. When we were actually sitting on the plane, strapped into our seats and waiting for takeoff, Martha and I looked at one another for a few minutes without saying anything. I think I know what was going through her mind, the same thing that was in mine. We were both understanding, perhaps for the first time, that we had truly cut ourselves loose from everything we had known except each other, that we were going off together and alone together. And perhaps this is the right place to describe what we each saw, the pre-Guatemala aspect of us, so to speak.

What Martha saw, of course, was me, and I cannot say exactly how I appeared to her. Solid and self-contained, I would guess. I had short curly brown hair, and I was a little bit overweight. I had a fairly round face and a few freckles, slightly unexpected in someone of my coloring. And I would have been wearing long earrings. People generally found me comforting before they found me attractive, a combination, I suppose, of my relative smallness and plumpness, my almost constant knitting, and my lack of glamour.

Not that Martha had much glamour. Although at times in my life I had wished to be taller and thinner, with long straight blond hair, I had not seen myself turning out to look like Martha. Martha was bony-thin and very pale; her dark blond hair looked brown against her skin. She played constantly with the ends of her hair, twisting them around her fingers, even chewing them, and I had noticed that Tara did the same with the ends of her shorter, darker hair. Martha looked fragile and nervous, and the competence I knew she possessed, in housekeeping affairs if in nothing else, would not have been at all obvious to anyone watching her. And then there were her children, with whom she also seemed quite competent; I, who was forever mothering my friends, had had almost nothing to do with children before we left for Guatemala, and I was generally impressed by the mixture of constant solicitude and casual patience with which Martha treated Adam and Tara. Both children were plump and dark; they looked more like mine than like Martha's, though in fact they merely resembled their father. Tara was bossy and Adam was shy; occasionally he rebelled against her leadership and a fight flared up, but mostly they seemed to function as a unit, a unit in which it was agreed that she was director.

I looked at the three of them: my new family group. Flying off to Guatemala didn't seem any more aimless than the life I had been leading in Cambridge. At least there would be new things to see. And Martha smiled at me, and I wondered if she had followed similar thoughts to a similar conclusion.

The flight turned out to be a pleasure because Adam and Tara were so desperately excited: the takeoff, the headphones, the meal, the bit of turbulence which might have frightened them except that Tara was unwilling to show fear in front of Adam and he accepted her authoritative assurances that nothing was wrong. I found myself feeding off their excitement, glorying not in the idea that I was flying, but in the sense that I was flying to a new life.

And so we got to Miami, and then to Guatemala. Early in the morning we hurried through the Guatemala City airport, passing closed shops in whose windows I could see those Indian fabrics on display. It all went amazingly smoothly, as we passed through customs and located a taxi which took us to a hotel the name of which I had circled in the guidebook to low-budget travel in Mexico and Guatemala. After our arrival everything was so completely new that I doubt I can describe it. Neither Martha nor I had been out of the U.S. before. It was even a shock to see everything written in Spanish. Guatemala City seemed endlessly spread out, and rather jerry-built in its low-to-the-ground sprawl. Later we would learn that it had been rebuilt after a severe earthquake.

We spent only two days in the city. We had already looked through our guidebook for possible settling places, and in the hotel we met plenty of other travelers who were eager to give advice. The guidebook and the travelers agreed: The most beautiful place in Guatemala is along the shores of Lake Atitlán. And the town to head for is Panajachel. You can rent a house near the lake. It's really cheap. And there will be some other gringos around to help you get started. The other travelers also gave us directions to the bus station. It all kept on going smoothly; everything was much easier than I would have expected. Within a week of our arrival in Guatemala, we were settled in a small house set in the hills above Panajachel, ours for what seemed, after Cambridge, a ludicrously small rent. We had done it, Martha and I said to each other.

I could walk out our door in the morning, go up a little rise, and stand looking out over the lake, the perfect bowl among the volcanoes. My life seemed to be made up of new blues and greens: the tropical sky, the lake reflecting the sky, the mountains, even our little front yard. I could walk down into Panajachel and come back with avocadoes and fresh bread, bananas, and corn. We all four went together down to the beach to swim and lie on the sand. Tara could swim a little, and I began to teach Adam how to float. Gradually we were accumulating household goods, replacing the makeshift with pottery and pillows bought in the Indian markets around Panajachel.

Actually, we learned fairly quickly to scorn Panajachel itself. "Gringo City," said all the gringos who had taken up residence in the neighborhood. In Panajachel there were discos, restaurants that catered to the granola-and-yogurt crowd, concrete and glass hotels. It was, for all that, a very little town, hardly one of your glamorous resorts, but by local standards it was Gringo City. The hills contained a number of little houses, most of them rented out to people from the U.S., and though we "settlers" were grateful for the resources of Panajachel, we tended to consider that we were in some sense natives.

The actual natives, I suppose, regarded us all as part of the Panajachel phenomenon. The natives I mean were the Indians, who lived in little villages around the lake. I took a boat trip across the lake to one such village during my second week in the rented house. As I walked along the one street, past the rows of low tin-roofed houses, a girl appeared and beckoned me into her doorway. I stood with her in a rectangular mud-walled room, with a roof only a few inches higher than my head; I had already noticed that I was as tall as or taller than most of the Guatemalan Indians I saw. At one end of the room was a woman making tortillas; she smiled and nodded to me without losing her rhythm: Pinch a piece of dough off a big ball, slap it flat, snap it down onto the griddle. The whole time I was in that room the sound of the damp little pats continued. The girl who had beckoned me in, whom I guessed to be about fifteen, produced a large piece of material and asked in Spanish if I wanted to buy it. I had been resurrecting my high school Spanish with the aid of a secondhand textbook I had picked up in Cambridge, and I found to my relief that I could follow her. Only later did I realize that Spanish would not have been her first language either and that she had prob-ably known only the same few elementary words I did. The Indians in those villages spoke the indigenous Indian lan-guages.

The cloth was white, obviously handwoven, and embroi-dered with a multitude of tiny figures, some of them human, others clearly animals, though it was not always possible to tell which animals. The dominant color in the embroidery was red, though there were many others. I instantly wanted the cloth, and the price she named embarrassed me. I had worked in a store in Cambridge which sold small numbers of hand-knitted and handwoven items, as well as wool and pattern books, and the general attitude of the people who made the sweaters and wall hangings we sold was that no price was too high for handwork. We salespeople would point out to the customers that each item was completely unique, that hours of hard work as well as years of accumulated skill had gone into each one, and most of us believed what we said. And here was this girl offering me a large piece of cloth, almost covered with intricate embroidery, for six dollars. Later on, of course, I learned to take this in stride, even to bargain, but that first time I just stood there. The girl said something else. At first I didn't understand, but after explanations and gestures I gathered that she was offering to make the cloth into a shirt for me on the spot. She produced a large pair of scissors.

"No," I said, and I took the cloth from her. I didn't want her to cut into it. She tried to insist on making me the shirt, almost as if she felt she was cheating me otherwise. When I left with the folded piece of cloth, the woman at the stove smiled at me again and then called sharply to her daughter, who left my side and ran to the back of the room; as I walked out blinking into the sunlight I could hear the two of them laughing. And that was my first purchase of Guatemalan cloth.

I kept on buying cloth. I bought large pieces of the handwoven material with the varicolored stripes, of the patterns that reminded me of bargello with their repeating W formations, even of the solid colors when I liked the feel of the cloth. I didn't try to make anything out of the cloth, I just hung a few favorite pieces up in my room and let the others sit and glow on open shelves or even on the floor. With Martha it was different. She bought shirts and skirts and shawls; by the time we had been living near Panajachel for a month, she hardly ever wore her old U.S. clothes. I sometimes saw Indians smile as she walked by, and I began to imagine that I knew what they were thinking: She looked so anomalous, so tall and blond, in those clothes made for and by small, dark people. And she wore them wrong too; she wore men's shirts and funny combinations of colors and patterns. I saw the same thing when I looked at other gringos living around us in the hills. It embarrassed me a little, but I told myself that the Indians must be glad enough to have the market for their fabrics.

I think that for a while I was completely happy. The business of keeping the household going, keeping us all fed, and keeping our clothes clean occupied a good part of the day for Martha and me. The rest of the time we filled in at the beach, at the market, or playing with the children, reading, and of course, for me, knitting. I made sweaters for both children. I made myself a little jacket. I would knit in the evenings when it was not too hot. Martha would read aloud to Tara and Adam while I was knitting and of course I would listen too. That was one of the first things I noticed when things started to go wrong: Martha stopped reading aloud in the evenings. She began to skip evenings, saying she was tired or her throat was sore, and gradually she just let the whole thing drop. I continued to knit in the evenings, but the children played together in their tiny room and Martha read to herself or else walked into Panajachel "to get out of the house for a while."

I found I was taking on more and more of the care of the children. Martha seemed to want to spend a lot of time by herself. She wasn't eager to go to the beach with the rest of us. If I offered to do the marketing, she would ask if I would mind taking Adam and Tara along. I didn't really mind any of it. I was a little in love with both of the children. My initial impression of Tara as the bully and Adam as the occasionally rebellious victim had been refined; I understood that Tara protected Adam and took the trouble to understand his rather complicated fears, and I also saw that Adam could manipulate Tara very effectively, using tears and the other prerogatives of babyhood. I found it fascinating to watch the two of them as they adjusted to our new life. The ease with which they picked up alien place names. The speed with which they had mapped important playing places around our house. The calm acceptance of all the changes. The only thing they missed, predictably enough, was television. For the first few weeks there had been regular complaints about programs they longed to see. But that faded very fast, and after a month or so they talked about their Cambridge lives in tones that suggested they had moved to Guatemala years ago, or perhaps that Cambridge was a place in a book, like Oz.

I liked being with them. I was glad they liked being with me. But I began to find it disturbing that Martha was so very eager to let me have them. She seemed to me at times to be reverting to some earlier Martha, one who had existed before I knew her, the childless unmarried Martha. I could see the children very quickly picking up the idea that I was responsible for their meals, for buying them new clothes. Adam took to coming into my bed at night sometimes when he heard noises that made him afraid.

Tara and Adam and I came home from the market in Sololá, a town near Panajachel, to find that Martha had a visitor. I had bought a small piece of old embroidery at the market, and carved wooden toys for the children. We also carried bags of food. Martha was sitting talking to a red-haired man who was dressed in Indian fabrics. He was smoking a cigar and the room smelled awful. Martha greeted the children offhandedly and asked what I had bought at the market. When I showed her the embroidery she said to the red-haired man, "Jenny never wears any of the cloth. She just buys it and keeps it in her room. She thinks it's disrespectful to wear it."

"Hey," the red-haired man said to me, "Indian culture is alive. You can't put it in a museum."

His name was Mike, it turned out, and Martha had met him in Panajachel. He was just traveling around, he told me, as he stood in the kitchen watching me make avocado-yogurt soup. He was traveling around learning. He had apparently not learned enough to offer to help me cook or set the table. Martha, in the meantime, had disappeared; when she returned she had on a whole new ensemble of living Indian culture. All through dinner Mike lectured us, telling us things I already knew about the Indians, about the repressive Guatemalan government, about how he despised Panajachel. Martha seemed fascinated by his store of conversation. Adam and Tara were restless since they were not able to talk. After dinner I took the two of them out to look at stars, leaving Martha and Mike to do the dishes. When the children and I got back, the dirty dishes were still on the table and the door to Martha's room was shut.

Mike stayed with us for three days. The smell of his cigars permeated the house. He seemed to consider it his duty to educate me about all matters Guatemalan, and I had to tell him several times that I knew everything he was trying to teach me. Not that I knew much, just that he didn't either. His pieces of information were on the order of "You know, each region has special patterns for weaving cloth. People who know can like recognize where a piece of cloth is from." The third day he was with us he tried to kiss me in the kitchen and I told him to get out and not come back. Martha came into my room to talk to me later that day and told me she was glad Mike was gone. "He got to be sort of a pain," she said.

I thought that perhaps Mike had provided something necessary in Martha's recovery from her husband's desertion. I hoped she would now return to normal. Adam and Tara had minded her lack of interest much more, it seemed to me, when

Mike was in the house. Her general distraction they had perhaps ascribed to the mysterious ways of adults, but a rival
was something they could understand. And for a little while
it did seem that Martha had gotten something out of her system. She began to bake more and she played with the children.
But within a week she was back to her pattern of going to
Panajachel alone in the evenings to get out of the house. And
then she began to bring people back with her. I would hear
them come in, usually after I was in bed. Usually Adam would
be in bed with me; his fears seemed to be increasing. In the
morning some man would emerge from the bathroom to eat
breakfast with us, some man from the U.S. or Germany or
France.

I think most of these men thought that the children were
mine. Martha did nothing to disabuse them of this idea, and
the children spoke mostly to me, the children were cared for
by me. I came to judge the men by how they reacted to the
children; I liked the ones who took the trouble to learn and
remember their names, who managed to make a little conversation with Tara. I did not like the ones who ignored the
children as if they and I were an inexcusably tactless intrusion
on a romantic little breakfast.

I tried not to be too hard on Martha in my thoughts. She
was entitled to a period of promiscuity, if that was what she
wanted. I didn't mind taking care of the children. The men
weren't really so bad, I told myself. One problem was that
the men really were pretty bad, most of them. Mike was one
of the worst, but there were others I could barely stand to eat
with. Sometimes Martha would remark to me that this man
or that one had been a real asshole, or alternatively, a really
interesting guy. But we did not discuss the general arrange-
ment. I went on taking care of her children. I went on shopping
for Indian fabrics. I was not as happy as I had been, but I

loved the children and I loved the fabrics. It sounds silly to put it that way, but those were the two things I really cared about. I was afraid that if I raised any serious issues with Martha, she would go away and take the children with her. I found myself pretending that they were indeed my children and Martha was a friend, a single childless woman staying with us as she went through a difficult time. I got the feeling, foolish though it may seem, that Adam and Tara were pretending the same thing.

Tara moved her mattress and Adam's into my room. She told me she had also become afraid of the dark, of the night noises. I would listen to the syncopation of the two of them breathing at night. For the first time since we had come to Guatemala, Tara began to talk to me about her father. Did I think he would ever come and get them? Where did I think he was? I didn't know where he was, I told her, but I was sure he thought about her. I was sure he still loved her. And though I didn't say it, of course, I hoped he would never come and get her.

The first sign that Martha's husband had arrived in Guatemala was a postcard mailed from Guatemala City. It told us that he was planning to come to Panajachel in a week and hoped Martha would be "willing to talk things over." He sent love to the children. For the first time in weeks, Martha and I had a long and serious talk. What should she say to him, she wanted to know. Should she tell the children? She did, and their joy actually hurt me. And the day of the proposed visit, as I watched Martha mix the batter for banana bread, I suddenly understood that she was now fulfilled. She had been waiting for this, for the return of her husband. She would go home with her husband, taking the children. While he was away, she had stored up some powerful ammunition with which to pay him back for leaving her. She would tell him about what she had done, and she would make it his fault: Because he had left her she had gone all to pieces and done crazy things. Of course, I suppose that was partially true.

Anyway, I was right about her going home with her husband. He came that night and admired our home and ate banana bread. I went for a long walk after dinner. I walked into town and stood by the lake thinking of my own husband and the life I did not want restored to me. I pictured my collection of cloth and wondered how long I could live on in Guatemala before my money ran out. In my head I said good-bye to Adam and Tara and wondered when I would get the chance to have children of my own. I imagined the Indian village across the lake, the woman making the tortillas. I could not see any lights across the lake. A young man came walking along the beach and stopped to talk. He was from Oregon. He thought Panajachel was a really great place. He invited me to come have a beer.

Instead I walked back up the mountain alone. The restored family group was gathered in the living room. Martha, I noticed, had provided her husband with an Indian shirt.

Theme and Variations

I get in the shower and start the water going, and I can hear Mark moving around in the bathroom.

"Don't blast off without me!" he yells.

I begin to count down, "Ten, nine, eight—"

He keeps me waiting.

"Three, two, one, one half, one quarter, one eighth—"

Finally the frosted glass door slides open and he is beside me, embracing me.

"Zero, blast-off!" I yell.

"Wait, we have to go back. I forgot something!"

"What?"

"My sandwich." Naughty-little-boy voice, we are both of us giggling.

"Okay. Houston, Houston, we're turning back for just a minute—oh, look, Markie, there's your Mommy, running up to the launching pad, carrying your lunch box!"

"Hi, Mommy!" Mark begins to soap my back. "How do you think my parents would have felt about my becoming an astronaut?" We both laugh. His parents wanted him to be a doctor, second choice lawyer, settled reluctantly for art historian, would-be artist. I, their almost-daughter-in-law, am at least a scientist. But not a real doctor and, for that matter, not a real daughter-in-law.

We talk for a while about the space missions we both remember so clearly from our childhoods, waking up at four or five in the morning to watch the blast-off on television, the preliminary hours of newsmen counting down and interviewing crew-cut technicians in rooms full of screens and computer terminals. Counting aloud with the television for the final ten seconds, the absurdly slow climb of the rocket with the ring of fire around its base. We know that both of us took away from these space flights a picture of science which now seems by turns touching in its idealism and frightening in its chauvinistic single-mindedness. Mark and I have in fact discussed this before, in Disneyland of all places, where the rides take you through outer space, or through the miraculous human body, and the authoritative voices booming about you as you progress from heart to lungs carry the same sort of faith in American Science, in Science and America. We discuss it again now in our shower. We both felt this, growing up, but I am the scientist.

Sheepishly, Mark picks up the bottle of special shampoo. We have both been suffering from an infestation of pubic lice, crabs, which can probably be traced to a little interlude Mark shared with a grubby boy he picked up in a bookstore, who was probably underage anyway—or at least, that is how I describe it back to Mark, to make him feel even more ashamed of himself. He feels deeply guilty, though I am not actually upset at all. The crabs are apparently gone, the shampoo was highly effective—but Mark goes on using it and using it, trying, no doubt, to wash away his guilt.

2. METONYMY, THE PART FOR THE WHOLE

Thus, we see that even in small and not particularly significant episodes, it is possible to find symbols for a whole story, a whole relationship—two whole lives. What I mean is, there you have it: the silliness, the parents, the infidelity. Are Mark and I so very much ourselves in everything we do? And is that because we shape life so completely to our own personalities, or is it rather that we have worn each other down, over the last four years, to simpler, more clichéd versions of the people we once were?

3. MOISTURIZER—THE MOST IMPORTANT THREE MINUTES IN A WOMAN'S DAY

Mark waits in bed after the shower while I rub on the cream that his mother gave me. For my last birthday, and she meant well, I assume. Mark was offended on my behalf, but I solved the situation and saved the evening by liking the present. I like the rich feel and smell, though I have no faith that it will ever mean a wrinkle less, or even a wrinkle deferred. I am, after all, the biochemist; I know what protein is, and what collagen is, the words have distinct meanings for me, and I almost cannot believe my eyes when I see them billed on a label as miracle ingredients. I know that rubbing these things into my skin will not keep me young, but I rub the cream in every night, peering into the mirror as if I were indeed checking for wrinkles, though perhaps only others with ugly adolescences behind them will believe me when I say that I am enjoying watching my skin age, even from the early twenties to the late twenties, that I am looking forward to my thirties and forties. For me, and for people like me, youth and beauty have nothing to do with each other.

For Mark's mother, on the other hand, aging is a battle to be fought, and I think she believes that if the creams that are available now had been available twenty-five years ago when she was my age, she would now have fewer wrinkles. Useless to tell her there were just as many creams then, and their claims were every bit as fabulous. It's like the question I used to ask myself when I was a teenager, leafing through the ads in magazines: If they've really made the big breakthrough, if they've really found the answer to oily skin and acne, then how can there still be some of us walking around with pimples? It's silly of course; I knew even then why those ads worked, because I could feel them working on me, and I know now why Mark's mother's skin cream is worth the money she pays for it, even though her skin continues to age.

When I get into bed next to Mark, I am aware that by now the light scent of the moisturizer is part of the way I smell at bedtime, and I wonder if he is even conscious of it, and I even wonder briefly whether it is some peculiar loyalty to his mother that keeps me putting it on night after night, and whether there is something even more peculiar which makes him glad to smell it on me.

4. AN EYE FOR AN EYE: AN OVERDUE INFIDELITY

I don't want to make myself out to be a saint. I may not get too upset when Mark picks up a boy in a bookstore and catches crabs and gives them to me, but I have my little ways of getting even. For one thing, as I mentioned, I tease him unmercifully and I reinterpret his little misadventures as particularly sordid self-indulgences. For another, well, there is always paying back in coin of the realm.

An old friend is in town, someone I knew three years ago, and in fact found very attractive three years ago. Nothing came of it then; I was much less casual about cheating on Mark (he had never cheated on me, though I rather saw it coming), and this old friend, Albert, was I think much too young and innocent himself to be able to take it in stride. But now, three years older, more attractive, Albert is back in town for two weeks, staying in the apartment of a faculty couple gone to Spain for the semester. Albert calls and we talk and he invites me to dinner. And I accept without mentioning Mark, and afterward I do not mention Albert to Mark, and I am not such a hypocrite that I would pretend not to know what all this means.

Sure enough. In this cramped efficiency apartment, decorated with bad abstract art and a few overly folkloric items brought back from other trips to Spain, Albert serves me salad and chicken baked in wine. I wonder why men, as they learn to cook, have to all learn the same dishes. But I don't say anything. I do, during dinner, mention Mark; I make it clear that he and I are still an item. Albert is perhaps a little puzzled, but now sophisticated enough to take it in stride. I drink a little too much wine, which has the effect of making me morally scrupulous in an unexpected direction. As we sit on the scratchy green couch, drinking brandy, I mention that I am just getting over an attack of crabs. I feel it is my duty to warn Albert; I am almost positive the little monsters are gone, but you never know. And maybe I am not so morally scrupulous after all, because that particular piece of information of course has another effect; it counteracts the figurative ring on my finger.

"Crabs?" Albert says, flirting with me over this highly unpromising material. "How did you get those in such a monogamous setup?"

"Well, maybe it isn't as monogamous as all that."

"You do think they're all gone?"

Continuing the romantic tone of the evening, after we are locked in an embrace on that horribly uncomfortable couch, Albert murmurs in my ear, "Well, at least it wasn't herpes."

5. A PROSPECTIVE DINNER WITH THE ALMOST-IN-LAWS

Mark's parents are planning to come up and visit us, take us out to a very expensive French restaurant where Mark and I would normally never eat and where, to tell you the truth, I would just as soon never eat at all. But we have cultivated the myth that it is a great treat when his parents come and take us out there. Mark, in anticipation of their coming, wants to finish a painting of me which he is pretending to himself will please them. How we do deceive ourselves. I am posing naked for this violently colored voluptuous portrait, wondering whether I still believe he is a good painter. Certainly there is some strong emotion painted into this one, but that may have more to do with Albert than with Mark.

Mark has not taken my affair with Albert at all well. I go and see Albert evenings for a couple of hours and then I come home to Mark, who, of course, tortures himself by asking me where I've been. No use pointing out that in three more days Albert will be gone. Mark asks me to stop, even begs me to stop, and I want to say, yes, my point is made, and then when I hear myself not saying yes, I have to wonder, have I outsmarted myself, fallen in love with silly old Albert?

I have this awful feeling, as I contemplate the advent of Mark's parents, that I know what I am finding in Albert. I am escaping from the semi-respectability of my life, revenging myself on Mark for that boy in the bookstore, who was, after all, his own escape from the same thing. Mark's parents approve of me too much for either of us to stomach. They are too ready to see us married. Perhaps we both fantasize about the same thing: that at dinner with his parents, I will suddenly let slip some detail about Albert, he will mention a boy in a bookstore.

6. FAITH AND FAITHFULNESS, OR, THE SUM OF ITS PARTS

In the end, Albert will go home to Oregon, and neither Mark nor I will shock his parents at dinner, and they will pretend to like his painting, and I will have to decide whether I like it too or not, and none of this is nearly as sad as I make it out to be. Both Mark and I seem to know what is episode and what is theme. It is not completely clear to me how we can know this, how we can possibly have managed to agree on a conclusion. What are we building on, what laws of motion propel us forward? Find your metaphors where you can: space missions, moisturizing creams. It is all a question of believing in them.

If we have a future, Mark and I, it has nothing to do with science and progress. We cannot depend on lotions, whatever their miracle ingredients. Whatever faith we have comes only from the conviction that somewhere in our symbolism is a structure so natural and essential to us both that we will continue to develop it, even while we wonder what it is. And somehow that is enough: It is satisfying to believe, and satisfying also to marvel at our own belief. And so we invoke an element of irony which is missing in Disneyland, and which we need if we are to permit ourselves this unreasonable faith, this sentiment, this romance.

Murderers Don't Cook for Themselves

Alice stands in the little grocery store, daring herself. She examines what people are putting in their red plastic baskets. One thin blond man in running shoes reaches past her to take four Budget Gourmet frozen dinners, and Alice decides no, not him. Then she trails down an aisle watching a large solid man with a red beard; he buys a granola cereal, rice, a couple of packages of spaghetti. Alice draws closer. The man turns the corner and adds a big bottle of Bloody Mary mix, and Alice hesitates, and then the man gets on line at the cash register and she abandons him. Alice drifts to the little produce section, mostly lettuce and onions, a few other vegetables. If I had a car, she thinks, I would drive to a real supermarket, and she imagines a long, blindingly lit aisle lined with piles of broccoli and cabbage and scallions and rhubarb. She would walk up to a boy who was stamping prices on cans, and she would say to him, excuse me, do you have any fresh dill, and he would put down his stamping machine and lead her to it. On her own, she finds a few rather dispirited bunches of fresh parsley behind the shiny cucumbers and adds a bunch to her own red basket.

Next to her, a youngish couple is having an argument. You always used to like iceberg lettuce, the woman is saying, furiously. This is much tastier, really, the man says, holding up some dark green lettuce. No it isn't, it's bitter and I don't like it, says the woman. And you wouldn't like it either if you hadn't read that iceberg lettuce is déclassé. Then suddenly they both look up rather fiercely at Alice, and she moves along, wondering which lettuce they will buy.

The meat section is a waist-high refrigerator. If I had a car, I would drive to a real supermarket, with a butcher who comes when you ring the bell, and I would say: Can you tell me the best way to cook these ribs? But here there are no ribs, and so Alice picks up a steak with a silver sticker on its plastic wrap, "Special Today." A man in a tweed jacket stands next to her, turning over packages of chicken breasts. Alice looks at him more carefully—he has very bad skin, all pitted and scarred from acne. She thinks about it, then sees him reach with his left hand to get a second package of breasts. A ring and a dinner party. He drifts away but she remains, thinking, what I need is someone who comes and buys himself a steak. Nothing fancy, just someone who cares enough to broil himself a little steak. She puts back the steak she is holding. A woman with two long brown braids comes to check out the meat and then buys a package of extra-lean ground beef. Alice sneaks a look into her basket, sees two tomatoes, a chunk of extra-sharp cheddar, and a jar of marinated artichoke hearts, and immediately she wants for her own dinner thick hamburgers with melted cheese on top, tomato and artichoke heart salad, everything extra-sharp and extra-lean. She follows behind the woman, waiting to see what the rest of her purchases will be. The woman hesitates in front of the Pepperidge Farm cookies, and Alice grabs a bag of Capris; no one is going to change her mind about those. Then she sees a man in jeans and a button-down shirt who is looking over the various canned tomato products. Finally he chooses a little can of paste and a big one of whole Italian plum tomatoes. Then he heads off to the pasta section, and again he spends a while looking things over. Alice likes the way he seems open to different things; he doesn't just reach for the spaghetti. In fact, he chooses a box of shells.

She is so sure he will go to the meat counter that she doesn't follow him; she goes the long way around, through another aisle, and meets him there. Sure enough, he is hefting one package of chopped meat after another. He has short black hair and a friendly face, perfectly nice skin. As she joins him at the meat counter, he smiles at her briefly, acknowledging that a moment ago they saw each other in pasta.

"Not a really great meat selection," Alice says.

"No, I guess not." He does not seem surprised to be spoken to. A nice friendly man, probably people are always starting conversations with him. "They have most of the things I know how to cook, though." He selects one particular pack of chopped meat and drops it in his basket.

Alice thinks of saying, "Is it noodles with meat sauce or with meatballs?" Which at that moment is what she most wants to know, but he is about to turn away, so she makes herself say instead, "Listen, this is going to sound kind of weird."

"Yes?" He looks pleasant but now wary; she could be a Moonie, she supposes he is thinking, or someone who wants money.

"Well, you see, I'm new in town and I'm having a house-warming party tonight, except I don't know many people, so I promised myself I would just walk up to someone I didn't know, but someone who looked nice, and invite them. See, that way I get to know some people in a new place."

"Well," he says. "Well, that's very nice of you. And it seems like a good idea."

"I like what you're buying," Alice says, a little helplessly.

"I like people who make their own tomato sauce instead of getting it out of a jar, and people who use other kinds of noodles besides spaghetti, and I have a recipe for meatballs that makes these tiny ones."

"That sounds good," says this nice man, and for one second Alice thinks, he's going to say, I'd be glad to come to your party, or even, why don't you forget about the party and come make supper with me?

"The thing is," he says, "I really have to get home. Otherwise I'd love to come to your party, and I really think it's a good idea. But the thing is, I have a new baby, only two weeks old, so I have to get home."

"Oh, sure, no problem," Alice says.

"I mean, if the baby was older—"

"No, sure, I know what you mean."

"It's just we haven't taken her out at all, not in big groups of people, and there's this cold going around that I don't want any of us to catch."

"No problem," Alice says, again, and he says thanks again, and then he heads off with his basket, and Alice thinks angrily that he's probably going now to buy paper diapers and formula and baby food.

She starts to throw things into her own basket, things she can imagine eating later that night, all by herself. A jar of macadamia nuts, very expensive. If he had said yes, she would have found a couple of other people to come so it would have seemed like a party. Called up some of the people from her new job, she can tell which of them are lonely, available on half an hour's notice. Walked up to a group of strangers in the street, people who seemed as if they might be up for a party, college students maybe. Or else just let the man show up and find her there waiting for him alone. A package of heat-and-serve egg rolls. A large bag of ruffled sour-cream-and-onion-flavored potato chips. She is new in town, relocated

by the chain of fancy furniture stores she works for, a promotion, a raise, and a relocation she actually requested, for
reasons which made sense at the time. She is a small roundish
woman with short dark hair, and she is very lonely. She feels
much older than the college students who are thick on the
streets, moving in gregarious bunches, but she does not feel
any adult strength. An adult would not need frozen Boston
cream pies to get through the night.

When she gets on line at the register, she is no longer angry
at that man. She is only depressed, thinking, it isn't really so
much, to want someone who knows how to take care of himself, who would show me how. To her tremendous embar-
rassment, the man comes and gets on line behind her. She
can't believe that he would do that; why isn't he trying to
avoid her, this crazed desperate woman? She feels him looking
at her purchases and suddenly thinks that maybe the nuts and
the potato chips and all will convince him that she really is
having a party. She doesn't look at him; she takes her bag and
leaves as his things are getting rung up. But even as she is
leaving, she notices that he has bought a fancy kind of ice
cream and a box of paper diapers, newborn size.

He overtakes her before she has turned the corner, puffs
up behind her, carrying his own bag. "Listen," he says to her,
"listen, are you really having a party tonight? I mean, are
there other people coming?"

"Of course not," Alice says, angry again; was this really
necessary? "I told you I don't know any people here. I'm just
lonely so I did something crazy. You probably never felt that
lonely in your whole life."

"What I was wondering," the man says, "I was thinking
maybe you would like to come and meet my baby—and my
wife. I mean, I was thinking you probably just wanted some
company, and the baby is very nice."

And so, disbelieving, Alice walks beside him, the two of

them clutching their brown paper bags. He lives only two blocks away. They have time to exchange names, Alice and Billy.

She follows him into his building, up the stairs to the second floor. As he unlocks the door, she is starting to say: Listen, I don't know what your wife will think of this, maybe I should just go home. But then the door is pulled open, away from them, and his wife is standing there holding the baby, who is crying.

"I think she's sick," his wife says. "I think there's something wrong with her. She feels all hot to me and she won't stop crying. I thought you were never going to get here."

"I bought spaghetti," Billy says, and Alice thinks, no you didn't, it's shells. Then he says, "What should we do?"

"I think we should call the pediatrician," says his wife.

"This is Alice," Billy says. "Alice, this is my wife, Monica. I brought Alice home to have dinner with us."

"I think you should call the pediatrician *now*," Monica says. "She really feels hot to me."

Alice stands there, uselessly, while Billy makes the phone call. Monica does not look anything like what she expected. Monica has short hair combed to one side in carefully arranged curls and dyed an obviously fake yellow. Monica is wearing a green skirt and a pale blue sweater with little green stripes knitted into it. The baby is very very tiny and is wrapped in a blanket; under other circumstances, Alice thinks, she could ask to see it, but that doesn't seem appropriate; she doesn't even ask its name.

Finally Billy gets through to the pediatrician, who tells them to take the baby's temperature. He gives them careful instructions over the phone, and Alice finds herself assisting, holding the tiny pink legs down while Monica guides the thermometer in.

"I don't know how they expect you to know what to do," Monica says to Alice. "I've only been doing this for two weeks, after all."

The baby does indeed have a fever. Alice expects the doctor to tell them: Nothing to worry about, some bug or other, give it aspirin. Instead, Billy hangs up the phone and says, "He says we have to take her to a doctor. He says with a baby this young you can't take any chances."

They don't have a car, it turns out. So Monica carries the baby, carefully wrapped in a blanket, and Billy runs around the corner to see if he can find a taxi, even if it is only six blocks or so to the hospital, and that leaves Alice to carry the big bag with BABY on it, full of spare diapers and spare baby clothes and heaven knows what else. Billy comes running back toward them; there is no taxi to be found. Then, anxiously, he dashes ahead again, as if to prepare the way. Monica and Alice trudge along, with baby and bag, and Alice notes that she is once again following Billy, burdened down.

They don't have to wait long at the hospital. In the waiting room, Monica and Billy bend down over their baby, who has been silent for the walk but is now screaming again. At one point Monica looks up from the baby and says to Alice, in perfect smooth social tones, "So, where do you know Billy from, did you say?"

"We just met, really," Alice says. Billy is paying no attention; he is making little fuzzy noises into the baby's ear. "I'm new in town, you see," Alice says.

"Do you like it here?" Monica asks politely.

Then their name is called. Alice stays in the waiting room, holding the baby bag and all the coats, and a few minutes later Billy comes out and sits beside her. "They have to draw blood," he says. "I don't want to watch. They might have to do a spinal tap." He looks upset and helpless, and Alice wonders, why did I ever think he was someone who could take care of other people?

Another family comes into the waiting room, a big fat father and mother and a little shrimpy boy with a big cut on his forehead. They take seats and immediately begin to argue in very loud voices.

"I don't want him ever playing with those lousy children again," the father says. "Do you hear me, you are never going to play with those lousy children again."

"I am too," says the boy.

"Listen to your father," says the mother. Then to the father, "This is all your fault, anyway. If you had fixed that cellar door like I told you to."

"A bunch of hoodlums," says the father.

"I'm playing with them again tomorrow and again the day after and again the day after that and every day forever."

"And just because it wasn't fixed doesn't mean they had to play on it."

"But it should have been fixed. I told you a long time ago."

"I'm *always* playing with them."

They fall silent and all three stare at the color TV set, eternally on for the benefit of people in the waiting room. The reception is very bad, and there is some kind of game show on. They watch for a few minutes, and Alice and Billy watch too, and then the boy says, "I hope I need a lot of stitches."

Monica comes out into the waiting room. They want to put the baby in the hospital; they think she has a urinary tract infection and they want to start giving her intravenous anti-biotics. Monica's yellow hair is a little rumpled and her eyes are bigger.

"I held her while they did those things," she says. "They wanted me to leave, but I couldn't just leave her there. The worst was when they wanted a urine sample. They took this enormous needle—"

"I don't want to know," Billy says. Across the room, the other family is listening attentively.

"It's called a bladder tap," Monica says. "I hated it."

Alice pats her on the back, rather awkwardly, and Monica looks like she might cry, right there, on Alice's shoulder.

"What do we do now?" Billy asks.

"I can stay with her in the hospital. They let mothers stay twenty-four hours, they'll put a bed in her room for me. So let's just get the two of us settled, and then you go on home and come back tomorrow morning."

Alice trails them upstairs. She would like to just leave and go back to her quiet apartment, but no one has offered to take the BABY bag from her and she cannot bring herself to thrust it at them and run. She still doesn't know the baby's name.

The baby is tiny in a big crib, a tube already dripping into her. A nurse with long red hair is helping Monica get settled, and it is she who finally takes the BABY bag from Alice and begins to sort out its contents.

"You'll need some things," Billy says to Monica, who is hanging over the crib, watching the baby, who seems to have gone to sleep.

"Oh, don't worry about Mother," says the nurse. "We can give her a hospital gown to sleep in, and we have toothbrushes and towels. We'll make her very comfortable indeed, and the best thing you can do now is to go on home and get some sleep so you can help out tomorrow."

"I could stay too, I don't mind," Billy says.

"Oh, now, doesn't Mother have enough to do without taking care of you too?" says the nurse cheerfully, teasing. "We like to have just one parent stay, and you'll find you can do a lot more good by getting some rest and coming in tomorrow to help."

"Billy, why don't you go home and have some dinner," Monica says. "And take—I'm sorry, I seem to have lost track of your name?"

"Alice."

"Take Alice along and the two of you make something to eat."

And so once more Alice trudges along, though this time she is not carrying anything. The time to bow out is past; Billy responded to her cry for help, so how can she leave him now? When they get back to his apartment, the first thing he does is call the hospital, as if to check that the number they gave him will work. He and Monica talk briefly, and Alice goes off to use their bathroom so he can have privacy, but as she leaves the room she can hear him murmuring, I love you, I love the baby, we'll all be home together again soon and everything will be wonderful.

Billy and Alice boil water for the shells, and together make a spaghetti sauce with meatballs. Alice rolls the meatballs, making them very small and perfectly round.

"This is really nice of you," Billy says. "I guess I meant it to be really nice of me, but it's really nice of you."

"I really did just move here," Alice says, pinching off another bit of chopped meat. "Soon I guess I'll know people and all. I don't want you to think I was just trying to pick up a man."

"I didn't," Billy assures her, and she is suddenly irritated.

"A grocery store would be a good place. Because you wouldn't have to worry so much about getting a murderer. I mean, don't you get the feeling that murderers don't cook for themselves? They all eat fast food, I guess."

"Yeah, I know what you mean," Billy says.

"That's what I was thinking, I guess. I mean, I really was trying to pick up a man, so I figured the grocery store would be a good place."

The sauce and the meatballs are simmering, the shells are dumped into their boiling water. Billy paces up and down the kitchen. Alice reaches into her bag of groceries and gives him the jar of macadamia nuts, and while he paces he eats the whole expensive jarful. Alice feels at peace; it is good to take care of someone, even if it is not exactly what she had in mind.

They eat the shells and the tomato sauce and the meatballs. It all tastes good, and Alice is glad she is not at home alone finishing off the sour-cream-and-onion-flavored potato chips. "I'm glad I talked to you in the store," she says.

"I am too."

After dinner they watch television together. Billy gets up once to call the hospital again, and Monica tells him the baby is sleeping peacefully, but please don't call again because the phone might wake her up. So Billy and Alice watch until the end of a complicated spy movie, full of actors they are both sure they have seen before but cannot identify, and then Billy says, I'll walk you home. By the end of the movie, they were sitting together on the floor and he had his arm around her, but Alice knows it doesn't mean anything.

He walks her home, carries the bag of groceries she bought. She is thinking that in front of her building she will kiss him once, gently, and then she will take her bag and turn away and go up the front stairs. And he will go home to his apartment and think about his wife and his baby, and maybe spare a fond and grateful thought for Alice, and she will think fondly of him. And so she does.

Two
New Jersey
Stories

I. Stealing

Saturday morning in New Jersey, October 1971. Rachel went to the bus stop and met Jan and Robin. Rachel's mother had given her fifteen dollars and told her to get a nice shirt. They waited ten minutes and then the bus came. They paid and headed down the aisle toward the empty long backseat where they could all sit together. Jan went first. She tripped slightly and had to grab the side of a seat. A tall boy pulled his foot out of the aisle and snickered. The girl sitting next to him looked at Jan and wrinkled her nose.

"Stupid freaks," she said, loudly enough for everyone on the bus to hear. She wore a bulky jacket made of blue and white felt. On each sleeve was a megaphone and the number 1974, on her back was written in script "Lakehill JV." "Stupid freaks," she repeated. Jan looked frightened and moved to the back of the bus. Robin paused a minute, smiled, and said, "Hello, Donna."

The couple in the seat began to laugh, and Robin and Rachel went to sit in the back of the bus. Rachel was afraid, even though she, Jan, and Rachel outnumbered Donna and her boyfriend. But the fear came from a much larger feeling of being outnumbered, a feeling which was with her whenever she was in school, and which she sometimes enjoyed. She looked at Jan and saw the same fear, but Robin seemed to feel she had won the exchange and was sprawled out on the seat, her hands jammed into the pockets of her enormous old suede jacket, singing to herself,

> *"Put your arms around me*
> *like a couple on the sun,*
> *You know I'll love you, baby,*
> *when my easy ridin's done."*

Jan and Rachel joined in, softly,

> *"You don't believe I love you,*
> *look at the fool I've been,*
> *You don't believe I'm sinkin',*
> *look at the hole I'm in."*

They rode for almost an hour, first through some small towns, then along Route 17, past Gino's hamburgers, and Pathmark, open twenty-four hours a day, and the biggest center for do-it-your-selfers in all New Jersey, and Pizza Hut, and Hillman-Kohan optometrists. They knew the stores along the highway as well as they knew the supermarket, two card shops, pizzeria, delicatessen, dress shop, and TV repair shop which made up the shopping district of Lakehill.

The last stop was the Bergen Mall. Donna and her boyfriend got off first and headed for Bamberger's. Rachel and Jan and Robin walked past a few of the smaller boutiques. Most were quite stylish, specializing in mixable matchables and accessories to highlight any outfit. But one was distinctly oriented toward jeans and incense, candles and long skirts, and even displayed a small selection of rolling papers.

The three girls went in there. The salesman wore jeans and a shirt made of Indian cotton, and his hair was appropriately long. Jan began looking through the skirts; she was fond of pretty clothes and had thirteen dollars to spend. Rachel wanted a new pair of jeans. The salesman recommended some Land-lubber hiphuggers with extra-large bells, and she went behind an Indian bedspread to try them on. When she came out, the salesman was telling Robin about a new product.

"It's this aerosol spray, and it like covers up odors. You spray it in your room after you've been smoking and no one would ever know." He handed her a can of the stuff.

"What a useful little thing," Robin said, turning to look at Rachel. "Those fit you pretty well." Rachel bought the jeans and paid fifteen cents extra for a large shopping bag with the name of the store on it.

They went into Alexander's, and wandered around the stationery department. Rachel looked through a large selection of greeting cards with slightly obscene messages: "You're the top . . . " said the front of one, "When I'm on top!" it said inside. She was pleased with her new jeans. Her mother would be a little angry.

"Don't you ever want to wear anything else to school? Don't you want to look like a girl?" she would ask. Even if she wanted to, Rachel thought, she could not wear dresses to school, because all the greasers and cheerleaders would make a point of noticing and probably of shoving her around. It was clear to her that once you had set an image, even if it was an image that most people disliked, you had less trouble if you stuck to it.

She went over to a table of candles. She saw one she really

liked, a dark red cylinder with shades of pink and white almost hidden in it, and quickly moved it over to the edge of the table, close to her stomach. Then she leaned over to reach for a fat calendar candle and with her elbow knocked the red candle backward into her shopping bag. As it fell, her hands became slightly sweaty and her movements speeded up a little. She stood a minute more, tapping her foot and considering the calendar candle, then ostentatiously set it back on the table. She picked up her shopping bag and wandered over to join Jan and Robin. They left the store.

"Hey," Rachel said to Robin when they were outside, "I brought you a present." She pulled out the candle.

"Well, well, well. And I brought you one too." From her coat pocket, she produced a pair of socks, made of bright red wool. There were separate compartments for the toes, and each toe was a different color. Rachel put the socks in her shopping bag and they continued to walk. She felt very good, proud of herself and set apart from the people around them, high school couples, buying caramel popcorn at the little Plexiglas booth, parents sitting exhausted on the scrolled metal benches while their children chased each other screaming around the colored cement patterns in the pavement, and groups of boys who did not shop but stood and commented loudly as girls walked by.

Rachel thought they should go to Bamberger's and she would get a shirt. She had only two dollars left, so she would steal it. She wondered if her mother would ask how she had been able to afford the jeans and the shirt both. Perhaps she would ask Robin to take the jeans home with her and keep them for a couple of days and then just hang them up in her own closet; her mother would never notice an extra pair of blue jeans. They walked past a bunch of boys who called out,

"Hippies!"

"Get a bra, blondie, you're flopping," one of them said loudly as Jan passed, and Rachel saw her cringe and pull her coat closed. Rachel and Robin both reached out and put their arms around Jan and the boys called after them, "Lesbos!"

Jan hated to be looked at that way, Rachel knew; she reacted to any kind of meanness or hatred as if to actual pain. She was the only person Rachel had ever actually protected, drawing the fire of some of the girls in school who insulted the clothing, bodies, and hygiene of girls they didn't like while they were dressing for gym, insisting to the social studies teacher that it was she who had been passing the note to Jan and not the other way around. Robin could take the abuse and the dislike; she seemed to expect it and therefore take it when it came as a confirmation and an intellectual victory. And Rachel herself was alternately terrified and defiant, but occasionally powerfully happy.

"Did you say you wanted a shirt?" Robin asked, when they had gotten a little way past the boys and taken their arms off Jan.

"Bamberger's, I think," Rachel said, and they went in and up the escalator. She found a blue cotton shirt with an appliqué of the sun on the front and a rainbow on the back which she thought might even please her mother. It was soft and looked a little like a Peter Max design, and was definitely made to be worn with jeans. She couldn't try it on, of course, but it was her size, twelve. Rachel was wearing a loose pea coat. She put the shirt she wanted in a pile of packaged flannel shirts on another table. She pushed her coat apart so it fell open as she leaned across the table, then in a quick motion pushed the shirt under the shirt she was wearing, tucking it into the waist of her jeans. She straightened up, pulling the coat closed and buttoning it as they went down the escalator. She was very frightened and very excited, and the familiarity of the feelings delighted her. The feelings stopped as soon as the three girls were a short distance away from Bamberger's. Rachel produced the shirt and Jan and Robin both admired it, and they folded it up and put it in the shopping bag. They all bought ice cream cones at Friendly's. They went and looked at the puppies in the cages in Puppy Palace, and at the lizards in Terrarium World. They browsed in Brentano's, and Rachel bought *The Bell Jar*. Robin slipped a copy of *Do It!* under the edge of her jacket and held it there with one hand.

After they had left the store, she said, "Did you see how they keep *Steal This Book* right by the cash register? I was going to try to get that, but forget it!"

"Did you know it was called *Fuck the System* first, but they wouldn't print it?" Jan asked, and they laughed. Jan looked in a store window. "Let's go in there," she said, and led them into a fairly expensive women's clothing store. Rachel and Robin went to look at the party dresses and make amazed noises about the prices; they were followed and closely watched by a salesgirl who every few minutes asked if she could help them. Rachel noticed that Jan was sorting through a pile of sweaters. A sign above the table said BARGAIN 100% CASHMERE TURTLENECKS ONLY $40. Rachel wondered if Jan was going to try to take one. She walked away from Robin and began to look at some small silk scarves. The salesgirl who had been watching Jan turned to look at Rachel, and Rachel saw the edge of Jan's movement; the same quick tuck under the shirt, then pulling the jacket closed. She casually dropped the silk scarves back onto the table, and they sauntered out and around the corner.

"That was a little crazy," Rachel said nervously. "They were really watching us."

Jan was smiling, not with pride but with pure pleasure.

"They were so soft!" she said happily. They turned another

corner, and found a little blind alley, between the back of Kresge's and the side of the movie theater. Jan took out the sweater. It was light purple, and she buried her face in it and stroked her neck with one of the sleeves. Rachel and Robin petted it gently, and Rachel thought that neither of them could wear anything that expensively soft and standard. Jan, with her blond prettiness, would wear it to school with faded jeans and it would be almost all right. Not exactly all right, because other girls would look at it and wonder and perhaps say something hesitant and complimentary, but almost all right. Jan took off her jacket to try it on.

"You think you're pretty smart, you little thieves!"

The three of them turned. Donna, the cheerleader from the bus, stood a little behind them, her blue and white arms folded across her chest. Her boyfriend stood a little distance away, not really watching. "I saw that. You think you're pretty smart. I think I'll go tell the people in that store."

Rachel felt helpless and terrified. Donna would tell the store, the store would tell her parents; for a moment she was convinced that by concentrating she could make this interruption disappear and take them all back to ten minutes ago. Jan had leaned back against the wall of Kresge's and her eyes were closed. Robin seemed to be looking for a reply, but she said nothing. Donna took a step forward.

"Sluts!" she said, just as she said it in gym when they undressed. "Think you're getting away with it!" She took another step forward, and Jan, trying to move farther back into the brick wall, held out the sweater, as though it would shield her. Donna took it, wrinkling her nose. "I guess we'll all go back there with this and tell them the whole story."

"Hey, look," Robin said weakly, "you're not going to get anything out of reporting this."

"I'm not going to let you get away with taking it," Donna said. She stroked the purple wool. "This is an expensive sweater."

She looked Jan over. Jan was shivering slightly in her yellow cotton shirt, and her breasts were shaking, just a little. "I suppose you were going to wear it like that"—a finger pointing—"like that to school so all the boys could look." She continued to stroke the sweater. Rachel looked over at the boyfriend, who was still not really watching.

"Look, you can have it," Jan said, "please just take it."

Donna made a fist. "I'm no thief, you dirty little freak!"

"No," said Jan, frightened that she had offended instead of appeasing.

"You tramp!" Donna looked at her boyfriend. Her fingers played in the sweater. They all waited. Suddenly she pushed the sweater under her cheerleading jacket and stepped away from them.

"You just better not ever say a word about this!" she said fiercely, and then she turned and walked to the boy, who put his arm tightly around her and walked her away.

Rachel and Robin and Jan walked toward the bus stop.

"Bitch!" Jan said, pulling her jacket closed. "Bitch!" She clamped her teeth together. Rachel put an arm around her and Jan shook her head violently, then smiled a little.

"I can't wait till she wears it to school," Robin said.

"My mother would've wanted to know how I could afford it anyway," Jan said. Rachel nodded.

"Hey, look," she said, "why don't you take that shirt I got?"

"No, that's okay. You don't have to do that."

"Come on, you've earned it. It isn't like it cost me anything." The three of them grinned at each other. Rachel pulled the shirt out of her shopping bag. "Here," she said, "I brought you a present."

II. Hudson Towers

The winter that we were all fourteen, Jan ran away from home. She didn't tell Robin or me that she was going, but we weren't very surprised. She had been fighting steadily with her mother, who wanted her to get a part-time job and stop running around all the time with boys and "those hippie friends of yours." I found out she had run away when her mother began to call my mother to ask if we knew where Jan was. She called every few hours for a whole weekend, and Monday Jan was not in school. Robin and I cut third period (French) to sit in the snow behind the bleachers on the football field and discuss it. We smoked a joint that Robin's older brother had given her.

"To her father's place, maybe?"

"No, her mother said she called there. Besides, can you imagine running away to Jersey City?"

"I suppose not to Chuck's house; his parents wouldn't let her."

"And her mother has been calling there almost as often as she's been calling me."

"What was the name of that older guy?" I asked. "The one you thought looked like a rich Mafia boss?"

"Oh, Lenny. But I don't think she was really having much to do with him. He's pretty old, thirty or so."

"I hope she's okay," I said.

"Yeah," Robin said, "I worry about her. She isn't too good at taking care of herself."

"She probably didn't go far."

Robin and I could both take care of ourselves. We had a common tough and angry attitude, and we did not easily trust anyone. Jan fell in love easily, smiled hopefully at the captain of her basketball team in gym after she had lost the ball, and cried often over the things her mother said to her.

She didn't call me; she called Robin a week later. Her mother had brought in the police by this time, who had told her, she reported to my mother, "The cop said, 'I tell you the truth lady, we got fifty of these kids run away in this town every six months.' " Her normally shrill voice sank in ungrammatical imitation. " 'Most of them come back by themselves, if they don't we can't hardly ever find them. They just go across the bridge into New York City and they can disappear completely. Probably she'll come back.' Then he asked me, does she use drugs, and I said, I don't think so, maybe marijuana but I doubt it. He said, does she have a boyfriend, and I told him about that boy Chuck in Teaneck, with the long blond hair and the car, but I already checked there." I listened to this on the upstairs extension. Jan's mother did not really like my mother, because she did not like me, but my mother was being sympathetic and Jan's mother needed sympathy.

Robin told me in school that Jan had called.

"Where is she?" We were standing near my locker while the rest of the high school settled down for homeroom. Since we weren't in the same homeroom, we had to stay in the hall to talk.

"She's in Fort Lee, in an apartment. It sounds sort of strange."

"Whose apartment?"

"I'm not sure, I think it might be Lenny's. But I'm not sure if he's living there."

"Well, what's going on?" Robin did not answer right away, and a teacher came along. Mr. Calvarese taught American history and coached the wrestling team.

"What are you girls doing out here? Didn't you hear the

bell for homeroom?" Robin and I stuck our hands in our jeans pockets and didn't smile. "You aren't allowed to stay in the halls talking during homeroom. Do you realize you've probably been marked absent?" He looked at us for a moment more, then said sternly, "You'd better answer, young ladies, if you have anything to say for yourselves." He smiled slightly and I realized he had thought of a sarcastic remark. "If you are young ladies, and I must say you certainly don't dress like it."

Robin looked at him with open hatred, mixed with a little scorn.

"Yeah," she said, "well, we were just leaving." We still had our jackets, because we hadn't opened our lockers, so we just ran down the stairs and out into the street. Mr. Calvarese did not compromise his dignity by chasing us, but he called, "I'll report this!" after us.

"I don't think he knows our names," Robin said when we were outside. "Good thing we don't take American history till next year."

"Good thing you didn't go out for wrestling. But you know, we're sure to run into him again."

"So what's a few detentions?"

"Look, what is this about Jan?" I asked. We didn't often cut whole days of school, because they usually notified your parents for something like that, but the uncertainty about Jan made it very important to me that we keep talking. Robin seemed embarrassed again.

"Well, the thing is," she said, "she didn't exactly say it, but I gather she's hooking."

"What?" I said, then processed the word and said, "Oh God. You mean for Lenny?"

"I think so. She sounded like she was doing it a little bit and he was getting her the people."

I thought for a minute, then said, "Do you know where she is?"

"Yeah, I have the address. It's in that big high-rise."

"Figures. I always said that was built by the Mafia." We kept walking, kicking the snow with the toes of our boots.

"Well," I said, "do you want to go visit her?"

"She said it was fine to come during the morning," Robin said, as though she had been waiting for the question. We turned onto the street that led to Fort Lee. We stood by the curb and stuck out our thumbs. Normally we were careful about hitching too near town, because we were forbidden to hitch and we got into trouble whenever someone saw us and mentioned it to our parents; that day we took the risk without discussing it.

"Jesus," Robin said from behind me, "I really feel bad."

"I know," I said, "I know what you mean. I sort of expected her to turn up in Greenwich Village, out of money." It had begun to snow just a little bit, and the wind blew the flakes right into our faces.

A car stopped, driven by a man in a business suit. I got into the front and Robin into the back.

"How come you girls aren't in school?" he asked cheerfully.

"My cousin's sick," I said, answering because I was sitting in front. "We're going to visit, and the bus didn't come, and we were cold."

"Where's he live, your cousin?"

"She lives in Fort Lee, in that new high-rise building. Are you going anywhere near there?"

"Yeah, I could let you off a couple of blocks from there, I guess." He did, and we walked toward the tower of the building. There were three more high-rises being built in Fort Lee. The apartments were very expensive and very much in demand because Fort Lee was so close to the George Washington Bridge. We walked through the parking lot (RESIDENTS ONLY said a large sign) and Robin pushed open the glass door.

The lobby was warm and carpeted in green. There were big mirrors with gold frames and three elevators. There was also a uniformed doorman sitting on a chair at the end of the hall, talking to a couple of young men who wore New Jersey Bell Customer Service jumpsuits. The doorman looked us over and seemed about to challenge us, but one of the elevators arrived and we got in. We went up to the ninth floor and found apartment 9S. Robin rang the bell. We heard Jan's voice, "Who's there?"

"Rachel and me," Robin answered. Jan pulled the door open and hugged us, first me, then Robin. She closed the door, locked it, put the chain up, and led us into the living room. She sat down on the couch, which was electric-blue velvet. Robin and I sat in matching armchairs and looked at her.

Jan wore a nightgown made of pale pink nylon. It had a few ruffles around the bottom and was cut fairly low across the top. Her blond hair covered the shoulders of the nightgown and turned into wisps over her breasts. She looked very beautiful to me, and also very young. She was nervous.

"Well, hello," she said, "would you like to smoke?" Robin and I nodded, and Jan got up and went to the glass coffee table. She opened an aluminum egg and took out three joints. She seemed about to hand us each one, then smiled, shrugged, and put two back on the table. We passed the joint around slowly, and finally I said, "Is this Lenny's apartment?"

"Yes. But he has another one in New York."

"Do you really like him?" I asked. It seemed like a silly question, but two weeks ago it had been the question to ask Jan about any boy.

"Yeah," she said, "he's really pretty cool."

"Are you working for him?" Robin said, too loudly, and Jan turned her face.

"So what if I turn a few tricks?" she said, and it sounded

ridiculous to me, like a five-year-old trying to sound tough, like someone quoting a bad novel. "Like Lenny says, I was giving it away free, wasn't I?" I couldn't stand the effort behind the things she was saying, and tried to make the conversation more comfortable and gossipy.

"Well, who do you, I mean, which men?"

"Oh, Lenny gives them the number. Lots of straight fathers of families—someday I'm sure some father I know is going to turn up here." We all laughed.

I asked timidly, "Do you think you'll come home?"

Jan began to cry very quietly.

"Like I really miss you all. Lenny's really cool, but he doesn't really love me. But he gives me lots of money, and he buys me a lot of stuff. And all the dope I want, and he says pills if I want them. But I'm even beginning to miss my mother."

"She's really upset," I said. It did not occur to me that Robin or I could tell Jan's mother where she was, but I hoped we could make Jan come home. "Maybe she'll go easier when you come back."

Jan sniffled and shook her head.

"You know she was even slapping me and all, because she doesn't like you, or Chuck, and she wants me to work at the luncheonette, and I don't know what she'd do if she ever found out about this. If she told my father, he'd kill me."

"You missed a test in English," Robin said, and we all laughed.

"Lisa gave Adam a blow job last night at Suzanne's party, in the clothes closet," I said, remembering that I had thought Jan would find that funny.

"Lisa! Really! Shit, I thought she only kissed in her room with the door locked! How come?"

"Oh, she was stoned and he asked if she felt like it."

"And you realize, I hope, that we're missing a very important pep rally this afternoon," Robin added, also trying to make the conversation normal. I went to use the bathroom, not looking into the bedroom as I passed it. The bathroom had the same sort of gold-framed mirrors as the lobby, a hair dryer with curling and setting attachments, and two bottles of Femme perfume. I dried my hands on a thick red towel and went back out to the living room.

"You have to be going," Jan said, "you know, because it's almost afternoon." She hugged us good-bye and I whispered to her, "I wish you'd come home," and then Robin and I were in the hall and Jan had disappeared back into the apartment. We got into the elevator, pushed the bottom button, and got out when the door opened. As it closed behind us, we realized that we had come to the basement instead of the ground floor. There was a fairly large supermarket, a sauna, and a nursery; all the doors said RESIDENTS ONLY. We rang again for the elevator and went up to the main floor and out of the building. It was snowing harder. We got a ride back almost immediately with two high school boys who wanted us to come with them to a bowling alley for the afternoon, but Robin explained that our parents were waiting for us, and we hadn't been able to get a bus, and they were going to be very anxious about us as it was. They let us off back in Lakehill, and we went to Robin's house. Both her parents were at work, and we went to her room and played records.

"I feel like this is really awful," Robin said. We were eating Oreos for munchies, lying on her bed. "I feel like she's really doing something awful, and I don't know why."

"She's so pretty," I said pointlessly.

"I know, I kept thinking, I bet he charges them plenty. I'd like to kill him," she added in a very hopeless tone.

"She could leave if she wanted to," I said, and Robin began to cry. I hugged her and she cried, and then she said, "Still, I bet she comes home in two weeks or so."

Actually, she came home one week later, walking into her

living room and telling her mother she had been staying with a girl she knew from YMCA summer camp. Her mother had hysterics, hugged her, and begged her never to run away again. She came back to school and sat quietly with a frightened look on her face. She had lost a little weight.

Robin and I walked home with her.

"Good to have you back," I said, being funny.

"How come you came back?" Robin said, still with a slightly sarcastic tone, as if to say this was not a serious question.

"Oh, you know, I really didn't like it all that much," Jan said, playing with the ends of her hair. "It was sort of boring there all day. And Lenny started wanting me to do more, you know, work more. And he said if I didn't want to I could just get out."

"Good to have you back," I said.

Officemate
with
Pink Feathers

This new woman, this new coworker, gets moved into Elton's office, and what he thinks, on first seeing her, is, well at least this one won't get me all tangled up in her life. The woman who had worked there before, at the desk facing his across the burnt-orange carpet, had been quite a tangle. She had been desperately terribly in love with some schmucky taxi driver who slept with her but didn't like her much, and Elton talked to her on the phone by the hour at night when the taxi driver didn't show up. He worried that she would try to kill herself one of those nights, and he would end up at San Francisco General sitting by her bedside. In the office, Elton answered the phone on her desk in feeble attempts to awaken the jealousy of the taxi driver, who never called. Elton, whose life had been calm and uneventful at the time, had rather enjoyed all the tumult, but the constant cycles of worry and despair and infatuation had worn thin after a while. And then his officemate had suddenly gotten into Yale Law School and gone East, and all he had gotten from her since was a birthday card which arrived inexplicably one day in September—his birthday was in March.

Anyway, they move in this new person, and Elton looks her over and feels she does not compare well to her predecessor, who was quite dramatically beautiful in an overtly high-strung and crazy sort of way. This new one is distinctly plain, a rather short, solid woman with round unremarkable features, shoulder-length mousy hair, big brown-rimmed glasses. And she is wearing bizarre clothing, a tight skirt of suede, dyed lemon yellow, slit up both thighs, a black blouse with cascades of lace down the front.

Grasping his hand with enthusiasm, she says, I'm Portia, can we do something about that carpet?

It turns out to be kind of pleasant, sharing an office with Portia. It's nice to have someone to talk to during the day, and it's also nice not to have to answer her phone to make an idiot taxi driver jealous, when he never calls anyway. When it comes to their work, Elton and Portia understand one another; the government is paying them well enough to sit there and assemble reports about the piles of forms and applications they read. In an hour's hard work it is possible to accomplish all that is necessary for any given day. Neither of them has any desire to rise faster than the inexorable course of civil service advancement permits. And politely, they do not discuss what has brought them to this job.

Portia's clothes continue to be peculiar. No single item she wears is at all indistinct; sweaters and blouses and skirts and dresses and scarves have all clearly been selected with tremendous care and attention. She wears vivid colors, large emphatic prints, leather and silk and taffeta and fur. And through it all, her face is resolutely clean of makeup, she makes no attempt to do anything special with her hair. It is almost as if, thinks Elton, she views her admittedly unremarkable body and face as a display dummy for various triumphant objects of art. And she never mentions her clothes. In she will walk in a flounced electric-blue satin skirt and a brilliant magenta sweater, trimmed with fur tails, and Elton will wait for her to make some reference to her costume, so vivid in the drab little room. And when she says nothing, he will venture, "I like your sweater," and Portia will look down at it with affection, even with love, smooth the fur, and turn her remarkably practical mind to the business of the day.

Elton himself wears khaki pants, button-down shirts, and ties. He allows himself to indulge in nice pastel shirts and expensive ties, ties made out of silk and Scottish wool, but otherwise his clothes are not terribly noteworthy. Not that he doesn't think about them; he is in fact rather vain, but he is also tremendously self-conscious, and would not care to leave the house dressed in anything that might excite comment.

The office in which the two of them sit all day long is in a very pretty Victorian house which deserves better than the treatment it has been given. It has been used by several government agencies to contain overflow offices and overflow staff, and so it is all fitted out with cheap metal desks and filing cabinets, and that awful burnt-orange carpeting, of course.

Eventually, Portia invites Elton home for dinner. Actually, it is not just something which happens to happen; it comes about because Elton is very depressed, and since for a change he has an officemate who is not totally absorbed in her own love affair, she notices that he is down, and he ends up telling her all about it. There ought to be other people he can tell, but he has been going through one of those periods which happen every so often in San Francisco, where everyone you know seems to be moving away. Besides his old officemate moving to New Haven, he has lost several other good friends and a number of acquaintances, who have moved to New

York, or Seattle (every lesbian in America is moving to Seattle apparently, including one of Elton's oldest friends), or in one case to Paris, to paint. So everyone is moving away, which adds to Elton's depression. The real reason he is depressed, though, is that someone is moving back to San Francisco, to be specific, his old lover, George, and George's new lover, who is apparently extremely rich, and they are going to live in a penthouse on Telegraph Hill, and all in all, Elton doesn't want to hear about it. But he and George are locked into one of those ridiculous pretenses that they are really friends, which gives George license to call Elton up and gloat, and Elton is depressed.

Portia listens patiently, then invites him to stop by for dinner on Saturday night. Her apartment is quite blank, not well lit, not well arranged, not full of interesting things, not even full of clutter. Elton feels somehow disappointed; he cannot tell whether he and Portia are on their way to becoming good friends, but if they are, he would like her to be someone with an interesting life, an interesting apartment, the kind of apartment you would like to get to know better. Portia is wearing a jet-black jumpsuit embroidered with bugle beads and sequins; Elton has a sudden desperate desire to check out her closets.

The kitchen is the nicest room of the apartment, warm and full of pleasant smells. On the walls in here are framed prints of Victorian women in elegant gowns, tiny-waisted silhouettes, flounces and ruffles and rosettes. Elton pictures Portia in a ball gown, in a century when women's clothes were so extravagant that a plain woman could be almost lost inside a glorious construction.

There is only one big pot on the stove. Two places are set at the kitchen table. Elton feels happy to be where he is, to be with a new friend. He feels suddenly sure that Portia has something to teach him, even if he doesn't know quite what it is.

This is the meal she serves him: First she fills his soup bowl with broth from the top of the big pot on the stove. Wonderful rich meaty broth, with tiny bits of vegetables, all a deep winy red color. Then she dips the ladle deeper into the pot, and the next course is a thick vegetable stew, carrot and chick pea and potato and tomato and mushroom and cabbage and onion and other things too, all cooked in wine and broth and sharply spiced. And finally the last course is from the very bottom of the pot, thick meaty bones permeated with all these other wonderful flavors he has tasted on the way down. It is maybe the best meal Elton has ever eaten. He is dazzled. Portia for her part makes no mention of the meal, taking it for granted as she does her jumpsuit. You would think she was wearing a sweater and a pair of jeans, and serving him hamburgers.

After that meal, Elton finds he thinks about her a lot. Portia's life, he thinks, is a work of art. Probably she doesn't need lovers at all, only clothes and food and probably all sorts of other details he can't even imagine. He cannot help wondering, though, whether she ever sleeps with anyone. Finally, one day when they have been discussing his ex-lover George, whom he has begun to run into all over the city, Elton asks Portia, casually, and how's your love life? She answers him with one of those evasions of pronouns: This person I used to be involved with who moved away, probably all for the best since, you know, not really the kind of person I do well with. Elton has to wonder: Is she really referring to some woman who has gone to Seattle? Or is she being deliberately perverse and using this double-talk about some goofball man? He doesn't find out, not then and not ever, not exactly.

What he does find out is that she is pregnant. This comes

as no small surprise to Elton. One day he compliments a velour tiger-skin print skirt, and Portia, looking down at it, says ruefully, soon I'll need maternity clothes and they're all so cutesy.

Finally he asks her: Who is the father of this baby? Like that, formally, sounding to himself like her outraged father or brother, holding in his anger. He waits for an expression of rage or regret or satisfaction from Portia: Someone who hurt me, someone I loved, someone I used. But all he gets is a quick and apparently genuine smile: Nobody you know, she says. Some guy.

Elton turns to his ex-lover George on the Geary bus and says, I can't believe how I keep running into you.

I'm following you, George says. Elton looks into his eyes, and realizes that this is the same old George, that there is no way to know when he says something like that, lightly and slightly sardonically, whether he means it or not.

Well, you can follow me home if you want to, Elton says, and George does.

And so begins a life, which Elton finds he rather likes, as the secret afternoon love of a rich man's pampered darling.

Portia remarks upon this: You're pretty well fixed, aren't you, she says to him one gray day. Her stomach is starting to show. She is a little gray herself, Elton realizes, a little sad-looking as she sits at her desk in a bright red tent dress printed with giant turquoise lilies.

Solicitous, Elton perches on her desk, expecting she will confide any one of a number of things: How can I take care of this baby alone, I'm so afraid, why did he leave me.

Portia smiles at him, a little sadly. Actually, I rather had someone in mind for you, she tells him, but it seems you're all fixed up.

He presses her, naturally, to tell him who it was, but she smiles again and ostentatiously picks up a form she has to fill out for the government employees benefits survey, and anyway George calls right about then to arrange one of his highly conditional Byzantine little rendezvous.

Elton has a fantasy in which he and Portia set up housekeeping together. He likes small children. He rather relishes the idea of George exposed to her calm, amused scrutiny. George, who would think he was in on the joke just because he would laugh at her clothes. George, who would never appreciate that some artists create their own art forms.

Instead of offering this fantasy, what Elton does offer is to go with her to the hospital when she goes into labor. Are you sure, Portia asks, looking unexpectedly touched.

Actually, he was rather expecting her to refuse. Can it be that she, like him, is somehow bereft of all her close friends? (Seattle?)

As if in gratitude for the offer, the next day she brings him a plastic bag full of what she calls turnovers, flaky pastries stuffed with mushrooms, cheddar cheese, fried fish, and jalapeño peppers. There must be twenty of them in the bag. George, predictably enough, can't eat them because they're too spicy and weird besides, but Elton eats them all over the next three days. He has never eaten anything so delicious.

One day after a rather bad fight with George, another afternoon together canceled, you don't give a damn about my feelings, et cetera, et cetera, Elton goes out for a walk and sees, on the other side of the street in Chinatown, Portia and the most beautiful man in the world. Or at least one of the top ten. Blond, tall, dark Byronic eyes, and all the rest. He is carrying a number of packages, walking slightly behind Portia, like her pack animal. The baby's father? Elton wonders, and then immediately, could this be the person she had in mind for *me?*

He crosses the street and trails along behind them, pauses as Portia steps into a store and comes out with another little bag which she adds to the man's burdens. Then bravely Elton catches up to them and is introduced. The name is Brad, which is, Elton thinks, a little much. The two of them accompany Portia to a hole-in-the-wall noodle joint, where she consumes three enormous bowls of Chinese noodles, one with pork, one with shrimp, one with strange-taste chicken.

Then, as they stand out on the sidewalk, Portia reclaims all her packages and says good-bye. Her parting words are: Go to a movie, you two, why don't you. And so they do.

Specifically, they go see *North by Northwest* and they end up making out ferociously through most of the film, and then they go back to Elton's place, and when George calls later, Elton thinks very gratefully of Portia as he cuts off the call saying, I can't talk now, someone's here.

Portia's stomach has slowly but surely taken on that unmistakable hump. In the office, she props her feet up on her desk, leans back, and rests her hands on her stomach, feeling the baby move. Elton spends hours sitting on her desk, sometimes feeling the baby, sometimes just watching Portia rub herself gently. They talk about books and movies and food, and every once in a while about Brad. Elton is embarrassed to find out that he is Portia's old officemate. It seems a little too pat to him, her fixing the two of them up like this.

Elton's life is now, to tell the truth, a little more complicated than he would most like. He and Brad are moving too fast, he knows, both of them too ready, as Portia suspected, for true eternal all-embracing love. And yet he and George continue their stolen moments, more balanced now that both of them are stealing. George is meaner and more sharp than Brad.

In his worst, his very worst most in-love most ridiculous moments, Elton imagines that Brad is the father of Portia's child and that there is a conspiracy against him. And in his almost worst somewhat more clear-sighted moments, he acknowledges that it is hard to imagine Portia taking Brad seriously enough to get into bed with him.

Toward the end of her seventh month, Portia stops coming to the office. First she is on leave, then she has quit. Elton is left to work alone in the office, waiting to see who will be moved in with him. He calls Portia every so often, but she sounds distracted, absorbed in the coming of the baby, and their conversations are short.

Things are turning sour with Brad; that may be one reason he doesn't really want to talk to her. Brad has become both possessive and invasive: Where do you go Saturday afternoon? Why weren't you home late last night when I called? George, on the other hand, is beginning to talk about leaving his rich lover; he says flattering things about missing Elton's sharpness, which are much like the things Elton thinks about George. When he is with Brad, they argue and fight and then they behave ridiculously tenderly to make up; when he is with George, they laugh and have sex and tease each other by mentioning their other lovers.

During the day, Elton sits at his desk and he finds himself thinking about Portia's clothes. The yellow chiffon blouse. The black dress with the rhinestone stars. The chartreuse skirt with the three inches of beaded fringe around the bottom. They drift slowly through his mind like lovely fragments of a more beautiful time. He thinks about her stomach growing. And he finds time in those long empty days to wonder: How will she support this child? What will she do? And who is the father, anyhow?

Also, alone in the office, he finds his mind returning to that dinner she cooked him, the three courses out of the single pot. Whatever he could learn from her, he is sure, he could learn from thinking about that dinner. He sighs and puts his feet up on his desk, leans back in his chair, and almost absently rubs his own almost flat stomach.

The phone call that he always vaguely expected would be at night comes instead during the day, to the office. In labor, says a rather officious voice, she asked that you be notified.

Moving as fast as he can, Elton gets a cab, runs through the hospital to find Labor and Delivery. He feels tremendous urgency; whatever happens, he must not miss this, he must not fail her. They leave him in the fathers' waiting room, which is completely empty; all the fathers are in with the mothers. It seems appropriate to pace, and Elton paces, up and down, up and down, thinking, the red and gold Lurex skirt. The orange silk dress with the deep V neck. The purple stretch pants.

He paces and paces, and finally a nurse comes to tell him: A baby boy. Perfectly healthy, ten fingers, ten toes, she keeps saying, in obvious uncertainty about who Elton is. But he is allowed into the recovery room to see Portia. She is wearing a pale blue hospital gown, lying back on a gurney. And exhausted as she plainly is, she is also, no question, glowing. And the reason is the bundle she clutches, an unexpectedly unhuman face, round and solemn, and maybe just a tiny bit smug and superior. Elton is suddenly washed, left weak, by an enormous wave of love. He feels overwhelmingly glad that this new life is in Portia's hands. He kisses her on the top of the head, and she looks up at him and smiles.

In my bag, over in the corner, she says, speaking with some effort. In her bag is a nightgown, slinky hot pink lace and ruffles, and a matching bed-jacket trimmed with feathers. Portia hands Elton the baby. Take him over to the window, she says. You can be the one to show him his first sight of San Francisco. Feeling deeply honored, Elton carries the baby across the room, while Portia wriggles into her nightgown. Elton and the baby look out at the city, and Elton says: Someday all this will be yours.

He carries the baby back to Portia and she receives him gently against the pink feathers.

"Someday all this will be yours," she says.

Not a
Good Girl

Men nowadays can be very strange, if you ask me. I went to bed with one I had just met when I was up in Boston for two days. This is not something I do ferociously often, jump into bed with men I've just met. In fact, for the last six months or so, I haven't jumped into bed with anyone. Not that I've been celibate on principle, or anything like that. It's just that I've been pretty busy lately.

This man I went to bed with in Boston was a graduate student in biochemistry at Harvard who had come to my seminar, the first of the two I was going to give. (You would never say, would you, "the man with whom I went to bed"? I suppose the whole phrase has its roots in such a cute, euphemistic view of things that it has to be kept schoolgirlish and ungrammatical.) Anyway, he was a graduate student in my field, which is immunology. That, of course, lends itself easily to crude sexual analogies, since it is concerned with the body's defenses against foreign intruders, but never mind all that now. I didn't take any particular notice of him at my seminar, except when he asked a reasonably intelligent question. Then he turned up again that evening, when the people who were "hosting" me took me to an Italian restaurant; there was a big group of junior-faculty types and graduate students, including this one, Eric. After dinner, which was extremely so-so and which seemed to leave everyone feeling a little discouraged, my hosts wanted to take me out drinking, but I said I thought I would just go back to the hotel, and Eric said he had a car and would drop me off. In his car I was conscious of our different clothes, me in my give-a-seminar outfit, blazer and wool skirt and stockings, Eric in very worn corduroy pants and a workshirt frayed at the cuffs. We stopped for a traffic light, he put his hand, ragged cuff and all, on my stockinged knee, and asked perfectly straightforwardly if I wanted "company for the night." As simple as that. I considered for a minute, maybe less, aware that I wanted his hand to travel further up my leg, and said okay, appropriately nonchalant.

I could not possibly have been more than four or five years older than he, though, of course, there was that infinite spiritual distance between still-in-school and out-of-school-and-working. Still, I was inclined to put his lack of romantic finesse down to his callow youth. I don't mean the come-on in the car; that seemed to me very acceptable and even sweet and disarming. And of course I wasn't expecting genuine romantic feeling and wouldn't have welcomed it if it had materialized, but once we were in the hotel room, I was less than thrilled when he kissed me and said, "Well, why don't you take your clothes off?", then started to pull off his own. It would frankly have done more for me if he'd unbuttoned even one or two of the buttons on my shirt. He did switch off the light, which might have indicated a romantic awareness of the full moon coming through the window, but more likely just meant he wanted the conventional darkened room. We fucked on the professionally large and accommodating hotel double bed, in the romantic silver splash of the full moon.

It just knocked me out how good he was, which shows that she who doesn't expect much is sometimes richly rewarded. But then, afterward, when we were exchanging bits of information to give our mutual nakedness some small base of intimacy (how we had no boyfriends, girlfriends, husbands, wives, how much he respected my work, that kind of thing), he said to me, "Women nowadays can be very strange, if you ask me." And he went on to tell me that women nowadays expect men to be gentle and tender but still to go on filling all the traditional male roles, by which he meant, for example, expecting the man to get out of bed and investigate noises in the night. I was protesting halfheartedly that I personally could imagine nothing worse than being left alone in bed to listen to night noises, when it occurred to me that this "complaint" was Eric's way of letting me know how sensitive he was, that he took seriously what he thought were feminist expectations of men, at least seriously enough to complain about them. A scientist who truly cared about his human relationships. I felt, with some irritation, that we had omitted all the traditional first-night trappings; there had been no false tenderness, no ersatz romance, and neither had there been any hard-bitten bedpost notching. Eric and I seemed to have skipped emotionally to some point later on in a relationship (and not a very appealing relationship), when sweeping generalizations about "men" and "women" were just another way of attacking each other.

But I didn't want to worry about any of this. Isn't the point of a one-night stand that you get off on the novelty and the adventure without having to worry about the other person?

In any case, it didn't turn out to be exactly a one-night stand. It turned out to be a two-night stand, though something should be said about the day between the two nights. I was supposed to go visit some labs, but it was a beautiful morning, and as Eric was driving me past the Boston Common, he suggested that we stop and enjoy the sunshine. So we got out of the car and went to the Public Gardens. I sat on Eric's wool lumberjack jacket which he had spread for me in deference to my costume, stockings again, and a different wool skirt and a different shirt, the same blazer. He, of course, was wearing exactly the same clothes he had worn the day before. I was feeling tension about the seminar I had to give that afternoon, and mindless pleasure in the sun and the smell of the earth, and I had half-forgotten the details of Eric's after-sex conversation, except that something about it had been faintly disagreeable. I also retained somewhere, between my legs perhaps, the impression that the preconversation sex had been distinctly agreeable. Overall, though, I was finding Eric today rather less attractive than I had the day before.

Mentally, I redesigned him, giving him truly curly hair instead of vaguely wavy tendrils, making him taller and thinner to entitle him to his awkwardness, while knitting his body more carefully so that the awkwardness would be more superficial. Though, in all fairness, I had to admit that he hadn't been the least bit awkward in bed. Suddenly he put his arms around me and kissed me. I let him, first amused, then aroused, though I don't really believe in making out in public. Soon, we had gotten each other pretty thoroughly worked up, and then without any apparent reason, certainly nothing as definite as anyone's orgasm, we slacked off and began to relax. I began thinking about my seminar again. Then, three boys, who apparently had been watching us climb all over each other, began to call things out at us, encouraging us to finish what we had started. They couldn't have been more than ten years old, maybe less, and they were all three small and thin and pale and should have been in school. One of them carried an enormous portable radio, a ghetto blaster, as they say, though they were as white as Eric and I. After a moment, when they still hadn't gone away, Eric got to his feet and ran toward them, running with rather surprising grace for someone engaged in such an awkward and ridiculous bit of behavior. I supposed that his motive was simple irritation and a desire to protect me from the jibes of these children, but he must have realized almost immediately, finding himself running across the grass, that he could only look sillier and sillier. The children retreated, slightly scared but triumphant in having provoked him, and he gave up the chase, veering around in a would-be casual semicircle, as if he had just been running a little ways to work off his exuberance at the feeling of spring in the air.

Needless to say, I was not fooled. I was annoyed with his silliness and more annoyed because I had just discovered a run in my stocking, which I attributed to our making out. Now I would have to stop at a drugstore sometime before my seminar and replace the stockings. Again I felt, watching him lope shamefacedly back to me, that we were somewhere deep into a relationship, maybe someone else's relationship, certainly not mine. The man making a fool of himself in public, attempting to defend his woman's honor against the onslaughts of smart-ass ten-year-olds. Someone else's relationship, someone else's man.

I might not have slept with Eric again if my second seminar had not gone so exceptionally well. I had been much more nervous about this one than the first, since I'd given the first one many times before. The second seminar, though, explained my very recent work, including work still in progress. I felt vulnerable and a little unconvinced about some of the material, but it went almost devastatingly well, the applause at the end was genuine, and the questions had a slightly awe-struck air, even the challenging questions, the ones that were

meant to suggest major gaps in my thinking. I had no trouble
with the questions. And I felt that one reason it had gone so
well was Eric's presence; I was showing off particularly for
him and also trying to intimidate him and dazzle him and so
on. And so then I felt a little in his debt; also I enjoyed the
tentativeness of his offer: "Do you want me to come with you
tonight?" It was much more tentative than you would expect,
considering that I had slept with him the night before. It took
us out of the middle of all those other relationships.

Once again, things turned out very well in bed, and we
were both satiated and asleep at 2:30 in the morning, when
the phone by the bed rang and it turned out to be my friend
Eleanora, calling from New York to say she'd broken my big
blue platter. Eleanora and her husband lived two floors up
from me, and I had given her my key when I left for Boston
and asked her to feed my cat. She had had company that night
and had needed a big serving platter and had taken mine and
broken it while she was washing it. Then she cried and drank
steadily, until she was drunk and miserable enough to call me
at the hotel in Boston.

She was crying over the phone. Don't cry, it doesn't matter,
I told her, aware that it mattered, that I would not forgive
her. I had not told her she could take the platter. Eleanora, I
kept saying, why are you carrying on like this, it doesn't
matter, I'll buy a new platter. The rhyme was becoming a
refrain. Eric was awake and had turned on the bedside lamp.
The sight of him was reassuring; he was calm, and we were
not emotionally mixed up with each other. I wanted to hang
up on Eleanora and see if Eric could get it up again. I was
angry about the platter and angry with myself for caring about
the platter, and angry with Eleanora for having judged me so
correctly that she knew I would be angry about it.

I'm so messy, she was saying. Everything I touch turns out
to be a mess. My life is one mess after another. After the

platter broke, she had a fight with her husband, a plump and pompous man. He had gone to sleep without forgiving her, she told me, and she was in the living room, with, I assumed, an empty bottle of Southern Comfort in front of her. I know Eleanora's tastes. Why did you have a fight, I asked wearily. Eric was lying back against his pillow, watching me, looking a little surprised. Eleanora said something incoherent, dinner had not gone well, things had not come out right, important guests. For heaven's sake, Eleanora, I said, this is right out of some TV sitcom when the husband's boss comes to dinner. Don't take it so seriously. But then I had to listen to a long speech about how awful her life was and how I couldn't understand. I had no husband, after all. Immunology. Fancy hotels.

Are you alone? she asked suddenly. Well, no, as a matter of fact, I'm not, I said. But it's okay. By which I meant, go ahead and keep me on the phone, we were only sleeping when you called, the sex was over and done with. Immediately, Eleanora's voice took on a giggly quality. She assured me that she hadn't meant to interrupt, that clearly I had more important things to worry about than a broken platter. I'll tell you all about it when I get home, I said. Eric raised his eyebrows; I shrugged. You just bet you will, Eleanora giggled, I'm not going to let you off without a full description. And she said good-bye in high spirits, so I guess I really did manage to do a good turn and cheer up a friend in distress.

I explained a little to Eric, feeling he deserved it. He seemed a bit off balance. It was the sudden awareness of my real, tangled life, which he did not know anything about, in which he had no place. He had asked me all the wrong questions, it seemed—did I have a husband, a boyfriend?—and should have asked, instead, if I had a cat and if I had a friend named Eleanora who broke things.

"What's your cat's name?" he asked me, after I explained

why Eleanora had the key to my apartment; then, after I told him, he said, "You have a cat named Carmen?" I wondered if he thought that was a ridiculous name, if he would, after all, turn out to be some kind of kindred sensibility, so I said, "Someone else named her," leaving him free to make fun of the name. But he had no particular opinion; he had perhaps begun to wonder who had named my cat—an ex-lover, someone I used to live with—and I thought of telling him that my little sister had chosen the name; giving me one of her own cat's kittens, she had thought to please me, knowing I like music. I didn't say it. Instead, Eric and I investigated and discovered that he could indeed get it up again, though, to be honest, it took him so damn long to reach orgasm that I lost interest. But I kept my eyes wide open; it is very bad manners to fall asleep in such a situation.

As if in return for his unexpected glimpse into my life, he offered me a confidence the next morning as he drove me to the airport to catch the air shuttle to New York. He told me that sometimes he was afraid he wouldn't be able to write his dissertation. All I could say was that I was sure he would be fine. I wondered whether he actually would be fine and whether I would see his name on articles or run into him in the future at scientific meetings. "Can I ask you something?" he said. I nodded. "If we lived near each other, would you have an affair with me?" I was silent too long to make it convincing before saying that we'd certainly give it a try, didn't he think? Fortunately, we got to the airport very soon after that and, instead of letting him park, I just got out in front of the terminal and kissed him good-bye and escaped.

Later, on the plane, I was thinking about all the little pieces of far-advanced and none-too-pleasant relationships that I had sensed between myself and Eric. I was wondering what my two-night stand might have to teach me; in science, of course, you have to learn from your experiments, and one valuable lesson is that you can never control all the variables. It can be scary when an experiment gets out of hand, and back at the airport, I'd had the distinct feeling that Eric was ready for all sorts of complications. I suspected there was something to be learned from this interlude with him about the nature of entanglements that occur between lives, the extremely fine line between no relationship and all relationships. And then suddenly, I began to smile to myself, almost to laugh, because it occurred to me that Eric had wanted to follow this experiment to wherever it might lead us, but that I had prevented it. I'd kept it to something more like a seminar—short, controlled, ending neatly on schedule. But it had been educational, I decided; it's hard to learn major lessons in quick little seminars, but they can serve to expose you to new ideas, to start you thinking. The most important thing about seminars is that they should surprise you a little. You shouldn't know, walking in, exactly how you'll feel walking out. And if, in addition, you enjoy them while they last, then you have to consider them successful, I suppose.

The
Almond Torte
Equilibrium

Karen and Marla have a problem. Marla has returned from a trip to California pregnant by her ex-lover, Richard. Karen, her current lover, is not pleased about this. In addition, the day Marla finds out she is pregnant they have an elaborate dinner party to cater, so they have other things to worry about too. That is how they come to play out one of the most important scenes of their life together in the WASP Republican kitchen of Mrs. Prescott, on a gracious tree-lined street in a quiet wealthy part of Cambridge.

This is an unusual party for them to be catering. Usually Karen and Marla, who together constitute Alice B. Caterers, do parties for the young and well-off and hip, or the old and well-off and hip—lots of professors since this is, after all, Cambridge. They make Mongolian hot pot, or elaborate curries, or rijsttafel. But here they are in the kitchen of Mrs. Prescott, who heard about them somehow and hired them to do this party she is giving in honor of her son and his new Ph.D. in engineering from MIT. Perhaps Mrs. Prescott chose Marla and Karen to do the catering because she thought it might please her son: young caterers, a party in a free and adventurous sort of spirit. Unfortunately, Mrs. Prescott was not prepared for unlimited adventure, and she did not respond at all well to Alice B.'s menu suggestions. Paella or couscous, she thought, might be just a trifle exotic for some of her guests. Finally she told them she thought she'd like beef stroganoff, so that is what Karen and Marla are now concocting for forty. It will be an excellent stroganoff; Marla is genuinely a brilliant cook, and she is enjoying herself. Karen is less cheerful about it, but maybe that's because she's upset about that other issue, Marla's pregnancy.

"This kitchen has seen too many goddamn cream sauces," she tells Marla that night, as they get to work in Mrs. Prescott's house. "Stupid WASPs." Karen herself is, naturally, a reformed WASP; Marla, who is Jewish, is more inclined to be charitable.

Karen has ruled that they should serve this dinner in black dresses with demure little white aprons tied around their waists. Karen determines matters of protocol and handles the clients; sharp-tongued in private, she is smooth and easy with customers. She inspires confidence. Marla does most of the cooking and Karen handles the desserts. Karen is a genius at pastry. The dark chocolate almond torte, the apricot filling, and the eggs for the meringue topping sit in Mrs. Prescott's kitchen, to be assembled later. Or rather, the six tortes.

What Karen really wants to ask is whether Marla got pregnant on purpose. She feels this is very important, though she isn't sure what answer she would prefer. They have in the past talked about having a child, raising it together, and there has never been any doubt that Marla would be the one to bear it. Marla is magical with children; this may be simply a version of Marla's general physical magic—adults who meet Marla want to touch her, to sleep with her, and children want to climb all over her, to hoist themselves up on her shoulders and peer down over her head into her face. No one can watch Marla with children without thinking that she should have a child of her own. Karen likes children too, but it's much more tentative. She'd like to raise a child, but she'd just as soon not go through a pregnancy. So, given all that, there is really one very obvious question to be answered: Should Marla have this baby? But Karen isn't ready for that question, and neither, she suspects, is Marla. What Karen wonders is: Did Marla plan this? Did Marla go to bed with Richard without using birth control?

Marla is, as always, superbly well organized. She takes plastic bags of asparagus out of a carton. The asparagus is already trimmed and picked over. Only the best for Mrs. Prescott and her son the Ph.D. and their guests. On one mental level, Marla is working out the logistics of the dinner: the time needed to steam the asparagus perfectly, the number of burners available, the coordination of asparagus and stroganoff and water for the noodles. On another level, she is rehearsing the hollandaise sauce she is about to make. "Cream sauce and more cream sauce," Karen had said disgustedly. Marla plans to put a lot of dill in the hollandaise so it will at least not be white. All that lavishness of perfect asparagus pleases Marla. After almost two years of catering, she is still astonished by the way some foods look in enormous quantity. Once they did crab for a hundred fifty, and Marla, looking over the trays and trays of neatly arranged crustaceans, was suddenly sure that spread before her was the very essence of crab, that even if she studied one crab very closely, learned all about its legs and its body and its life, she would never get the feeling of what crabs were the way she got it when she looked at crab for a hundred fifty. This need to understand the essence of foods is important to Marla; it is probably why she is such a very good cook. Now she thinks of asparagus, and her thought embraces at once the tender subtlety of asparagus properly cooked and the stringy resistance of too-old asparagus, which still yields on energetic chewing its faint ghost of a taste. She even remembers textureless frozen asparagus she has known, and of course, she pictures the asparagus she will steam tonight to an ideal succulence and arrange on silver serving platters. Marla is also very much aware that she and Karen are not discussing a certain issue.

"What do you think Richard would think?" Karen asks suddenly, and Marla understands her to mean, what would Richard think if you went ahead and had it, would he know it was his, would he care?

"Oh, Richard. He knows what I'm like," Marla says, a willingness in her voice to join Karen in making fun of Richard or even in making fun of Marla herself, if that will help. "He probably won't even hear about it, and if he does, he'll never be sure that it's his."

"He knows what you're like," Karen repeats, but without humor, feeling a certain sympathy with the absent Richard, whom she met once and disliked; handsome, certainly, but self-obsessed and a little didactic.

What Marla is like is this: It is almost impossible to know her well without wanting to know her sexually. She seduces the world. And people she likes enough to let them know her well are usually people she is happy to sleep with. The sexual joy and fullness people see in her are probably connected to her cheerful but casual attitude. She is, as Richard has told her bitterly, as Karen has not bothered to tell her, essentially promiscuous; she takes her own sexuality lightly, she is almost always happy to see an old lover. When she and Richard were involved, this was a constant source of quarrels. With Karen, because Karen is very important, a compromise has been reached, an equilibrium worked out. Two basic rules: number one, only out of town, and number two, only males. These seem unnatural to Marla, but Karen matters, so she tries to keep them, has in fact kept them successfully, with only two minor lapses, for the last four years. Only out of town, so Karen never has to sit and wonder if some night Marla is late coming home for dinner. And only men, because Karen does not worry about losing Marla to a man.

Rules or no rules, Karen could not quite take it in stride, for example, when Marla came back from California and mentioned that she'd seen old Richard in Los Angeles. There was, in fact, a certain amount of coolness after the initial warmth of homecoming. But they've been through that before, and they came through it this time, and everything was fine and back to normal by the time Marla found out she was pregnant.

Mrs. Prescott's son, Denver, comes wandering into the kitchen, all dressed up and waiting for the guests to arrive. ("WASPs," Marla remembers Karen saying, "they all have two last names. Denver Prescott, Prescott Denver.") Denver is, Marla sees, extremely awkward. He is a very tall young man, going prematurely bald in a funny pattern, and he walks with a graceless stoop. He has pale blue eyes but no glasses. He is wearing a gray linen suit, obviously expensive, but already wrinkled and disarrayed. The conservative striped tie does not align properly with the buttons at the front of his shirt, the jacket shoulders are somehow off center. Karen, seeing him, moves her delicate cake layers off the long counter and out of harm's way.

"So, how's the cooking going, ladies," he says, in what Marla imagines is meant to be a cross between suggestive banter and the proper tone to use with servants.

Karen answers, smooth and professional, telling him how well everything is going. She compliments him on what a nice kitchen his mother has and he looks confused; probably, Marla thinks, he has never thought for a minute in his whole life about kitchens and what they look like and what makes one nice. He is an obvious candidate for space food, meals-in-a-pill; an engineer whose food should be engineered, not cooked. She feels a sudden abrupt sympathy with his mother, going to so much trouble to give a party that Denver will like, when he would probably be happier with a beer and a computer terminal and no one to force him into nontechnical conversation. Marla is prejudiced; once, long ago, during her time with Richard, she slept with a tall blond graduate student in computer sciences from MIT. He made love as if he were programming, or maybe, as if he were programmed.

Karen suspects that Denver is responding to Marla, who, Karen thinks, is never more beautiful than when she is cooking. Marla is starting the stroganoff going now, setting two enormous pans of finely chopped onions to sauté. Marla always insists on cooking the food at the home where it is to be served; she claims that she can taste the difference in any dish. The filet of beef is already sliced and pounded, the mushrooms are sliced as well. Expertly she shakes her giant pans of onions; nothing must stick. The smell of onions cooking in butter fills the kitchen.

Marla is not actually beautiful in any conventional way; she has a shock of dark wiry hair around her face and strong, almost harsh features, but she has a rounded, thrillingly graceful body and a smile that Karen could not even try to describe without becoming maudlin. Marla is smiling now as her onions turn golden. Actually, what she is smiling at is her scornful memory of that computer sciences graduate student all those years ago, but, probably just as well, Karen doesn't know that. Karen herself is small and neat and her hair is almost light enough to be called blond, and she somehow gives the impression that she is athletic, though in fact she hates all forms of exercise. It must be her fine family tradition of golf and tennis and horseback riding and sailing which has left her looking like she should be wearing white shorts and carrying a racquet; that same tradition is, or course, exactly what has left her so completely opposed to sports. She watches Denver, wondering whether he is watching Marla, she thinks of Richard, and all the while she is smiling socially at Denver and her nimble fingers are cracking and separating one egg after another for her meringue topping.

Karen is a purist about meringues; she doesn't believe in making them ahead of time. Denver is, in fact, watching Karen, not Marla, and finally he asks what she's doing, and she explains about separating eggs.

Mrs. Prescott comes bustling in, wearing a rather severe ice-blue dress and an elaborate diamond necklace. She asks nervously if they don't think they should be putting out the hors d'oeuvres now, the guests might start arriving at any minute. Karen and Marla actually know there is probably still half an hour, but they tactfully take out the less perishable hors d'oeuvres, already arranged on the platters. Mrs. Prescott takes Denver away with her, perhaps to correct his costume, and Marla and Karen are left alone in the kitchen. Marla adds her mushrooms and meat and Karen continues to separate eggs, each egg opened neatly over a tiny bowl, then, after she is sure that no yolk has contaminated the white, dumped into an enormous metal bowl to await beating.

They do not discuss Denver. There is really nothing to say; they are both aware of the joke. Karen finds herself thinking about the two of them with a child. Marla, not surprisingly, is thinking along the same lines, and finally she says, "Well, at least it would eat well."

"You want to have it, don't you?" Karen asks, in a casual

tone of voice, exactly as if they have not been avoiding this question all day.

And "Yes," Marla answers calmly—as if she were announcing that the stroganoff would be ready in plenty of time.

Marla wonders, turning off the heat under her pans and going to start the hollandaise sauce, why she is so sure that she wants the baby. If it meant losing Karen, would she still want it? No, absolutely not. But what makes her so sure that she can have the baby and Karen too? Probably Karen would come around in time to accepting the fact that it was conceived before they had made a decision to have a baby together rather than after. Probably in the end Karen wouldn't really mind that it was Richard's, especially since Richard will never know. Genetically, Richard should be all right, Marla thinks, good-looking, and both his parents still alive, no bad family diseases. She almost says that aloud, but when she looks over at Karen, she sees that Karen is about to say something.

"I'm just not sure I'm ready for it," Karen says. "And especially this way—"

"I know this isn't the ideal way," Marla says apologetically. Karen is still suspicious; deep down she believes it is possible that Marla planned this, that Marla was afraid she, Karen, wouldn't agree if she had been consulted first.

At this point the first guests do arrive, and Marla goes out to start serving hors d'oeuvres while Karen finishes her meringue toppings in the kitchen. Marla smiles and offers hors d'oeuvres automatically, noting that most of the guests are closer to Mrs. Prescott's age than to Denver's. This is not a happy family, Marla thinks, moving through their elegant living room, Oriental rugs and grand piano and shelves of highly unread books. Something is wrong in this family, and she wonders if there is a Mr. Prescott, and if not, what became of him, and whether Mrs. Prescott has any other children.

Marla hopes she has at least one grateful, gracious child, but has to remind herself that a child whom Mrs. Prescott considered satisfactory would probably be a person she, Marla, did not care for at all. This is a well-dressed crowd, she registers—no surprise there. They take fried shrimp balls or hard-boiled eggs stuffed with caviar without exchanging undue remarks with Marla; this is a crowd used to being served. And they all seem to arrive within ten minutes of each other. A homogeneous well-heeled crowd.

Clumsy Denver takes an egg and drips caviar onto his tie. He doesn't notice it and Marla doesn't point it out. An unhappy family, she thinks again, heading back to the kitchen for another tray, and of course she thinks of herself and Karen and a baby—what kind of family would they make? A happy one?

Karen, in the kitchen, is beating her tub of egg whites with the enormous electric mixer she carries to people's homes so she can make their meringues on the spot. Marla reports briefly on the party, then heads out again. She knows that when she comes back, ring-shaped meringue toppings for six tortes will be in the oven. And Karen will be getting ready to help serve the main course. The dinner will be buffet, and at one end of the long table, on the spotless white linen tablecloth, Mrs. Prescott's elegant but uninteresting china and crystal await her guests.

Marla is actually rather hungry; she is strict with herself about not snacking too much when she is catering—it would be so easy to get fat, all those enormous heaps of delicacies. Anyway, usually all that cooking takes away her appetite. She wonders whether this sharp hunger is connected to her pregnancy. Eating for two, she thinks. Particularly she is hungry for Karen's fabulous chocolate almond torte, the dark richness of the cake, the slight tartness of the apricot filling, the sat-

isfying sweet dissolution of meringue on her tongue. A relationship has a certain equilibrium, she thinks. Bringing a baby
in has to change everything. Suppose it destroys their equilibrium and they cannot find another? Are they actually ready
for this? Will they ever be? Will Karen be willing to adjust
to a new equilibrium, Karen who is sometimes jealous of mean-
ingless old boyfriends like Richard, Karen who cannot stand
old meringues, let alone a cake with too much flour in it, or
not enough apricot filling? And what about Marla herself?
Could she find that balance just within herself if Karen left?
She can't even bear to think about it.

Sure enough, when Marla comes back into the kitchen the
meringues are baking. They look at each other, Marla and
Karen. Karen thinks about all the people who see Marla and
want to touch her, adults and children. How can Karen feel
so sure of Marla, allow her to go out of town, knowing what
that means, believe that she and Marla are each other's future?
Well, perhaps people who can create perfect dark chocolate
almond apricot tortes with perfect meringue toppings have
some special kind of confidence in themselves.

Marla checks the stroganoff, which is heated through but
not boiling: perfect. The noodles, the asparagus, the hollandaise sauce. She and Karen carry out platter after platter, and
when the guests have served themselves and settled down at
the little tables arranged all through the living room and dining
room and sun porch, Karen and Marla have a moment of
genuine peace in the kitchen. The meringues are cooling, beautiful snowy peaks and valleys. Karen smiles at Marla, recog-
nizing that they have both performed properly; after two years
in the business, they are no longer nervous every time they
do a party, afraid that something terrible will go wrong, but
still, it is always gratifying to see things go smoothly. That,
of course, seems like a funny way to describe an evening during
which they have both been in turmoil.

Karen begins to assemble her tortes. Marla watches her, searching for something to say. She doesn't exactly want to return to the subject of her pregnancy, but she can't leave it alone. What she wants to say is, I want to have this baby, I want to raise it with you, I want us to stay together forever and ever. What she actually says, and what is, miraculously, the right thing to say, is this: "You know, I really didn't plan this at all, not for a minute. I made him use a condom, really I did, I had no intention of getting pregnant. I wouldn't have picked this way for it to happen. But now it's happened, can't we go ahead and have the baby?"

Karen turns to face her. "I suppose," she says hesitantly. "It's very frightening, though. Everything will change."

"Everything," Marla echoes.

And there are six perfect chocolate almond tortes, each topped with a perfect meringue ring, sitting in a row on the counter in Mrs. Prescott's kitchen.